RULED

AN OUTLAWS NOVEL

ELLE KENNEDY

piatkus

PIATKUS

First published in the US in 2016 by Berkley,
an imprint of Penguin Random House LLC
First published in Great Britain in 2016 by Piatkus
This paperback edition published in 2016 by Piatkus

1 3 5 7 9 10 8 6 4 2

A CIP catalogue record for this book
is available from the British Library.

ISBN 978-0-349-41196-5

Printed and bound in Great Britain by
Clays Ltd, St Ives plc

Papers used by Piatkus are from well-managed forests
and other responsible sources.

MIX
Paper from
responsible sources
FSC® C104740

Piatkus
An imprint of
Little, Brown Book Group
Carmelite House
50 Victoria Embankment
London EC4Y 0DZ

An Hachette UK Company
www.hachette.co.uk

www.piatkus.co.uk

To J,
for all the love, support, and endless phone calls . . .

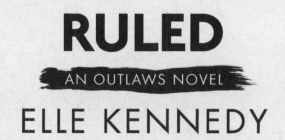

RULED

AN OUTLAWS NOVEL

ELLE KENNEDY

1

"Everyone's in position. Just waiting on your word."

At the sound of the deep male voice, Reese shifted her gaze from the high-voltage electric fence in the distance to find her most trusted friend emerge from the shadows. Sloan wore black from head to toe, and he was armed to the teeth. So was she. They all were.

She bit the inside of her cheek. *Just waiting on your word.* Because it all came down to her. Her word. Her plan. Her decision to rob this munitions depot.

The weight of leadership was heavier than normal tonight. The crushing losses she'd suffered, the unceasing guilt she harbored . . . they were light and airy compared to this burden. Before, her raids had involved teams of three at the most, but this one consisted of more than triple that. She was holding too many people's lives in her hands, and she didn't fucking like it.

"You want to abort?" Sloan studied her face, his hazel eyes piercing through the armor that always turned from steely to flimsy when he was around.

He knew her well. Too well. Four years ago, when

this strong, silent man joined up with her small band of outlaws, it had taken mere seconds for Reese to trust him. Something about Sloan had compelled her to confide in him, to lean on him, to seek him out whenever a decision needed to be made.

It was no surprise that his simple prompting lifted the lid on the self-doubt she'd been trying to contain. "This could backfire on us. People could die."

"We all die eventually." His tone didn't hold a trace of emotion. "If it happens tonight, at least it'll be for a good cause."

"Will it?" Her teeth dug deeper into her cheek. What cause was she *really* fighting for? Freedom?

Or was it vengeance?

She wanted the Global Council to burn. She wanted to kill every single council member in the Colonies, every single Enforcer who carried out their dirty work. If she succeeded, the citizens living behind the city walls would be free. The outlaws living in secret outside those walls would no longer be hunted. But Reese would be lying if she said her motives were selfless.

The council had stolen everything from her. Every goddamn thing that she'd ever held dear. She despised them for it, and when that red-hot hatred burned as hot as it did now, it stripped away all notions that she might be doing this for anything other than pure revenge.

As usual, Sloan read her mind. He chuckled. "Doesn't matter that the cause—for you, anyway— might be tangled up with a bunch of other shit. It's still a cause, sweetheart. It's still something we all want." He jerked his head toward the small warehouse several hundred yards away. "We want those guns. We want to kill the bastards who are guarding those guns. And we're going to succeed."

A smile ghosted across her face. "We will, huh?"

"We've been planning this for weeks. Those mother-fuckers don't stand a chance against us."

The rare flicker of humor in his eyes wore away at her hesitation. If Sloan was confident this could work, then she had to be too. He was right—meticulous planning had gone into it. They knew where every perimeter guard was posted. They knew exactly how many Enforcers were manning the interior. They knew the codes to deactivate the fence. They knew how to disable the cameras and the backup alert that the Enforcers would try to dispatch.

If they followed the plan to the last letter, they *would* get out of this alive.

Probably.

Maybe.

Fuck. She was doubting herself again.

Reese stared at the warehouse and wished there were more places around it to use for cover. The wooded area spanning the rear and east side was advantageous for only half her people; approaching the front of the building would be impossible to do covertly. The warehouse's location was completely isolated, which made sense because the structure, for all intents and purposes, was a gigantic time bomb. With all the potential ammo, weapons, and explosives inside, one tiny accident could kill everyone in the vicinity. The blast barriers might absorb most of the damage, but either way, an explosion wasn't the outcome Reese hoped to get out of this.

She wanted those weapons.

But she also wanted her people to stay alive.

"Maybe we should do this alone," she told Sloan, wincing at the note of panic in her voice. "You and me. Send the others home."

His handsome features creased. She couldn't tell if he was worried or annoyed. Probably the latter. God knew she was pretty fucking annoyed with herself right now. Why was she acting like a scared little girl?

"They know what they're doing," Sloan assured her. "We made sure of it."

They had. Reese had assembled her best-trained people for this raid. And Connor Mackenzie, the leader of a small camp not far from hers, had sent three of his best men as well. Rylan, Pike, and Xander were used to these types of dangerous missions. In fact, Xan's technological prowess was what made the entire plan possible.

"Give the order, Reese," Sloan said softly. "We've wasted enough time."

She swallowed. Then she reached for the radio strapped to her belt. One shaky jab of her finger and she was addressing her soldiers. "Go time," she murmured. "The front guards will be switching rotation in three minutes. Xan, disable the fence now."

"Copy," came Xander's faint reply.

There was no outward sign that the fence would no longer zap anything that came in contact with it, but Reese trusted Xander when he reported a moment later that they were all set. The fence and cameras had been taken care of.

"Rylan, get ready," she said into the radio.

"Born ready," the bane of her existence drawled back.

She pictured him lying flat on his belly like a snake, hidden behind the small rise in the landscape that was hardly considered decent cover but was their only option. If the night breeze rustled even one strand of his hair, the Enforcers at the front gates would spot him. Though Rylan probably got off on that. From what Reese had seen, the man was addicted to danger.

She really wished Connor hadn't sent Rylan to join the party. The gorgeous blond outlaw got on her nerves, big-time. But he was also one of the most lethal fighters she'd ever met, thanks to the years he'd spent training recruits for the now defunct People's Army, an outlaw military group that had risen decades ago to fight the GC right after the war.

She might not like Rylan, but she needed him.

She glanced at Sloan, who was getting his rifle in position. "Let's do this shit," she said with a sigh.

His mouth quirked up in an almost smile.

The radio crackled to life again. "Shift change about to happen," Pike reported.

Reese took a breath before voicing the command. "Go."

There was only a split second of silence between her orders and the gunfire that blasted through the night.

Reese and Sloan burst out of the tree line, rifles up, fingers on the triggers. All her people had been given the same order: shoot to kill. They weren't taking prisoners.

Four Enforcers stood at the back gate, identifiable by their black tactical gear with red stripes down the sides of their pants. Two were behind the fence; two were posted at the gate beyond it. Reese didn't hesitate as she took aim on her enemies and opened fire.

Between her and Sloan—and the element of surprise—the guards at the gate dropped like flies, dead before they even hit the pavement.

The two behind the fence were a different story.

"Take cover!" Sloan shouted as they charged toward the fence.

Reese dove for shelter behind a military Jeep parked nearby. Sloan threw himself beside her as bullets whizzed above their heads. The Enforcers were shouting sharp, muffled orders to each other that Reese couldn't make out over the gunshots. The odor of gunpowder filled the air and she breathed it in as she repositioned her rifle and turned to Sloan.

"Head for the gate. I'll cover you."

He nodded, waited for her silent count, then flew forward with a surprising amount of grace and dexterity for such a large man. Reese popped up and provided cover fire, crowing in triumph when one of her bullets connected with her target. The assault rifle clattered out of the Enforcer's hands as a pained shout left his mouth. She'd hit his shooting arm. Good. That meant one less weapon being aimed at Sloan as he stormed the gate.

Shots continued to explode from all directions, but she refused to think about what was going on outside her assigned quadrant, refused to consider that her people might be caught in the crossfire she was hearing all around her. She focused on backing up Sloan, protecting Sloan.

"Clear!" he called less than a minute later.

Adrenaline surged through her blood as she hurried toward him. The cameras affixed to the tops of the fence weren't blinking green, but she still angled her face away from them, ducking her head as she ran.

Sloan trained his rifle on the rear doors. Reese did the same. She expected those doors to fly open at any second. The Enforcers guarding the interior would panic once they realized their lockdown procedures had been thwarted, a notion that brought a cruel smile to her lips. This station and its security protocols were wholly dependent on the technology that kept it operational. Thanks to Xander, all systems were down.

Her smile widened when muffled gunshots sounded from inside the warehouse. "They're in," she murmured to Sloan.

He didn't look as thrilled by that. "We should be in there too." But he didn't make a move toward the doors.

"We stay in position," she told him. "Stick to the plan, remember?"

And the plan required them to secure the rear and take out any Enforcers who tried to flee. Rylan and the others were doing their part inside.

It felt like an interminably long time before the gunfire died down and her people began reporting in.

"All clear." Beckett, who was with Nash on the west side of the warehouse.

"Clear." Davis and Cole from the east.

"All good here." Xander, who was monitoring the tech from one of their trucks.

"You guys can head inside now." The final report came from Rylan, sounding mighty pleased with himself.

Reese clicked on the radio. "Any casualties?"

A chorus of *no*s rang out, though she didn't miss the note of hesitation in Pike's voice. Shit. She hoped all her people were in one piece.

"Let's go," she said brusquely.

Weapons drawn, she and Sloan raced toward the two metal doors that swung open at their approach. A beaming Rylan appeared, his blue eyes dancing with mischief. "Hey, guys. Fancy meeting you here."

Sloan rolled his eyes.

"Is everything a joke to you?" Reese asked irritably.

"Gorgeous, we just raided a weapons depot and didn't die. I think I'm allowed to be in a good mood right now."

He had a point.

As they followed Rylan into the fluorescent-lit corridor, the ringing in Reese's ears eased, replaced by the wild hammering of her pulse. Holy fuck. They'd done it. They'd actually done it.

"Everyone okay?" she asked Rylan.

He shrugged. "More or less."

"What the hell does that mean?"

"Your girl Sam took a bullet, but she'll live."

A rush of concern overtook her, spurring her to walk faster. Damn it. She'd been torn about bringing Sam along, but the woman was one of the best sharpshooters in Foxworth, the small town Reese had commandeered years ago.

"Where is she?" Reese demanded.

Rylan gestured to the set of doors at the end of the hall. "Pike's stitching her up. Don't worry, everything's fine."

Reese only moved faster. She'd be a fool to take Rylan's word for anything—the man could be bleeding out from his femoral artery and still insist everything was "fine." She rarely saw him without some injury that was "no big deal, gorgeous", although he was always quick to ask her to kiss it and make it better.

She pushed at the doors and found herself in a cavernous room filled with endless rows of shelving soaring almost to the ceiling. The scent of metal, gunpowder, and blood assaulted her nostrils as she stepped through the threshold. She paid no attention to the bodies strewn all over the cement floor. Dead Enforcers meant nothing to her.

Apparently they meant nothing to Rylan too; he didn't even glance down as he carelessly stepped over the bloodied body of an Enforcer who'd taken several bullets to the chest.

"See? She's fine." Rylan sounded exasperated as he pointed across the warehouse.

Reese relaxed when she glimpsed Sam. The slender brunette was sitting on a plastic chair, wearing a stony expression as Pike tied what looked like a piece of his shirt around her upper arm.

"You okay, Sammy?" Reese called out.

"Peachy," the woman called back, then offered a thumbs-up.

Appeased, Reese walked over to the nearest aisle and poked her head around the corner. Stacks upon stacks of wooden crates met her eyes, and then she spotted Beckett already hard at work, prying a crate open with his crowbar. He grinned when he saw her, then shoved aside a sea of packing peanuts to extract a gleaming assault rifle from the crate.

"Nice, huh?" he remarked.

Her heart started pounding again, this time from

excitement rather than adrenaline. When she'd been gathering intel about this warehouse, all her sources were unclear about whether it would contain weapons or ammunition. Most depots weren't equipped to handle both, and it would have been pointless to get their hands on a shit ton of ammo when they had no weapons to use it with.

But Reese's gut had told her that West Colony's council members didn't have enough manpower to guard multiple munitions warehouses, particularly with the new colony that they were supposedly terraforming along the west coast. She'd banked on the council consolidating both weapons and ammo in one place, and her gamble had paid off.

These weapons were hers now. The endless boxes of ammunition were hers. It was all hers.

Her pulse sped up at the thought, but there was no time to bask in her victory. Once the Enforcers they'd killed missed their hourly check-in with headquarters, the city would send backup.

Reese clapped her hands together, and the sharp sound echoed through the massive space. "Load the trucks," she ordered. "We have fifteen minutes to take as much as we can. Let's not waste time, people."

2

Maybe he was a sick bastard, but violence got him hard. Really fucking hard. Which made for a very uncomfortable ride home. Rylan shifted restlessly in the passenger's side of the pickup truck, did some strategic rearranging down below, and hoped that Xander didn't feel the need to comment on Rylan's very noticeable hard-on.

But Xan's gaze stayed on the dark road beyond the windshield. He'd barely said a word since they'd settled in for the long drive back to Connor's camp.

Rylan reached into his pack and pulled out two cigarettes. "You want?" he asked, waving an unlit one in Xander's direction.

The quiet man gave a sharp nod.

Rylan lit the two smokes, took a long drag, and handed one over. Xander puffed his down to a nub before another mile passed. Without being asked, Rylan lit another one. He hoped his friend would pace himself on the second, because he only had one left.

Fortunately, it looked like Xan planned to make this one last, probably so he'd have an excuse not to talk. He didn't need one, though. Everyone knew the source of Xander's silence. It had been two months since the attack on Reese's town, two months since the death of Xander's best friend, Kade. In those two months, all of Xander's spoken words could've been written on a napkin. He'd never been one to crack jokes or run around with a big grin on his face, but the man's expression had two modes now—stoic or pained. He winced every time Kade's name came up.

And for all the success they'd experienced tonight, their excursions weren't picnics. They were battles with live rounds and a shit ton of ammunition. Rylan wasn't naive enough to think that Kade's death was the last they'd suffer before the end—if there was going to be an end.

Reese's plan to take down the Global Council was dangerous, risky, and only working because the outlaws on her side would rather bet their lives than sit on their asses, hiding from the world. Even Connor, Rylan's best friend and leader, had been brought around to Reese's way of thinking.

Strike first, strike often, and strike hard—that was their new motto, because as evidenced by the recent attack on Foxworth, the Enforcers who carried out the will of the GC wouldn't allow the outlaws to hide for much longer.

Rylan rolled his head around his neck, trying to ease some of the tension, but he knew it wasn't going away with any car-bound workout. There was only one way the granite in his pants would subside—with his hand working his cock while his mind fever-ishly played images of Reese.

Though if he were being honest, the solo act wasn't

much fun. He liked active, happy companions. More than one if possible, which was why he'd been a frequent visitor to Connor and Hudson's bed. There wasn't anything better in the world than driving a woman crazy in the sack, and he got the most pleasure doing it with another man in the mix. Two men, devoted to one woman's pleasure, meant everyone had a fan-fucking-tastic time.

But Reese's pleasure was off-limits to him, apparently. Seemed like she'd rather sleep with anyone but him. And he was good, damn it. He knew that if he had the opportunity, he could rock that woman's world. He'd do it by himself or they could have Reese's brick-faced companion join them. At this point, he didn't give a shit who was there as long as he finally got his hands on her. But the stubborn woman continued to resist his every attempt, every sugarcoated word. And in the last couple months, Rylan's desire for everyone else seemed to have tapped out like a dried well. His dick was raw from all the hand work it was getting.

He stared moodily out the window. It was cold outside, but there wasn't any snow. Technically it was still winter, but spring-like weather had come too soon, and with it, endless rain. The truck moved slowly in the mud and slush. He hated it.

After another ten miles of smoke-filled silence, Rylan had had enough. Enough of the shitty weather. Enough of the bleak landscape. Enough of the goddamn quiet. He didn't want to be in his head thinking about Reese, the weather, or the dire situation that the successful raid would no doubt spark.

"Nice work with the electronics tonight."

Xander grunted.

Okay, this wasn't going to work. No way could he survive another two hours next to this sullen soldier, especially when his own thoughts were wandering into melancholy territory. If he stayed in the truck with Xan, the two of them would end up singing dirges and wiping away man tears.

The rumble of a motorcycle roared next to them. As Rylan looked out the window, he made out long red hair streaming out the bottom of a black wool hat, and leather-clad legs wrapped around a man big enough to be mistaken for a mountain.

The fit of his pants became impossibly tight as he stared at Reese, the outlaw queen. There wasn't a man who saw her that didn't instantly want to fuck her. Or if there was, Rylan hadn't met him and didn't want to. He couldn't stand ridiculous jackasses who were turned off by a woman as strong as steel.

He wondered if Sloan could feel the heat of Reese's pussy as she plastered her body against the man's back. Now *that* was where Rylan wanted to be. Not cooped up with Mr. Sourface, but out on the open road with Reese wrapped around him. One of her hands would be attached to his dick, which meant they'd have to stop at some point so he could bend her over the side of the bike and fuck her until she was too weak to walk. Then, when they got to Foxworth, they'd shower, fuck again, get into bed, and fuck some more.

His cock couldn't get stiffer.

"You're gonna permanently damage something downstairs if you don't get yourself under control," Xander remarked.

"Shit, man, the condition of my hard-on is what gets you to talk? Why don't you reach over and do something about it?" Rylan waved a hand toward his lap. Anything but his own touch would be a welcome relief these days.

"Pass."

Beside the truck, Sloan gunned the motorcycle's engine and the vehicle jumped past them, heading for Foxworth. Reese didn't even look Rylan's way.

There was a name for men who constantly chased after what they couldn't have. Scratch that. Several names: *Idiot. Fool. Ass.*

But Rylan couldn't turn off his desire, even if he wanted to.

He had options, of course. Jamie might be off the table because she'd finally hooked Lennox—or rather, Lennox had woken the fuck up and realized if he didn't make his claim, he was going to lose Jamie. But even without Jamie, there were other options at Connor's camp. Layla. Piper. And Connor and Hudson would definitely invite him to join them. They both enjoyed his company—Connor, because he loved making Hudson happy, and Hudson, because, well, Rylan was shit hot in bed. But afterward, he'd still have to go back to sleep in his cabin and think about the fact that they were starting a war.

Or . . . he could throw himself at the tigress. Who cared if he got scratched up a little? Better than being dead. Besides, Xan was right. If he didn't do something about the spike in his pants, there was going to be damage. If not to his head, then to his body.

He rolled down the window and looked behind him. Ten lengths back was Beckett's vehicle. Beck was the mechanic at Foxworth. "Pull over and drop me off," Rylan told Xander.

The other man tilted his head. "You think she's gonna say yes this time after months of saying no?"

"You only lose the fights you never enter," Rylan quipped.

Maybe if he was lucky, Reese would finally throw him a bone.

Sloan didn't knock as he entered Reese's room. She would've laughed if he had, telling him he had as much right to the space as she did. But the space he wanted most was in her bed—the one she was sitting on as he closed the door behind him.

Her tanned, toned, bare legs stretched out in front of her as she toweled her hair dry. A faded blue T-shirt clung to her ripe tits. The skin at her throat, around her cheeks, on the tops of her silky thighs, was flushed from the heat of her recent shower. Her body was an unintentional invitation to feast.

He wanted to run his fingers over her legs. No, his tongue. He'd lick his way up, part her thighs, and . . .

Fuck. He shut down those fantasies quick before his wood became too awkward to hide. Then he strode angrily to the far wall and stared out the window— seeing nothing but golden skin, wet strands of red hair, swaying breasts, and whisper-thin cotton that teased rather than disguised.

"What's wrong?" she asked. "Is it the raid? It was almost too easy, wasn't it?"

Her uncertainty shamed him. She was shouldering a huge load, and here he was, feeling sorry for himself like a baby bitch. Swallowing his inappropriate desire, Sloan turned to face her. "No. It seemed easy because you planned it flawlessly."

She didn't respond, but he could tell by the look on her face exactly what was going on. She was tunneling deep into her own head, second-guessing herself.

He cursed inwardly, but gentled his voice. "Reese."

She pressed her lips together for a moment, and then the shield dropped. "I'm scared."

Sloan's heart turned over. He was the only one who got to see her like this, the only one she trusted enough to see her uncertain and frightened. Outside this room, she cloaked herself in impenetrable armor. She fought and fucked with verve. There wasn't a person better suited to lead this rebellion than Reese.

But inside, she quaked at the responsibility. She wanted to save everyone, mourned every loss. Even the ones she made with her own hands.

Her trust made him both the luckiest man alive and the most cursed. Reese would show him her vulnerability, but she wouldn't allow him to comfort her. And he never put her in the position of having to turn him down. That was one burden Sloan wouldn't place on her shoulders—the knowledge that he ached for her and her alone.

He knew how she felt about love. How she shied away from commitment and those tender emotions that glowed around couples like Lennox and Jamie or Connor Mackenzie and his woman. Reese would never say it to their faces, but she believed that kind of love didn't have a place in this world.

She was doing everything in her power to change that. To make it so the young girls and boys in her care would grow up without the need to foster their fierce, angry, wild sides in order to survive.

Still, all that change came at a cost. It meant putting

her people in danger. Their lives were in her hands and every mission she laid out had very real consequences.

"They trust me."

Even though her eyes weren't red, Sloan suspected some of the water in that shower hadn't come from the reservoir tanks. "They should."

"Should they? Should they really? Am I even doing this for the right reasons? We both know I want to bring down the council for my own personal pleasure. It has nothing to do with that pretty ideal of freedom." Reese's fingers clenched into a ball.

Sloan crossed the room and sat beside her. She leaned into him immediately, and the need in his blood spiked hard. With ruthless self-control, he tamped it down. Picking up her hand, he pulled her fingers apart, wincing at the sight of the bloody crescents in her palms. Yeah, there'd been plenty of tears shed in that shower, all right.

He allowed himself this touch, just as he allowed himself a million other small tortures. Because these small things were worth all the pain of not having her.

"You can want both—revenge and freedom—and still be on the side of good." He rubbed her fingers. Hard calluses met hard calluses. Reese was a warrior, not a soft-palmed woman of the Colonies. And the thickened skin at the base of her fingers, the weathered pads of her fingertips, the wind-burned cheeks . . . it all made her sexier than any woman had the right to be.

"I . . . worry that I'm not making the right decisions."

What she really meant was that she worried that

the number of lost lives would be higher than she would be able to live with in the end.

"You're overthinking this. Listen." He tipped his head toward the open window. Outside the building, people were starting to gather at the rec hall. Music had been turned on and the sound of laughter and singing and merriment mixed together. All of it existed because Reese was willing to put her neck, heart, and soul on the line.

Yes, there were going to be losses, but it wasn't healthy for her to sit up in her room and count them when she could be out there with the people she had saved.

"That's the sound of celebration. We need to have these moments too. All of us." Sloan pushed to his feet without letting go of her hand. "So get dressed, find a man tonight, and ride his dick until you're limp."

3

Sloan was right. She needed to be around people. Needed to let the voices and laughter and music drown out the doubts that were pounding through her brain.

And he was right about the other thing—she needed sex. A hard cock slamming into her until she was mindless would be the perfect antidote to her melancholy.

Any man in this room could help her out with that. It was just a matter of deciding which one to pick.

Her gaze swept over the small crowd as she moved deeper into the rec hall. The old building had once been a place where the long-since-dead residents of Foxworth had come to amuse themselves. Kids would pop in after school to play Ping-Pong and do arts and crafts. There'd been knitting classes and book club meetings, according to the faded flyers on the bulletin board near the door, and aerobics classes in the gym upstairs, though all the equipment was now covered in rust and essentially unusable.

Since nobody had felt like lugging broken tread-mills and exercise bikes down two flights of stairs, they'd decided to pretend a second floor didn't exist. On the main floor, they'd brought in furniture— couches, chairs, a pool table Jake had found in one of the wealthier homes in town.

The thought of Jake made her stomach roil. It was hard to look at anything in Foxworth without thinking of him. He was ingrained in every inch of this town. She was the one who'd found Foxworth and decided to make it a permanent base, but Jake had turned it into something better, something she'd never even dreamed of. It was his idea to raid the nearby factories for sheet metal, his idea to erect the gates around the main stretch of town. His idea to form alliances with the shadier Enforcers, offering them sex and booze in exchange for protection and invisibility.

Foxworth was their creation. He'd been its king, and she his queen. A queen who'd murdered him for the crown.

No, not for the crown. For *them*—Reese looked around at the thirty or so people filling the room.

A little more than eighty people resided in Foxworth, but not all of them were original members of the group. Some were nomads who'd wandered up to the gates long after Jake's death. Others were old acquaintances who'd found their way back to the area. But the ones who'd known Jake . . . the ones who'd suffered at his hands . . . they were the ones she'd saved from the man she'd loved.

Jake had needed to be stopped.

She'd stopped him.

"So who's it going to be?"

Reese tensed as Rylan came up beside her. He held

a tumbler of amber liquid in one big hand, tapping his thumb against the glass.

"Who's going to be what?" she muttered. As always, his presence threw her guard up a hundred feet.

"The man who'll be getting the gift of your pussy tonight." His blue eyes flickered with irritation. "I'd be happy if you chose me, but that's probably hoping for too much, huh?"

"You're right about that."

Rylan chuckled and handed her his glass. "Drink?"

"You trying to liquor me up, honey?"

He blinked innocently. "Nah, you looked thirsty."

A laugh slipped out, but she still accepted the glass and took a long swig. Bourbon, she noted as the alcohol slid down her throat. She wondered if Rylan had picked it because he knew she had a hard-on for bourbon, or if it was a coincidence.

After another sip, she handed the glass back. "Getting me drunk won't impair my judgment, you know. I'm even more stubborn when I'm wasted."

He laughed too, and the deep, husky sound tickled a place she didn't want associated with this man. She fought a smile, but it broke free when she noticed the very obvious bulge in his pants. Rylan seemed to sport a permanent erection, as if he expected he might have to whip out his dick at a moment's notice and always wanted to be prepared.

"Seriously, gorgeous, would it kill you to say yes?" Rylan leaned in so close that his lips brushed her ear. "You know I'd make it good for you."

She had no doubt. But Rylan was too damn dangerous to spread her legs for. Forget the fact that he physically resembled her ex-lover, with his golden hair and vivid blue eyes. That was an issue, sure, but not an insurmountable one. He and Jake might look vaguely the same, but Reese knew from experience that no man fucked the same.

No, it was the other resemblance between Rylan and Jake that scared her—the reckless streak. Rylan didn't seem to give a shit whether he lived or died. He breezed through life as if it were a game. One he evidently didn't care about winning, otherwise he wouldn't throw himself headfirst into dangerous situations without a single care for his well-being. And although he took orders from Connor Mackenzie, Reese knew he'd disobey his leader in a heartbeat if it struck his fancy.

Granted, he didn't seem to crave power the way Jake had, but the motives behind Rylan's actions didn't matter. Like Jake, he was too impulsive. Dangerously so.

A man who didn't think before he acted was a man who couldn't be controlled.

And for a woman who carefully planned every move she made, *that* was the issue. She refused to let another loose cannon into her bed, especially when she was well aware that men like Jake and Rylan were her weakness.

"You know who else would make it good for me?" she said sweetly. "Beckett."

Rylan followed her gaze to the tattooed man across the room. Beckett was laughing at something his friend Travis had said. "Beck's a decent lay," Rylan agreed. "But he's not what you need tonight. Too playful."

She raised an eyebrow. "And what do I need tonight?"

"With all the adrenaline from the raid still burning in your blood? You need a good, hard dicking, gorgeous." He nodded to their left. "Nash could probably give it to you."

Reese glanced at the man in question. Nash's rugged features and lean frame were definitely appealing, but she wasn't really feeling him tonight.

"It's too bad Lennox isn't here. He'd give it to you as hard as you wanted." Rylan grinned. "But he's a one-woman man these days, so maybe it's a good thing he's at Con's camp. This way your poor ego doesn't have to take a hit every time he rejects you."

She narrowed her eyes. But she couldn't argue with that. Lennox had made it clear that he was with Jamie now and not interested in screwing anyone else. And Jamie had made it clear what would happen if Reese made a play for Lennox's bed ever again—that little bitch had beaten the shit out of Reese the last time they'd crossed paths.

Not that Reese held a grudge. She'd be possessive of Lennox too, if he was her man.

"I don't mind rejection," she answered. "It's character building."

"Too much of it can crush a man's ego, though."

Reese ran her gaze over Rylan's confident frame. "Hasn't worked so far."

"Inside, I'm hurt," he said playfully. "I'm probably going to need someone to check me out later. Maybe if we danced, it'd soothe some of the sting."

Reese turned away from Rylan's twinkling blue eyes and searched the room for Sloan, who was never far from her side. Usually lurking in the shadows somewhere, his watchful gaze fixed on her.

When she couldn't see him anywhere, a pang of unease tugged at her insides. He must have ducked out right after he'd walked her over to the rec hall, which was odd, because Sloan rarely left her alone. Then again, it *was* late. He'd probably gone to bed.

The room felt unbalanced somehow without Sloan.

"Too stubborn to take a turn with me?" Rylan countered, drawing her from her thoughts.

Rather than give her the chance to reply, he took her hand and yanked her against him. Reese grabbed onto his broad shoulders by instinct, barely righting herself before he shoved one thigh between her legs and plastered their bodies together.

Her traitorous hormones instantly kicked in. The last time she and Rylan were in this position, she'd been seconds away from taking him to bed, a foolish decision that had been interrupted by the arrival of the Enforcers. The events that followed had been a total shit storm. People had died. Good people, like Arch, whose death had left his pregnant woman all alone in this world. And Kade, whose death had been the push Connor needed to join Reese's cause.

"Get out of your head," Rylan murmured against her cheek.

Damn. Was he reading her like Sloan did? She clenched her fingers over his shoulders, but, for some stupid reason, didn't shove him away. "I'm not . . ." She trailed off.

"Not thinking about your next move?" he mocked. "Planning the next attack? Mentally counting all the bodies you might leave in your wake?"

His faint laughter grated. And damn him for knowing what was eating at her. Before his extended stay at Foxworth two months ago to train her people in the art of guns and combat, she never would've used the word *perceptive* to describe this man. But he'd proven her wrong during that visit. Rylan was far more observant than she'd ever given him credit for.

His rough thumb traced a path up her neck to her mouth. He rubbed her lower lip, slowly, seductively. "You need to fuck," he whispered.

Tension gathered inside her, tightening her muscles, pulsing in her core. He was absolutely right. Sex was a surefire way to release all the volatile energy surging through her veins.

"Use me tonight, Reese." He buried his face in her neck as he continued to rub up against her. He wasn't moving in time to the fast-paced beat pulsing out of the rec hall speakers, but to his own slow, sensual rhythm. Each grind of his hips weakened her resolve. "Use me however you want. Fuck me however you want. Just . . . say . . . yes."

A shiver racked her body as his warm mouth latched onto the side of her throat. He kissed her hot flesh, then sucked hard enough to make her moan.

That got her a low chuckle. "You know you want to." He licked a path along her jaw and upward, until their lips were a mere inch apart. "We'll burn so hot together, baby."

She didn't answer. She couldn't, because her throat was clamped shut. God, of course they'd be hot together. Her entire body was close to going up in flames. The feel of his erection against her thigh made her weak-kneed and achy.

But . . . she didn't trust herself when she was around him.

The truth was, there was a reason she was drawn to loose cannons.

Because she *was* one.

She was only careful because she forced herself to be, but those wild tendencies that had gravitated toward Jake lived inside her too. She was driven by base urges just like Jake had been, and she struggled every second of every day to hold on to restraint and be the kind of leader her people deserved. The kind of leader Jake had failed to be.

Rylan tested that restraint, and she didn't like it.

Where was Sloan, damn it? Panic rolled through her as she peered past Rylan and once again searched the room. Sloan grounded her. He was the only one who—her panic faded when she spotted him near the door. A breath of relief slid past her lips.

"I'm down with Sloan joining us. The more, the merrier," Rylan said after he'd twisted his head to track her gaze.

Sloan stared back at them, steady and reassuring. *I'm here,* his eyes telegraphed from across the room. Reese watched as he settled his broad shoulders against the wall, crossing his arms and resting one ankle over the other.

She turned to Rylan, who took her renewed attention as an invitation. He shifted her around so she couldn't see Sloan anymore and nuzzled her neck again, whispering, "What's it going to be, gorgeous?"

No.

Yes.

Her body was a fuse waiting for a spark. Primed for sex. Aching for it.

She felt the unshakable gaze of Sloan at her back. Yeah, if she didn't pull out of this maelstrom of guilt and worry, she wasn't going to be good for anything.

Now, more than ever, she needed to be sharp and ready. She looked up into Rylan's heated gaze. He never took anything too seriously, was rumored to be one of the best fucks in West Colony. Sex with him would be the greatest distraction she could ask for.

Except . . . she still didn't trust herself. She didn't trust that she could give in to Rylan and come out of it unscathed.

But she did trust someone else.

Abruptly, she pulled out of his arms. "Follow me."

She turned on her heel, not waiting to see if he followed. The hard boots hitting the floor answered for him. Sloan straightened as she arrowed in his direction, and by the time she came to a stop in front of him, he'd reached his full, towering height.

"You said I needed a man tonight," Reese muttered. "Is he the one?"

Sloan's hazel eyes locked with hers. "I can't think of a better person in this room to pull you out of your head."

Rylan's breath was hot on her neck, and Reese had to fight to keep from shivering in sexual delight. She shook her head instead. "He's reckless."

Sloan nodded.

"It's not wise."

Sloan nodded again. "If we did everything that was wise, we would've been dead a long time ago." He lifted his hand as if to cup her cheek, but the touch didn't land. It never did. He always held himself back.

She knew, because she wasn't dumb or blind, that he lusted after her. He'd never made a move to scratch that itch, but it was always there between them, like the caress that never happened. Reese had become accustomed to it, as much as she expected the sun to rise and the rain to fall. Sloan was the one constant in her life.

Rylan coughed. "I'm right here, you know."

They both ignored him. Reese kept her eyes on Sloan. If he was with her . . . then maybe she could hold on to some shred of control. Maybe the fiery lust, the recklessness Rylan stirred in her, wouldn't spill over into other more vulnerable areas.

"Only if you're there," she whispered to Sloan. "I don't trust myself." In other words, she needed him to be the lifeline he'd always been and pull her out of the quicksand when it threatened to swallow her.

Sloan searched her face, but she wasn't sure what he was looking for. He went quiet, as if he was turning the proposition over in his head a few dozen times, until finally he nodded again. "If that's what it takes to ease your mind, then I'm there. Nothing will happen that you don't need."

"Interesting choice of words there, brother," Rylan noted. "What about giving Reese what she wants?"

Sloan's gaze hardened when it shifted from her to Rylan. "She gets it all."

4

Rylan had slept with a lot of women over the years. A helluva lot. But he could honestly say this was the first time a woman had consulted her . . . her what? Lover? Lieutenant? Whatever Sloan was to Reese, he was clearly important enough that she needed to ask him before making decisions about her pussy.

Which was all sorts of fucked up.

Other men might've walked away after that bizarre exchange in the rec hall, but Rylan wasn't other men. He was the man who'd wanted Reese from the moment he'd met her. The man who was finally going to feel her naked curves pressed up against him as she rode the cock that was downright aching for her.

If she wanted an audience, fine. He didn't have a problem with Sloan taking a front-row seat to what was bound to be some pretty spectacular sex. Hell, he'd be cool with Sloan joining in, if that was what got Reese off.

But the perpetually somber man gave no indication that he was interested in getting his rocks off.

When the three of them entered Reese's bedroom, Sloan flicked on the light, marched to the lone armchair near the bed, and lowered his muscular frame onto it. Then he crossed his arms and said nothing.

Rylan looked around the room. The bed and chair were the only pieces of furniture. And unlike in his cabin back at Connor's wilderness camp, there were no items of clothing littering the floor, no clutter, no guns and holsters and ammo strewn about. Everything was neat and orderly.

"Take your clothes off."

Reese's throaty command drew his gaze back to her. Her brown eyes were bright, glittering with lust. He didn't know if she was still riding the high of the raid or drunk off the bourbon, but he'd never seen a sexier sight. He could *feel* the sexual energy radiating from her body, the heat of it going right to his balls.

"Do it for me," he drawled.

She smirked. "You don't get to give me orders tonight, honey."

He smirked back. "Then you don't get me naked."

A smile played on her lush lips. She tilted her head and said, "Sloan."

The big man rubbed a hand over his dark, neatly trimmed beard. "Rylan," he said brusquely. "Take off your clothes."

Rylan's hand slid down to his zipper as if it had a mind of its own.

Fuck. What the hell was he doing, taking orders from this asshole? Yet he couldn't stop himself. Something about Sloan's low, steady voice was damn near hypnotic.

Reese's smile widened as Rylan unzipped his

jeans. He kicked off his boots, shoved the denim down his legs, and then drew his shirt up and over his head.

"Socks," came Sloan's restrained command.

Rolling his eyes, Rylan peeled off the thick wool socks and flicked them onto the hardwood floor. He was fully naked now, and he grinned when Reese's gaze fixed on his very prominent erection. He could see her studying the barbell piercing on his cockhead, as if trying to decide whether or not she was going to enjoy it.

He fisted his cock and gave it a slow stroke, thumbing the piercing with deliberate showiness. "What now, gorgeous? I'm naked and hard and it's all for you."

She didn't answer. And she remained fully dressed in skintight jeans plastered to her long legs and a tight sweater clinging to her tits. Those big brown eyes continued to gleam, darkening with pleasure as he gave his dick another pump.

The longer she stared, the closer he got to the brink. "I need to come before I fuck you," he muttered.

That finally got him a response. "Any reason you can't come *while* you're fucking me?" She toyed with the hem of her sweater, absently sliding the fabric up an inch.

His gaze tracked the motion of her hand, focusing on the narrow strip of flesh that had just been revealed. He swallowed a groan, resisting the urge to rip that goddamn sweater to shreds. He wanted her naked, but he was afraid that if he barked out another order, she'd kick him out on his ass.

"I'll last longer if you suck me off first." He shuddered out a breath. The thought of those pouty red lips around his dick almost caused him to shoot in his hand. He glanced at Sloan, whose faint smile told Rylan that the man knew exactly how close he was to losing it.

Rylan held Sloan's gaze and forced out a mocking laugh. "Seriously not interested in joining the party? You're just gonna sit there and watch?"

Sloan arched a brow. "Not if all you're gonna do is talk. Because if that's all you have to offer her, then she was right to turn you away before."

Rylan's nostrils flared. "Fuck you."

The man chuckled. "I already turned you down."

"Sloan," Reese chided without turning around, "be nice."

"Only if you're extra rough with him. He's annoying me."

She threw her head back and laughed, and the sight of her exposed throat summoned a growl from Rylan's mouth. He snapped his arm out, bunching his fingers in the soft fabric of her sweater to wrench her toward him.

"You wanna know what I have to offer?" he bit out. "I'll fucking show you." Then he crashed his mouth over hers before she or her guard dog could say another goddamn word.

Reese gasped, startled. The moment her lips parted, his tongue slipped past them, thrusting deep. She tasted like hot sin, fierce and wild, and the blood in his body pounded harder with a driving need to claim her as his own. He laughed internally at the utterly nonsensical thought. Tethering her would be like tethering the tide. Impossible. The minute you had her, she'd slide from your grasp, teasing you to come after her and try again.

But for now, he had her. He had her fevered lips clinging to his. Her tongue licking a fiery path inside his mouth. Her delectable body sliding against his.

He'd take it. He was a simple man. He liked to fight and to fuck and he'd wanted Reese for far too long to put conditions on this encounter.

They devoured each other with their mouths. He tunneled his fingers into her hair and pulled her head back with a sharp tug to get her mouth in a better position for his invasion. Her fingernails dug into his biceps and he shuddered at the thought of those marks on his shoulders, down his back, on his ass cheeks.

Reese kissed like she did everything else—with every ounce of energy and life she had in her. This was what *outlaw* meant. Living one's life to the very edge. If Rylan wanted a sedate, tame existence, he'd live behind the gates of West City and slowly kill himself with normalcy.

Nope. This passion—this *life*—was what he craved. And there wasn't more of it in all of the land than in this one woman.

The need for release throbbed in his cock. He tore his mouth away and shot a fierce look toward Sloan.

"No more waiting," he growled. The two of them were turning him into a reckless animal—Reese with her scorching body rubbing all over his bared aroused one, and Sloan with his impenetrable gaze and commanding nature.

The other man's eyes dropped to Rylan's cock and . . . lingered? Rylan felt himself swell even thicker, which wasn't that much of a surprise. He'd shared plenty of women and wasn't at all shy about showing his dick to anyone who was interested in looking.

But there was something electric in Sloan's gaze, something that spoke to Rylan directly.

Sloan's inspection moved from Rylan's body to Reese's. She stood flushed, panting, and ready. A lioness ready to pounce. But neither of them moved. It was as if they couldn't, not without Sloan's approval.

And Sloan withheld that blessing for long, silent moments while the air grew thin, Rylan's blood thickened, and his pounding heartbeat grew so loud it was all he could hear.

He was choking on his lust, goddamn it. Close to coming from Reese's mere proximity and the intensity of Sloan's stare.

Had he ever been this turned on before?

No. Not ever.

Not with all the partners he'd had before. Not with Connor and Hudson. Not with Jamie. Not with anyone.

If he didn't get his dick into something, he was going to shoot all over the floor. His hand drifted down to his shaft, a movement that neither Sloan nor Reese missed. Reese let out a whimper of need, which snapped Sloan to action.

"On your knees, Reese," the big man ordered. "I want to see his cock in your throat."

Holy shit. Rylan moved his hand to his balls and squeezed, hoping the sharp pain would drive away the urge to come.

His agony drew a rough laugh from Reese, who was lowering herself to the wooden floorboards.

Before her knees hit the ground, Sloan called a halt. "Wait."

"Goddammit," Rylan cursed, because Reese's mouth was inches from his pained shaft.

"What's wrong?" She looked at Sloan with concern.

He directed his answer to Rylan. "Put your pants on the floor. Her knees don't need to be torn up." Taking care of Reese was clearly Sloan's number one concern, and he showed it all of the time.

"She's not going to be on her knees that long," Rylan grunted, but he still reached for the pants he'd discarded and did as Sloan ordered, because he didn't want to mar any of that precious skin either.

Once the pants were in place, Reese knelt down and finally, *finally* put her capable hands around him.

Rylan closed his eyes and summoned up the last threads of his self-control. He didn't know how he did it. He truly didn't. When her hot, wet mouth closed around his tip, it was a miracle that he didn't shoot his wad immediately. But he wanted to feel exactly what Sloan had ordered Reese to do—her swallowing him whole.

Reese didn't spend a lot of time prolonging the torture. She obviously knew how close to the edge he already was, because she opened her mouth, made a bed of her tongue, and took him in. She paused, just for a second, when the pierced head hit the back of her throat. Long enough for Sloan to interject another command.

"Open your throat, sweetheart. Man wants to fuck your face. Let's see what he's got."

She laughed again, and this time Rylan felt the

sound reverberate around his cock. Jesus, he was going to embarrass himself.

"Rylan, eyes on me."

His eyes flicked open at Sloan's command, and Reese retreated.

"What?" He growled with impatience. His barely wet dick was twitching with need.

"You do not come until I tell you to. Reese has wanted this for a long time. You gonna ruin that for her by coming too soon?"

They stared at each other until Rylan found his head and his footing. He widened his stance, took a deep breath, and said, "No. I have a little self-control." He gave them both a rueful smile. "Not much, but enough to give you what you want."

He wasn't sure who he was talking to anymore. The two of them were more of a unit than he'd realized. No matter who Reese ended up with—if she ended up with anyone—Sloan would always be there. And Rylan found he didn't care much. Sloan was a good man. He'd pick that steady hand to be at his back any day of the week.

"Are you two done sorting out the rules?" Reese mocked. "If I knew this was going to be a production, I would've picked Beckett."

That got Rylan's attention. He'd waited too long to lose out now. He cupped the back of her head and threaded his fingers through her hair. "Suck," he said.

She sucked. Hard. The hot suction made his eyes roll to the back of his head. Her tongue flicked over his piercing and then her teeth captured it, lightly tugging at the silver barbell and summoning a desperate sound from him. Oh shit. He wasn't sure he'd survive this.

His eyes stayed open as he watched her play with him. Then those gorgeous lips wrapped tight around him and she swallowed him down again. The noises she was making were unbelievable. Delicate whimpers and breathy moans, as she took him deep in long, lazy pulls.

Rylan registered the sound of Sloan's laughter. He looked at the other man with damn near helplessness, wanting to warn him how close he was, to beg him for permission to let go.

Permission. Since when did he ask for permission for anything, from anyone? He would've been angry about it if his dick wasn't in heaven right now, wet and worshipped by Reese's eager mouth.

She swatted at the hand he was using to cup his balls and took its place, squeezing his sac, kneading and toying and tormenting while her mouth tested every shred of his patience. When she released him abruptly, he almost wept.

"I want you to fuck my mouth," she said. "Don't stop until you come."

He stupidly looked to Sloan again. Asking for permission again. Goddamn it. When Sloan's head dipped in a nod, Rylan groaned and shoved his entire length inside Reese's waiting mouth.

His hips snapped in a ferocious tempo, both hands clamped on Reese's head as she deep-throated him hard and fast enough to bring stars to his eyes. He didn't last long. Five strokes. Maybe ten, before his orgasm stormed through his body and spilled into her mouth.

She swallowed it all. Every single drop. The convulsions in her throat as she drank him down sent a shuddering thrill through his body.

"Damn." Rylan licked his dry lips. All of the fluids had just been sucked out of his body. "Damn."

"You okay, honey?" Reese asked with a cocky smile. Her lips were bruised and her voice raspy, and damn if he didn't feel stirrings in his dick again.

His gaze slid toward the silent man in the corner, waiting for Sloan's next command. Reese on the battlefield drove him crazy, but Reese in the bedroom was completely and utterly irresistible.

If he didn't get a taste of her in the next five seconds, blood was going to be spilled.

5

Rylan looked way too tense for a man who'd just shot a gallon of come down a beautiful woman's throat. But Sloan knew exactly what would satisfy Rylan. It was the same thing Sloan wanted. The same thing Sloan fantasized about every spare minute of every day. He wanted to flip Reese onto the mattress, rip down her jeans, and lay his mouth on her until she was crying for him to fuck her hard and nasty.

And that was the one thing that Sloan couldn't ever have.

But this? He could have this. He could watch the woman he'd always loved find pleasure and release. The fact that Reese wanted him here, wanted him near her at all times, even in the most intimate of moments, made all his torture worthwhile.

Sloan turned his attention to the most important person in the room. "That feel good, Reese?"

"So good."

Her smile told him it had been exceptional. She'd always liked giving blow jobs. There was real power in it even though the woman was on her knees. The man was at her mercy. If she'd stopped in the middle of Rylan's face-fucking and asked him to go and kill Connor Mackenzie for her, he'd have found the nearest gun and calmly shot his friend and leader.

"Want more, don't you?"

"Always." A dark look passed over her eyes.

The need in Reese had always run deep. Sloan knew that Jake's ability to let his emotions fly out in the open was the trait that drew Reese the most. It was what she responded to in Rylan, and it was what she feared deeply. That her desire for more—more freedom, more pleasure, more joy—would endanger everyone around her.

It frustrated Sloan that Reese didn't recognize this as her greatest strength. Without her vision, her passion and drive, this haven in the middle of outlaw country wouldn't exist. Half the people inside the walls of Foxworth would have died at the hands of the Enforcers. Well, if starvation and lack of shelter hadn't done them in before that.

"Nothing wrong with wanting more, is there, Rylan?" Sloan prompted.

The other man cast an unreadable look at Sloan, then at Reese. Rylan could clearly sense that the conversation had changed from sex to something else, but also understood that asking questions was a surefire way to put an end to the evening's activities. By the way his recently sucked cock was making a miraculous revival, it was obvious that Rylan would rather have the building burn down than stop now.

"Gorgeous, there isn't anything more right in this world than you getting more." He reached out to cup her cheek, running a finger over her swollen lips.

"There isn't anything more right than me putting my face between your legs and making you see heaven."

"Take off her sweater," Sloan ordered.

Rylan's features grew heavy with lust as he worked the sweater over her head and got his first up close look at her breasts. Sloan's breath hitched too, because, hell, Reese had spectacular tits. Round and bouncy, with bite-size nipples. They were the perfect fit for a man's palm.

"On the bed, Reese," Sloan rasped. "Cup your tits and hold them out for Rylan. Show him how you like to be touched. How rough you want it."

She obeyed immediately, scrambling back onto the mattress and positioning herself so she was facing Sloan. Rylan moved to stand at the edge of the futon but without obscuring Sloan's view one inch. He appreciated that, more than either of them knew.

"Like this?" she asked. Her hands came up and curved around her flesh. She tugged and pinched her nipples until they were taut and erect, ready to be licked, nipped, and sucked.

Sloan's mouth watered. Exactly like that. He wanted. Oh fuck, he wanted. But he was going to have to make do with his proxy. "Now her jeans."

Rylan didn't hesitate. He dropped to his knees, roughly pulled Reese to the edge of the bed, and tore off the jeans, leaving her clad in a tiny scrap of panties.

"How wet is she, Rylan?" The words scraped along his throat.

Rylan ran his hands up Reese's strong, athletic legs. As his thumbs traced a path from inner ankle to inner thigh, Reese's eyes grew slumberous. Her face sharpened with desire as she watched Rylan's fingers slide closer to her center.

"Soaked," Rylan announced when he reached her panty-covered sex. "Soaked through. I'm dying to get my mouth on you, baby."

She tangled her fingers through his hair, tugging his mouth close to her pussy. "I'm dying to have it there."

Rylan reached on either side of her hips and tore the underwear in two with a jerk of his wrists. Sloan was surprised when Rylan didn't dive right in. Instead, he watched as the other man pushed Reese's thighs wide, opening her so Sloan could see every aroused inch of her gorgeous body—the narrow strip of reddish curls on her mound, the jut of her tiny clit, her swollen lips glistening with need.

"I could come just looking at you. You have the prettiest pussy I've ever seen." Rylan voiced Sloan's thoughts, then slid two fingers down either side of Reese's slit. He tilted his head to the side, glancing at Sloan. "You've never touched this particular patch of paradise? Because I gotta tell you, I don't know how you can sit over there watching when you could be over here feasting."

Yeah, it was torture, all right.

Rylan turned back to Reese. "I don't want to eat anything else but your pussy for the rest of my life. Morning, noon, and night. It's all the sustenance I need."

Reese laughed hoarsely. "You'd waste away then."

"I'd die a happy man." Then he laid his mouth against her.

Sloan couldn't see it. Rylan's blond head was in the

way, but he could hear the slick sounds of long fingers pumping in and out of her. Reese's fevered moans told him that Rylan was touching her in all the right places with all the right amount of force.

Sloan knew she was teetering on the edge of oblivion. Her head thrashed against the mattress and her toes curled as she dug her heels into Rylan's back. He'd seen her with other men before, but she was different with Rylan. Wilder, more out of control. Her nails gouged the man's shoulders, and her back arched off the bed as she strained to get closer.

Fuck. He was so damned tempted to join them. He could slide in behind Reese and rub his erection in the valley of her ass cheeks. Hell, he could lube up and fuck her ass while Rylan went down on her. And all the while, he'd be holding her against him, his arm banded around her waist, her neck turned so that he could ravage her mouth while she rode his cock and Rylan's tongue.

Sloan drew a shaky hand over his mouth and fought for control. He valued Reese's friendship, and because their past didn't allow anything more, he ruthlessly stamped out his base desires. Taking Rylan up on the invitation to join them would open a door that would only lead to heartache.

This would be enough for him.

And as Rylan took her over the edge with his fingers and mouth, Sloan convinced himself that Reese's pleasure would always be enough for him.

It had to be.

After her moans died down, Rylan lifted his head and kissed his way up Reese's toned stomach to capture her mouth again. When their lips met, it wasn't in quiet, leisurely postcoital comfort. These two were still tense, quivering with unchecked need. Rylan's erection hung heavy between his legs. Reese shifted restlessly beneath him, her legs swinging up to wrap around his body and pull him close.

Sloan could see her turmoil. She needed more but didn't want to ask for it. Didn't want to come off as needy. Didn't want to even acknowledge that one tongue-induced orgasm wasn't going to set her free tonight.

"That's all you got, boy?" Sloan mocked. "Reese gave you the blow job of your life, and you're just going to eat her out and go?"

Rylan tore his mouth from Reese and swung an angry gaze in Sloan's direction. "Your dick broken?"

Man didn't like having his performance critiqued like that. Tough shit. Reese deserved more than she was getting, and Rylan was holding back. Sloan would have to push them both over the edge while still serving as their anchor when they needed to be reeled back to shore.

"Leave him alone, Sloan," Reese admonished.

She sat up, her body flushed, but Sloan could tell by the fever in her eyes that she wasn't satiated. Far from it. Reese had a big appetite and he was tired of her denying herself.

"Why should I? This guy's been talking a big game ever since he moved into our orbit. He's been telling you he'll be the best lay you've ever had, but all he's done is get his tongue wet."

"I'm being a gentleman," Rylan protested, raking an agitated hand through his hair.

Reese coughed lightly in her hand to cover a laugh,

but Sloan went for the jugular. "Who wants a gentleman in the bed? Reese, you have a new kink I don't know about?"

"No, but I'm good." She slid toward the edge of the mattress.

Rylan caught her arm and dragged her back. "Fine. You want it hard? I'll give you hard." Then he flipped her over in one smooth motion, so quick and easy that Sloan barely saw it happen.

Reese yelped and then struggled as Rylan pushed her head into the pillow that she used for the few hours that she allowed herself to rest. One more move and her hands were clasped at the small of her back. Ass up and restrained, she'd never looked more tempting.

"This rough enough for you?" Rylan growled as he yanked hard on her hair.

Her response was to grind her ass into Rylan's groin. This time it was Sloan who raised a hand to smother the laugh. Or maybe it was a groan.

"Enough talking," Sloan rasped. "Give her your dick or get out."

Rylan snarled but tried to obey, as he'd done every other time Sloan had issued an order. But Sloan saw the problem immediately—Rylan had one hand around her wrists and the other in her hair.

"Then get over here and restrain her," the blond outlaw bit out. "I don't have three hands."

Sloan pushed himself out of the chair and approached the couple. Rylan's grip in Reese's hair loosened just enough that she could turn her head. The desire in her eyes started to cloud with worry as Sloan got closer.

"Give me your hands." His voice was harsh, implacable. He was her rock. Always, forever. Even in this. His brusqueness was what she needed.

Rylan released her wrists and immediately stroked her pussy with his newly freed hand, while Reese jerked and gasped.

Sloan caught her hands, pulling her forward, past the bed so that her upper body hung in the air, held upright only by his hold. Her delectable breasts swayed between them, like the pendulum on the big clock in the center of West City. Mesmerizing and beautiful, the vision held the men in thrall.

The hard-on in his pants pushed insistently against the zipper. Later, after Reese slept, he'd slip away and jack off so hard and long his dick would be raw for days. But tonight, his cock would remain restrained.

"Sloan."

His name. Her lips. The sound was so soft, it was almost a puff of breath. He raised his eyes to hers at the same moment that Rylan plunged inside her.

Reese's mouth opened. A gasp escaped. The hard slap of flesh against flesh filled the room as Rylan powered into her. His thrusts were measured but fierce, and Sloan couldn't help but admire the strong lines of the other man's body. The taut muscles flexing as Rylan knelt behind Reese and gave it to her hard.

Sloan's gaze rested on Rylan's tattoos, the random lines of black text inked onto that powerful chest. Some were done in an elegant script font; others were in block letters. No images, though. Just words that Sloan forced himself not to read, because he wasn't sure he wanted to know more about Rylan than he had to.

"You like that?" Rylan growled. "I've wanted this for so long. Just to push you down and drive into you until your whole world was my dick."

Sloan answered for her. "Tell him. Tell him how it feels. How you like it."

Reese dragged her lower lip between her teeth and bit down until the red plush velvet turned white. "I like it hard. Exactly like you're doing."

Her eyelids started to flutter closed, shutting Sloan out.

"Eyes up on me," he barked out.

Rylan pulled her hair until it was impossible for Reese to do anything but stare directly at Sloan. Her face came close to his each time Rylan jacked into her in an unforgiving and determined pace that went on for longer than Sloan—and Reese—had anticipated. Reese's hands grew slick. Sweat beaded around Rylan's forehead and dropped on Reese's ass. Both of them took on a sheen as the temperature in the room rose at least ten degrees.

And Sloan never moved. Not an inch. Not once.

Not even when Reese's mouth dropped open and she began to chant short, nonsensical words. Rylan's name, Sloan's name, God's name, until it was one rhythmic plea.

GodSloanYesRylanMoreFuckMoreYesMooooore.

Rylan wasn't much better. "Jesus, you feel like a goddamn miracle. You're so tight. So fucking tight. I'm not gonna last. Come, goddamn you. Come."

His command worked as effectively as any of Sloan's. Reese came with a scream, her body jerking and shuddering as Rylan kept hammering into her, seeking his own release. The two of them were mindless, and Sloan was so turned on he wondered, briefly, if he was going to come in his pants.

But his control was greater than he'd thought. Despite the agony in his groin, he kept his cool. Until Reese's eyes fluttered open and he saw the hunger in them, and he realized his restraint was about to be tested again.

She still hadn't had enough.

"Grab her some water," he snapped at Rylan. "And then come back and get yourself hard again. You're not done here."

Reese damn near purred at that.

Fuck.

It was going to be a long night.

6

Rylan woke up naked and alone. He blinked, rubbed his eyes, and realized he was sprawled on Reese's bed. Weird. He didn't even remember falling asleep last night. And he was genuinely surprised she hadn't kicked him out after the sex.

The mind-melting, body-numbing sex.

The best sex of his life.

A part of him wondered if he'd dreamed it. He'd screwed her, what, five, six times?

The amount of orgasms he'd had seemed biologically impossible.

It happened, though. It must have, because he could still hear Sloan's raspy orders in his head, commanding him to fuck Reese again and again and again.

Rylan sat up and arched his back to stretch it. Jesus. He was sore as shit. And pretty sure he'd pulled a muscle in his groin when he'd drilled Reese from behind that last time.

Unwittingly, his gaze moved to the armchair next to the bed. It was empty. But it hadn't been empty last night. Sloan had sat in that chair and watched . . . when he wasn't helping to hold Reese down.

Damn, that had been so hot. Rylan had known Reese was a passionate woman, but now he understood why men got that glazed look in their eyes whenever they talked about sleeping with her.

Last night had been . . . intense.

And he wanted, with every fiber of his being, to do it again.

He lazily climbed off the futon and did another stretch, a tremor of excitement rippling through him when he heard footsteps beyond the door. But, no. They were too heavy, the thump of a man's boots rather than the soft tread of a woman's.

Sure enough, the door swung open and Sloan appeared. "Morning," he said roughly.

Rylan raked a hand through his tousled hair. "Morning." He peered past Sloan's broad shoulders, but Reese was nowhere in sight.

Swallowing his disappointment, he focused back on Sloan. The man wore faded jeans that rode low on his hips and a red plaid shirt he was in the process of buttoning up, but not before Rylan caught a glimpse of defined pectorals and the hard ridges of Sloan's abs. The man was jacked. And a lot more attractive than Rylan had realized, though he hadn't exactly been looking.

But at six-four, with his dark beard and rugged face, Sloan was damn easy on the eyes. Which made it all the more bizarre that Reese wasn't screwing him.

"Where's Reese?" Rylan asked lightly.

Sloan snapped the last button in place, then rolled

up his sleeves, revealing his muscular forearms. "Visiting with Bethany."

Rylan's hand slipped from the top of his head to squeeze the back of his neck. He would've stopped in to see Bethany last night, but the raiding party hadn't reached Foxworth until late. He hadn't wanted to wake her up. Pregnant women needed sleep, right?

Or had she already had the baby?

Sloan must have read his thoughts, because he said, "She's ready to pop any day now."

Shit. Rylan wondered who was going to help with the delivery. Reese? Beckett? He doubted anyone in town had much experience with delivering babies.

Procreation was strictly forbidden in the Colonies; it was the council's way of controlling a population that had once been in the billions. Nowadays, the GC decided how many babies were born, and to whom. The female breeders and male studs were chosen based on genetics and traits that the council felt were desirable, and if you weren't picked to breed, you were shit out of luck. Sterilized like a defective mare.

Although nobody was monitoring who slept with whom in the free land, most outlaws chose to use protection rather than sire offspring. Life was already dangerous enough as it was. Add a screaming infant to the mix, or a toddler clutching his mama's skirts, a six-year-old throwing a tantrum . . . it was too risky. If an outlaw was caught with a child, the latter was whisked off to the city while the former ate an Enforcer's bullet for breaking the law. And if you did manage to hide your kid, there was an extra mouth to feed and an extra body to clothe. Kids were too much of a hassle, at least in Rylan's opinion.

His old friend Arch had disagreed. Rylan had balked when he'd heard that Arch and Bethany were having a baby. The couple had decided it was worth the risk, but look where that had gotten them. Now Bethany was nearly nine months pregnant and all alone, because two months ago Arch had died at the hands of an Enforcer.

So had Kade.

Rylan's throat tightened. The losses were still too raw, a wound that refused to scab over because the memory of Kade and Arch was everywhere. In Xander's grief-stricken eyes. In Bethany's huge swollen belly. He couldn't escape them, no matter how hard he tried to shove the painful memories aside.

"If I'm still here when she goes into labor, come find me," he told Sloan.

The man looked startled. "Why would I do that?"

"I grew up on a farm. When our animals gave birth, I was there helping with the deliveries. Had my entire arm inside a cow once, trying to turn a calf that was breeched. Fun times."

Sloan's lips twitched slightly.

"You're allowed to laugh, you know." Rylan rolled his eyes. "I won't tell your mistress if you don't want me to."

Immediately, the man's expression hardened. "If Bethy's in labor when you're here, someone will get you." Sloan turned toward the door. "Time for you to go. Reese won't want you in here when she gets back."

He bristled. "And why's that?"

"Because she got what she needed last night. She's not looking for a repeat performance."

Rylan slanted his head. "Yeah? And when is she planning on telling me this?"

"She just did."

Sloan's expressionless eyes grated on Rylan's nerves almost as much as the impassive words. He didn't understand their relationship. Sloan and Reese. Queen and . . . knight? Bodyguard? They weren't sleeping together. They weren't openly affectionate. And yet something bound them together. Sloan spoke on Reese's behalf, and Reese, a woman who never let *anyone* give her orders, allowed him to do that.

"What if I have a problem with that?" Rylan challenged.

Sloan shrugged. "What can I tell you, boy? She doesn't want seconds. Tough shit."

"Would you cut it out with that 'boy' crap? You're what, a year older than me? Two?" Sloan couldn't be a day over thirty, and Rylan was tired of him acting like he was older and wiser. He was also damn tired of staring at Sloan's smug face. "And I don't give a shit if Reese wants to use you as her mouthpiece. She doesn't want seconds? Well, fine. She'll just have to tell me that herself."

Not bothering to hide his annoyance, he muscled past Sloan and marched out of the bedroom.

Reese curled both hands around the cracked ceramic mug and breathed in the mint-flavored steam rising from the rim. It heated the tip of her nose and brought a much-needed rush of warmth. She'd felt chilled to the bone all morning, and it had nothing to do with the dipping temperature outside.

"So the raid was a success?" The very pregnant Bethany waddled over to the small sofa under the window.

Reese nodded. "We've got enough guns and ammo to start a war."

Bethany's eyebrows flicked up. "Or a revolution."

"Same thing."

"Is it?"

She didn't even know anymore. Reese lifted the mug to her lips and took a small sip, all the while doing her best to avoid looking at Bethany's bulging stomach. Seeing it reminded her of her own losses, the choice that had been stolen from her. And it reminded her of Arch, the ginger-haired giant who was never going to see his baby come into this world.

Arch had been a good man, an exceptional soldier. Everyone in town was still grieving for him, but none more so than his woman, whose brown eyes fixed on Reese now.

"What's going on?" Bethany stroked her belly in absentminded gestures. "You look worried."

Reese set down her mug. "Nah, I'm fine."

"Bullshit. Something's up."

She hesitated, because she didn't confide in many people. Sloan was the one she went to when she was feeling vulnerable. Sometimes Lennox. Tamara. But for all the others, she put on a strong front. She was their leader, which meant they weren't allowed to see her worrying, or vacillating, or drowning in self-doubt.

She'd known Bethany a long time, though. Shit, it had been almost eight years now. The two women were seventeen when they'd first crossed paths. Where the hell did the time go?

"I did something stupid last night," she found herself confessing.

"Yeah? What'd you do?"

"Rylan."

Bethany snorted. "Ah. So he finally charmed his way into your bed?"

The humor in Bethany's eyes was such a welcome sight that Reese's heart squeezed. In the two months since Arch's death, Bethany's expressions had alternated between completely vacant and raw with grief.

"How was it?" Bethany pressed.

How was it? Reese couldn't even begin to answer that. Hell, she wasn't sure there were actual words in the English language that could describe what went down between the two of them last night.

No, the *three* of them.

Her wrists were still sore from Sloan's punishing grip. He'd held her, restrained her so she was at Rylan's mercy. Sloan's mercy. The memory sent a rush of desire to her core, which only confused her body. She didn't even know who she'd been coming for last night. Rylan? Or Sloan? Or both?

What she did know was that she'd done a very bad thing. A dangerous thing.

Rylan had been as wild and addictive as she'd suspected he'd be, but . . . she'd crossed a line with Sloan. She'd stared into his eyes while she was sobbing in release. She'd clung to him while Rylan screwed her hard enough to make her see stars. She'd threatened their friendship, and for what? A few orgasms?

It wasn't fair to Sloan. She knew damn well that he wanted her—she'd always known—yet she'd selfishly asked him to be there last night, even though it must have been torture for him.

What kind of friend did that make her?

"You're worrying me again."

Bethany's quiet voice jolted her from her thoughts. "I'm sorry," Reese murmured. She picked up her mug and took another long sip. "My head is foggy this morning."

"Good sex will do that to you." Bethany's faint smile was betrayed by the sadness in her tone.

"I guess. Anyway." Reese finally lowered her gaze to Bethany's belly. "I came here to talk about *you*. How are you doing, honey?"

"I'm fine."

"Bethy."

The woman let out a shaky breath. "Okay, I'm not fine. I'm fucking terrified." She had both hands on her stomach now. "I have to pee every five seconds. This kid keeps me awake at night with all his kicking. My back hurts. And I'm dreading the birth, I really am." Her face grew ashen. "What if something goes wrong?"

"It won't," Reese said firmly.

"You can't be sure of that. I could die."

"You won't die, Bethy." She wasn't usually one to offer false assurances— especially when they all knew how fleeting life in the free land could be—but there was no way in hell she was letting Bethany even *consider* the possibility of dying in childbirth. "We have two medics who'll look after you. And the other camp leaders will be showing up in a day or two. That means Connor, which means he'll be bringing his woman. Hudson was a nurse in the city. If you feel comfortable having her around, she could be an asset."

"I don't feel comfortable about any of this," Bethany muttered. She paused, then released a strangled cry. "I can't do this alone! Why the *fuck* am I doing this alone? Arch was supposed to be here for this! He was supposed to hold my hand and mop the sweat from my brow and . . . and . . ." She trailed off, her entire face collapsing.

Reese instantly slid closer and took Bethany's hands in hers. The woman's fingers were ice-cold. "*I'll* be there," she said fiercely. "I'll hold your hand and mop the sweat, honey. You won't be alone, I promise you that."

The assurances fell on deaf ears. Bethany's eyes filled with tears, her dark lashes growing wet. "I miss him," she whispered.

Reese drew a ragged breath and tried to ignore the deep pain in her chest. She dropped Bethany's hands and picked up her mug, hoping the heat of it would warm *her* ice-cold body. It felt like someone was stabbing her heart with a rusty knife, each sharp thrust bringing the same scathing accusation: *Arch died because of you.*

The Enforcer who'd shot Arch had been aiming for Reese. That bullet was meant for her, but Arch had stepped in front of it. He'd lost his life protecting her.

Reese could barely breathe as the memory crushed her windpipe.

"I know you do," she mumbled. "We all miss him."

The tears slid out, staining Bethany's cheeks. "Do you ever miss Jake?"

Reese's head flew up in shock. Nobody in Foxworth ever said Jake's name these days. Most of the new folks hadn't known him, and the original members liked to pretend he never existed.

"No, I don't." The words were wrenched out of her throat, burning it on their way out.

Bethany brushed the tears from her eyes and said, "It's okay to miss him, Reese."

"No, it's not."

"Yes, it is." Bethany spoke firmly. "You loved him."

"Not by the end," she said sadly.

No, she'd loathed him by the end. Fucking despised him. And . . . and . . . goddamn it, yes! She'd also loved him. She'd loved *and* hated him, and she'd hated herself for being able to feel both emotions in equal measure.

Maybe if the hatred had been stronger, she could've stopped him sooner. Instead, she'd stood by and watched as his behavior became increasingly tyrannical. Cruel. Nauseating.

She and Sloan had both seen Jake losing control, but they'd been loyal to him. Too loyal. Neither of them had stepped in until it was too late.

Reese sucked in another breath, but it didn't help. She still felt dizzy, and she couldn't stop the grisly images from flashing through her mind. Couldn't shut out the screams she'd heard coming from her bedroom that horrible night three years ago. Her hands trembled as she remembered opening the door and seeing Jake with Cassie. Seeing the wild look in his eyes. And Cassie's stricken face. The blood . . .

"Reese."

She squeaked when she felt a punishing grip on her chin, when her head was yanked up.

"I'm sorry," Bethany murmured. "I shouldn't have brought him up. But you need to let go of that mug before you cut yourself, sweetie."

Blankly, Reese stared down at her hands and realized she'd been clenching the mug so tightly that the crack on its side had fractured, leaving two jagged pieces between her fingers and warm liquid on her lap and the sofa cushion.

"Fuck," she swore. "Let me clean this up."

Bethany started to get up. "I can do it—"

"No. Sit. I'll do it." She flew off the sofa and into the tiny kitchen. But the apartment Bethany had shared with Arch had an open layout, which meant the other woman could see Reese moving around in the kitchen, could see how shaken up she was.

Without a word, Reese dumped the broken mug into the trashcan, then grabbed a rag and hurried back to mop up the stain on the sofa. Her throat was tight with shame. Not just for ruining Bethany's couch, but for *everything*. Arch's death. Jake's death. Flaunting her naked body in front of Sloan last night when she knew he lusted for her.

She was a goddamn bitch. The way she treated him, it was a wonder that man had stuck by her side all these years.

"Listen, I don't want you to worry about the delivery," Reese said, finally meeting her friend's eyes. "I'm going to take care of you. We all will."

Bethany nodded.

"Anyway." She feigned a careless tone. "I've got to check in with Beckett about a few things, and then I'm heading over to the field behind the high school to check on the crops that Gwen is experimenting with. If you need anything, find Sloan, okay?"

"Okay."

She gave Bethany a quick, awkward hug good-bye, then ducked out the door before the woman could say another word.

On the front stoop of the two-story building, Reese took a series of deep, calming breaths. It didn't help. She was rattled. Mad at herself for falling apart in front of Bethany. She was supposed to lead, damn it, not slice her chest open and display all her fears and insecurities to the people who trusted her to be confident and unafraid.

"Reese," a timid voice called out.

She turned her head to find one of her teenage charges approaching. It was Christine, the quiet fourteen-year-old who'd joined them less than a year ago. Sloan and Beckett found her and her two older brothers living in the woods about a hundred miles south of Foxworth. The men had brought the three siblings home with them, but while Christine's brothers had adjusted to their new camp almost immediately, the girl remained shy and withdrawn even after ten months of living inside the town gates.

"What do you need, honey?" Reese asked.

"I didn't want to bother you, but"—Christine grimaced and then lowered her voice—"my, uh, time came."

"Your time?" Reese was momentarily confused.

The girl waved a hand toward her pants. "Yeah, you know. My *girl* time?"

Ahh. Reese got it now. Fighting a smile, she reached out to ruffle Christine's brown hair. "That's perfectly normal. Remember we talked about it before? Did you use your supplies?"

"Yes. I just . . ." There was a frustrated sigh.

"Are you in pain? Does it hurt?" Reese pushed.

Christine's face screwed up. "Yeah . . . is that normal? To hurt so much?"

"Unfortunately, yes. One of the many amazing perks of being a woman," she said dryly, then slid an arm around the girl's shoulders.

That was all the encouragement Christine needed—the teenager threw her slender body against Reese, wrapping her arms around Reese's waist. "Thank you for taking us in. We wouldn't be here if it weren't for you."

Reese allowed herself a moment to treasure this. This girl and her siblings. The people she'd sworn to protect.

This war she'd started . . . it wasn't simply about destroying the council for her own bloodlust. It was about making the world a safe place for Christine and all the girls who would come after her. It was allowing Christine to have the choices that the council had taken away from Reese.

"Go see Bethany and ask her for a pill," she said softly. "Take half of one, then get a hot water bottle and lie down."

Christine nodded.

"We'll talk more later, all right, honey? I need to go to the garage now to see Beckett."

Christine nodded shyly, then flitted away.

Reese had barely taken two steps down the sidewalk when another voice called out to her. Her shoulders instantly tensed. Shit. Rylan was making his way toward her.

She should've never given in to him.

"We need to talk," he said as he neared.

She kept walking. "Told Sloan to talk to you."

"Didn't take you for a coward."

That got her attention. She halted and swiveled toward him. "What was that?"

He planted his hands on his hips and gave her a half-amused, half-exasperated look. She itched to punch it right off his face.

"You heard me." He closed the distance between them. "You want to tell me off, then tell me to my face, otherwise I'm gonna assume that you're too chicken. Because we both know last night was the best sex of your life."

She forced out a laugh. "Don't flatter yourself."

A feral look spread across his face, sharpening his cheekbones and darkening his eyes. "It was."

Reese swayed on her feet, assaulted by the memory of his hands, Sloan's hands, Rylan's thick cock, the ache between her thighs. "I—"

"Enforcers at the gate!" someone yelled from the watchtower.

"Goddammit," Reese muttered.

Rylan reached for her, but she danced backward. She didn't need his touch right now, even if it was meant to be protective. There were more important things to worry about than whether she should sleep with him again.

But damned if it wasn't the one thought that lingered in her mind as she stalked toward the front gate.

7

As the gates opened with a loud metallic grind, Sloan couldn't fight the growing tension in his body. Couldn't stop from scowling either, though his inability to paste on a happy face was probably why he wasn't the leader of this town.

His queen, on the other hand, was all smiles when she arrived to face the West City Enforcers. Reese could be damn charming when she wanted to, but it was obvious to Sloan that charm wasn't going to cut it today. The team of men that marched into the courtyard wouldn't be appeased by a friendly welcome—they were giving off some serious hostility, which didn't bode well for the longstanding arrangement between Foxworth and the Enforcers.

For years, the town had reaped the benefits of the alliance. Foxworth offered good booze, a warm bed, and, if the ladies were willing, even warmer women to the Enforcers who spent weeks at a time patrolling West Colony. In exchange, they left Foxworth alone.

The bargained-for alliance had allowed Reese to build Foxworth into the fortified town it now was.

The main gate wasn't the only barricade; there was also one at the back, and each able-bodied man and woman patrolled every small space in between.

"Your color's high," Sloan murmured when Reese stepped to the side of the gravel-lined courtyard.

Her flushed cheeks told him that the arrival of the Enforcers had interrupted a seduction. Predictably, one night hadn't been enough for Rylan. Sloan didn't blame him. If Sloan could only pack away his guilt and fear, he'd probably need a full week between Reese's legs just to take the edge off. He'd want to wreck himself on her body, drilling her until they were both unconscious.

"I don't like this," she replied, ignoring his observation. "It's too soon after the raid."

"You suspected they'd come for you."

"Being right doesn't make me feel better."

Sloan shrugged unsympathetically. "Better get to it. They're waiting."

One of the Enforcers had climbed out of the two-truck convoy and was tapping his long gun against the distinctive red stripe along the outer seam of his trousers. Sloan could hardly tell those bastards apart with their buzzed hair and uniforms. They were like toys the council wound up and set off in motion every morning.

Despite her pasted-on smile, Reese finally revealed a hint of her true feelings in the rigid set of her shoulders. Both she and Sloan were well aware that the ten armed soldiers in front of them could kill everyone in the camp if they wanted.

"Is Bethany getting everyone situated?" she asked quietly.

"Her and Nash," he replied, and saw some of the tension ease out of her shoulders.

Since outlaws weren't allowed to have kids, the very pregnant Bethany and the few children in town were forced to stay out of sight during Enforcer visits. They hid in a tiny concrete bunker below the freezer in the restaurant. At one time, it might've served as a cellar for the kitchen, but it was now Foxworth's hidey-hole.

"Good. The last thing we need is another bloodbath."

Sloan nodded grimly. Two months ago, a West City crew had showed up at the gates seeking shelter and aid. Reese hadn't exactly thrown open the doors with glee, but she'd given them a place to bed down along with food and booze. Only problem was, one of them got it into his head that he needed a woman too, and instead of asking, he'd tried to take young Sarah against her will. Another teenager had shot the Enforcer dead, and the ensuing clusterfuck had left Arch dead, along with one of Connor's men.

Charlie, one of Reese's Enforcer allies, had tried to bargain for his life, but Sloan had known that if they let Charlie and the others go, one of them would've spilled the beans and Foxworth would've been torched.

Sloan had itched to kill them immediately, but he'd waited until Reese gave him the order. He'd always wondered if people realized that giving the order was always harder than pulling the trigger. And it broke his goddamn heart, because he knew just how heavily each kill weighed on Reese. But the thing about Reese was that she wasn't afraid of making the tough calls, even at her own personal expense, and that was the reason Sloan would follow her until he died. Why he'd do everything in his power, even if he had to come back from the grave, to protect and help her in whatever way he could.

"Why don't you fuck her and be done with it?"

Sloan turned to find Rylan approaching from his left. For a man that big, Rylan had a boxer's agility, which he'd used very, very effectively to pleasure Reese last night. Watching the two of them had been the most erotic experience of Sloan's life, he realized with a jolt.

"I'll hold your hand if you need it," Rylan offered.

"No."

"'No' what? No, you won't fuck her or no you don't need me to hold your hand?"

"All of it," Sloan answered.

He stepped off the curb of the broken sidewalk and headed toward the soldiers. Rylan followed closely. Both men kept their arms loose at their sides in case they needed to draw a weapon.

"Search it all. I've got nothing to hide," Reese was informing an unhappy-looking Enforcer.

"I'll be the judge of that." He seemed pissed that she was being compliant, but also unsure if it was a bluff.

Sloan got it—people who were hiding things generally didn't roll out the welcome mat.

"Sloan, this is Eric. He's part of the senior guard out of West City."

Shit. Sloan didn't like this. The deals they had in place were with lieutenant Enforcers that outranked the senior guard: Nestor, Hal, and Charlie, though their ties to the latter had been severed the moment

Sloan put a bullet in Charlie's head. The presence of this new guy made him uneasy.

Reese caught his eye and added, "He's aware of our arrangement with Nestor and has assured me that he's not here to change that. They're just following up on a raid that apparently happened at one of their ammunitions depots."

Sloan rocked slightly on his heels, trying to look casual and nonmenacing. At well over six feet, it wasn't always easy. "Heard about that. Must've been bandits."

Eric scoffed. "Right. A band of misfits rolled up to an ammo depot, took a huge cache of weapons and equipment, and disappeared."

"A bunch of bandits tried to rape one of our women a couple months back. We came across seven of them who were ransacking a town about three clicks north of here," Sloan offered helpfully.

"And where are they now?" Eric sounded skeptical.

"Gone is my guess," Sloan answered. "They tend to scurry off like the rats they are."

"And you think they scurried off to rob my ammo depot?"

"Maybe. I can't even begin to speculate about what those assholes might do." Sloan shrugged, but he could tell that Eric wasn't buying the bandit scenario. As he shouldn't—bandits didn't perform coordinated raids on heavily fortified compounds. They searched out the easiest prey, snuck in, stole shit, and ran off.

Eric swung his assault rifle off his shoulder and raised a hand to motion his team forward. "We'll be searching everything," he informed Reese.

"Be my guest, but I'd appreciate it if you'd keep your guns up," she said with a touch of impatience.

"Gates. Main Street. Park." Eric used the tip of his rifle to point out each part of the town to his men.

Sloan gave Reese and then Rylan a warning sign not to release the sarcastic remark that he knew was tingling the end of their tongues.

"You've got a real town here," Eric said, suspicion lining his tone. "When people dig in and grow roots, they start wanting to defend it."

"Is that against the council's rules?" Rylan interjected.

Eric swiveled around, the barrel of his rifle pointing directly into Rylan's gut. "Your entire existence is against the colony laws."

Rylan didn't even flinch. He merely raised his hand and pushed the barrel aside. "Yeah? Sure doesn't stop your lieutenants from popping in and drinking our booze every chance they get."

"I can't control what my superiors choose to do," Eric said stiffly, "but that doesn't mean I condone it."

"And you can't do a damn thing about it." Rylan grinned at the tense Enforcer. "Damn shame, huh? That your boss Nestor won't let you burn this place to the ground? I bet the thought of lighting that match gives you a raging boner."

Sloan almost snorted with laughter.

"Enjoy this place while it lasts," Eric warned. "Lieutenant Nestor won't be there to hold your hand forever."

"Are you guys done gabbing?" Reese muttered. "I'm sure Eric has other towns to terrorize today."

He gave her a thin smile. "No. You're it on my list." But he motioned for his men to move forward, and the search began in earnest.

Foxworth had plenty of nice houses on the farthest edges of the town boundaries, but the square in the middle was small. Along with the gravel courtyard and the park Eric had pointed out, there was one main street that led from the gate down the artery of the town, with two- and three-story buildings on either side. Everyone in Foxworth lived within shouting distance of one another, and the tight-knit physical nature of the community made it easier to protect and defend. It also made the search parameters smaller for the Enforcers.

Eric and his men were well trained. They paused outside each door, sticking their rifles through the entryway before moving in silently. These Enforcers were more careful than the ones Sloan and Reese had dealt with in the past, which reinforced what Eric had warned. The game was changing.

"Think he ever takes the stick out of his ass?" Rylan asked as they lagged behind the group.

"He's too uptight for assplay," Sloan said.

A bark of laughter escaped Rylan's lips, which he promptly turned into a coughing fit when a couple of Enforcers turned to glare at the two men.

Sloan slid a look of amusement toward Rylan. "Surprised I know what assplay is?"

"Kinda. The other night you were pretty resistant to someone's charms." Rylan tilted his head in Reese's direction. "But now that I know what the key is to getting you in bed with us, I'll be more persuasive next time."

"Save your persuasion for Reese. You'll need it."

Rylan shrugged, undeterred by the warning. "Wouldn't be worth it if it was too easy, brother." Then he quickened his pace to catch up with Reese, whose fake smiles were growing frayed around the edges.

If Eric or one of his crew pointed a barrel in her direction one more time, Sloan suspected Reese would pull the rifle out of the soldier's hands and beat him senseless with it. Sloan, of course, would hold everyone back while she delivered the well-earned thrashing.

Rylan ambled up to the front of the search team, pushing a rifle or three out of his way to take a place next to Reese. He was either making himself a target for the Enforcers or providing a buffer for Reese. Either one was good in Sloan's book.

Truth was, he appreciated Rylan's fearless confidence. The man would need it if he wanted to go toe-to-toe with Reese, and the more Sloan got to know him, the more he was becoming convinced that Reese needed Rylan. She needed someone to tease her out of her glum moods and fuck her hard whenever she got too tangled up in that web of worry and guilt.

Sloan tensed up again when the search party reached the last building on Main Street, which housed Christine, her brothers, and a few others. The soldiers had decided to crisscross their way down the street, instead of moving down one side and up the other as Sloan would have done.

Rylan had been cracking an inappropriate joke every few houses—"I haven't seen this many pricks since the orgy we held over at Mosby's camp" and,

"Eric, your ass cheeks are so tight, I'm worried about chafing. You got any special oils over at your Enforcer base?"

Sloan suspected Rylan was doing it mostly to keep Reese from losing it, but none of the Enforcers found his raunchy jokes funny. They wouldn't, because, as Rylan noted, they had sticks up their asses. Hudson, Connor's woman, swore that the Enforcers received all the benefits of being a citizen, including any woman or man they wanted, but these men were wound so tight that Sloan wouldn't have been surprised if they hadn't had sex since they picked up their first gun.

Rylan's jokes stopped, however, when the group walked into the remaining building. Sloan ducked in behind the last soldier and immediately understood the reason for Rylan's sudden change of demeanor.

Some of the Enforcers had gone upstairs, but the building's front room was tiny enough that Christine had found herself crowded into a corner. At fourteen, she was old enough to stay out of the cellar; there was only so much room in that small space, and she could easily pass as an adult.

But that was the problem. She was *adult* enough that every single Enforcer was openly leering at her.

Shit.

Christine had been washing clothes at the sink, and the front of her white dress was soaked. Even though she was fourteen, the wet cloth stuck to her chest, revealing womanly curves. The bare hint of sexuality was enough to make these boys pant like hounds hunting a bird.

"C'mere, Crissy." Sloan gestured for the girl to join him.

She sidled along the side of the room until she reached him. He planted his large frame in front of her smaller one and crossed his arms. A few of the Enforcers had the decency to look away, but one, a blond kid with a scar on his forehead, sneered in their direction.

"They were right. This place is a fucking dump filled with fucking whores." He kicked over a metal pail and the stench of rotted vegetables filled the air.

"Really think a crate of ammunition is going to be hiding under a composting pail?" Sloan asked mockingly.

The Enforcer started to lift his rifle, and Sloan instantly reached behind his back.

"What's going on here?" Reese's voice cut through the tension, but the kid didn't lower his gun. "Eric," she called at the staircase, "you've searched for three hours. Your men are tired. Come down and take care of this."

There were thumps upstairs and then a clatter of boots on the stairs. Eric appeared without delay and took in the scene before him: the trigger-happy Enforcer, Sloan with his hand behind his back reaching for his sidearm, the young woman crouching behind him.

"Stand down," Eric muttered to his soldier, before marching toward the door. "We're watching you, Reese. We know that a unit came out here about two months ago and never came back. I'd be careful if I were you."

"I'm always careful." Reese said lightly. "When you live out here, you're born careful."

"Don't know why anyone would choose this life."

"Because out here we actually have a choice." She gave him her caustic smile, the one a man would see before she put a bullet between his eyes. "We can choose to live how we want. We don't take people from their families and make them live with strangers. We can do what we want, when we want. That's why we choose this life."

"Don't get drunk on your freedom, Reese," Eric warned. "The ammo depot was only scratching the surface of what the council has. A few guns in the hands of certain parties don't mean shit."

"Hope not. We wouldn't want the bandits to get us," Reese replied with a straight face.

Rylan and Sloan exchanged barely suppressed grins as Reese ushered Eric to the exit.

8

Few in the camp breathed easily even after the gates closed behind the last Enforcer truck. The usual laughter and chatter in the community was replaced by tense silence and stiff shoulders as the residents applied themselves to erasing the council's touch from their belongings. Rylan's gaze caught on Reese standing in front of Graham's restaurant, halfway down the main road. Her eyes were fixed on the dust clouds the Enforcer trucks had left behind.

With the enemy gone, her guard was down and the worry radiating off her was so strong Rylan felt it a hundred paces away. He flicked his gaze to Sloan, who leaned against one of the front windows of the rec hall that hosted the town's communal gatherings. Like the one yesterday that had led to the hottest threesome of Rylan's life.

Sloan was staring at Reese with a narrowed, thoughtful gaze, and Rylan stepped off the curb and started toward him, wondering if the quiet muscle behind Reese's orders would give him some insight into how to crack Reese's shell. If Rylan believed that she didn't want him again, he'd leave her alone, but after last night it was going to take more than a few weak refusals to get him to stay away.

His plan to gather intel from Sloan was interrupted when Nash, one of Reese's men, opened the rec hall door and poked his head out. "Got a minute?" he called to Sloan.

"Yup, what do you need?" Sloan asked without taking his eyes off Reese.

"Connor's camp just radioed the inventory of what we took from the ammo depot. Con's on the sat phone, wants to know how we're going to distribute the weapons."

"I'll be right there." Sloan turned to follow Nash inside, but before he disappeared, he caught Rylan's eye and jerked his head toward Reese, who had just ducked inside her building.

If there was anyone who knew what Reese wanted, it'd be Sloan.

Rylan didn't waste time. He strode to the two-story brownstone on Main Street and entered behind her. He didn't bother to knock. Better to ask for forgiveness than permission and all that.

He found her upstairs in her small kitchen, arms braced against the counter as she stared out the window at the unkempt yard behind the building. It was empty, save for a decrepit playset in the back corner. The slide was long gone, but a single swing hung from a rusted bar.

"When you die," she said without turning around, "I'm going to dub you Saint Rylan, patron of lost causes."

Rylan stepped close enough that he could feel the

heat from her body, but far enough away that there was room for her to escape. "How'd you know it was me instead of Sloan?"

"Your footsteps are different."

"Huh." He chewed on that piece of information a bit. He was probably reading too much into it, but the fact that she could distinguish his footsteps from someone else's? That was all the encouragement he needed to stay. "You're a damn impressive woman, Reese."

"Is that right? Because I can tell you and Sloan apart?" She sounded tired, almost resigned.

Rylan experienced a pang of concern. Connor had never sounded like this before, but then again, Rylan's leader had never been in charge of eighty-plus people before either. Con kept his camp small. Even Hudson, his woman, had been an interloper he hadn't wanted to take in.

Reese, on the other hand, threw her doors open to any misfits, wanderers, and beggars that rattled on her gates.

Rylan briefly pondered what it would've been like growing up if there'd been a Reese around when he was young. Maybe then every night wouldn't have been filled with his mother's tears and his father's angry shouts, followed by mournful pleas for forgiveness and hollow exchanges of *I love you*.

"That, and because you've got a vision for the future that few people would ever try to make a reality," he said frankly.

"You and Connor think I'm nuts, don't you?"

"Nah, brave."

And maybe a little foolish, but hell, if it wasn't for

Reese's foot in their asses, they'd still be holed up in their isolated camp, avoiding Enforcers and scavenging for supplies. Reese's plan was big and bold and possibly suicidal, but the alternative was to cower, and Rylan had had enough of that.

She sighed and finally turned to look at him. "Did Sloan send you in here to cheer me up?"

Was that a dig? It kinda felt like one. But it was also true—Sloan *had* sent him. Or at least given him the signal that he wasn't totally barking up the wrong tree by running after Reese.

He searched her eyes for traces of derision, but he only saw fatigue with a side of melancholy. He wanted to scoop this tough woman into his arms and pleasure her until she was too satisfied to frown.

"I'm here because last night was the best sex I've ever had. Because walking away from you isn't an option for me."

She made a strangled sound—half laugh, half groan—and rubbed the back of her hand across her forehead. "Is that all you can think about?"

"Around you? Yup. I fuck and I fight. Don't scratch too deep because there's nothing there."

She snorted in disbelief. "Tell that to someone who'll believe you."

Rylan's brow furrowed. He'd always skated on the surface of intimacy, enjoying the physical nature of sex—the hot embrace, the rough friction, the sharp desire. What he'd just told Reese was absolutely true. He *didn't* feel deeply. He could appreciate it in others, but he'd witnessed firsthand the emptiness of love. What he wanted, and what he could give, was pleasure and nothing more.

"What're you talking about?" he finally asked, feeling slightly off-center that Reese saw something in him that didn't exist.

She studied him for a moment before waving her hand carelessly. "It's nothing. Look, last night was hot, but there's nothing left here for you." She presented her back to him and stared out the window again.

Was that a challenge? Sure sounded like one.

He placed a hand on the counter beside her hips and looked down at the top of her head. Her red hair glowed as the sunlight streamed in through the window. Reese had such a large presence that Rylan sometimes forgot how small she actually was. From this perspective, he understood Sloan's protectiveness a whole lot better.

Speaking of Sloan . . . "Do you need to have Sloan here?" he asked slowly. "Because I don't mind if he watches again."

"No, it's not Sloan. I don't have time for sex."

"Why? You running off to take down an Enforcer troop right now?"

"There's stuff to do," she protested.

"There's always stuff to do. You know, you don't strike me as someone who makes a habit of turning away from things that she truly wants. As you told old Eric out there, the number one reason to be an outlaw is to have choice."

He slipped a hand around her abdomen and pulled her flush against his body so that his erection was pressed into her back. He spread his fingers until his thumb reached past her breastbone and his little finger delved below her navel. With his chin, he nudged her hair to one side and ran his nose along her neck. The blood in her vein pumped wildly in response.

"You have a lot on your plate, gorgeous," he whispered into the delicate shell of her ear. "I'm a simple soldier. A weapon. You point me in the direction you need me to go and I'll execute your mission. I'm not much of a thinker but even I can sense when someone's head is about to explode. You're wound so tight right now, I'm worried you won't be able to breathe."

"You treat Connor this way?" she accused, her anger betraying some of the agitation that vibrated through her.

"Damn straight I would. I'd haul him off and get him drunk or, if he really wanted it, we'd fuck. If I had the choice, though, I'd pick the soft curves of a woman over the hard planes of a man any day." Rylan brought his free hand up to curl around her neck, tipping her head to rest against his shoulder.

"You think sex is the answer to everything, don't you?"

"It's not?" He dipped his knees, snugged his dick against her ass, and ground his hips against hers.

"Did you ask about Sloan because you need an audience?" she taunted.

"I asked because I want to make sure you've got everything you need." Still holding her neck, he reached up to drag his thumb across her lips, then pushed it through the seams. "Suck," he whispered.

Her lips closed around him, pulling him inside her mouth. She rubbed the flat of her tongue along the underside of his thumb, and the lick and suck went all the way to his cock. When she bit down, he almost came in his pants.

"Reese," he groaned as he slid his thumb out of her mouth. "I want you. Don't know why you're denying yourself."

"Because I'm an adult with a shit ton of responsibilities and I can't be spending all my time in bed with you."

They both knew that was a hollow excuse, but Rylan released her anyway. When she sagged against the counter, he almost took pity on her. Instead, he kicked one of the chairs out from under the kitchen table and sat down in it. The slow slide of his zipper caused her to turn around.

"What are you doing?" she demanded.

"I'm hard and horny and since you claim you're not interested, I'm going to take matters into my own hands."

His shaft was engorged and aching. The touch of his rough hand was familiar, but not entirely welcome, because his dick knew there were better, softer, wetter, hotter things in the room. His hand would have to do, though.

It helped a helluva lot that Reese's eyes were pinned to his crotch. With a slight smile, he palmed himself and used his thumb to spread the pearls of pre-come around the sensitive head.

"You know you want me," he murmured to her.

"Keep telling yourself that," she murmured back.

But every second she spent watching him reaffirmed his belief. After all, no one was holding her down while he was jacking off. Sloan wasn't standing behind her, arms locked around her waist, hand fixed on her chin, forcing her to look. She was there because she wanted him, damn it. Because she wanted to watch him.

"I haven't done this in front of someone in a long time," Rylan admitted. "Too many willing people around."

"Why don't you find one of those willing people, then?" she tossed back.

"Because you like this too much." The veins in his forearm rippled as he roughly worked himself. He paused, lifted his hand to spit on it, and then reached down to grip himself again.

Reese didn't take her eyes off his dick, not even once.

Grinning, he tilted his hips off the chair to shove his cargo pants to his ankles. He kicked one leg free, then spread his legs to give her a better view.

He stroked himself, root to tip and back again. Reese tracked every movement as if she was memorizing how he touched himself so she could either play it back in her head or figure out how he really liked his hand jobs. Maybe both.

"What was your favorite position last night?" he asked in a tone that could've been used to inquire about the weather.

"Nothing . . ." Her voice came out raspy. She cleared her throat and tried again. "Nothing I haven't done before."

"That wasn't what I asked," he said playfully. "It's all right. I can't pick a favorite either. It was all too damn good. I'm surprised I was able to get it up so many times, but then I had quite the inspiration."

"Sloan's an attractive man," she mocked.

"No doubt, but we both know I didn't mean Sloan." He reached down with his free hand to cup his balls. He rolled them gently between his fingers and then tugged with enough force that he felt the right amount of pain mixed with the pleasure. "I liked it when you rode me cowgirl style. You've got a gorgeous ass, baby. I loved looking at it, squeezing it. Your hair looked like fire licking along your spine. And I loved watching your cunt swallow my dick with each stroke. Every scrape from your nails as they dug into my knees only got me hotter because I knew you were really lost in the moment."

They both lowered their gazes to his knees. Sure enough, there were deep gouge marks on either side where Reese had gripped him while she'd straddled him. While Sloan sat in the corner and stared at them both.

Rylan's balls tightened at the wicked memory. He pumped harder. "I also enjoyed it when Sloan held you down. Actually, it'd be filthy as hell to have you entirely restrained while we both went at you. How wet do you think your pussy would get then? How wet is it now?"

Reese's cheeks were fiery red. And this was not a woman who blushed. This was pure arousal, and Rylan knew if he touched her skin right now, it would be scorching hot.

Sweat beaded at his forehead and ran down the side of his face. His large frame trembled with the effort of staving off the orgasm that pulsed at the base of his spine. "The real kicker would be taking you at the same time. Can you imagine how tight you'd feel? How full? There'd be no room in your head for any kind of guilt or worry or concern. There'd only be me and Sloan and every goddamned sensation we could wring from your body."

Her lips parted. Her jagged breaths matched the rough tugs on his dick. Jesus. He wanted her to crawl over, straddle his legs, and take his heavy, aching cock inside her welcoming body. He wanted her to seize his mouth in a biting, passionate kiss.

But he settled for her hot gaze instead, stroking to a hard finish as the seed from his body spilled into his hand and splashed his abs.

And not once did Reese look away.

9

Dealing with another outlaw leader was a headache. Dealing with four of them? It was a goddamn migraine. But Reese had only herself to blame for this meeting. Actually, forget that—*Rylan* was to blame.

Her frustration levels had been at an all-time high ever since Rylan's impromptu sex show the other day. She'd told herself that she was inviting the other camp leaders for strategy meetings because she was in a hurry to move forward with her plans, but deep down she knew she was just looking for a distraction. She was so eager for it, in fact, that she'd even allowed Beckett to fly their helicopter—wasting valuable fuel—to pick up Brynn from the coast and Mick in the south, rather than wait for them to make the long drive. Luckily, Garrett, the leader of a small northern community, and Connor, whose camp was nearby, were both less than a day's drive away.

Now she was regretting extending the invitations. For the hundredth time in the last hour, Reese wished she could send everyone home and go forward with her plans using her own people. But that was a foolish dream. If she wanted to destroy the council and take the city, she needed all the allies she could get.

The five of them—well, six, because Sloan was sitting in on the meeting—were gathered in the living area of Reese's apartment, poring over maps that each leader had brought to the table.

Notably absent was Tamara, an outlaw smuggler who Reese trusted with her life. Tam had connections all over the Colonies, but she was currently in South Colony recruiting other outlaws to the cause. Reese wished she were here, though. God knew there'd be a lot less bickering this afternoon if Tam was present. The woman was deadly with a knife and had a habit of pulling one out whenever anyone tested her patience. Then again, if Tam were here, she'd want to fuck Rylan, and that would piss Reese off even more.

"It doesn't make sense to spread out all our resources," Mick was arguing, his dark eyes flickering with annoyance.

Reese gave herself a mental head slap and returned her focus to the task at hand. "Why do you say that?"

He jammed one finger against the map in front of Connor. "We have the location of their headquarters. And your woman"—he scowled at Con—"is related to goddamn Dominik. You said they're still in contact, right?"

Connor nodded, but his expression held a trace of reluctance. "They communicate, yeah."

"How?" Mick demanded.

"Over a sat phone that Dominik gave her when he helped her escape the compound." Connor's features hardened before Mick could ask another question. "Don't get any ideas about using Hudson to get to the Enforcers. Dominik is keeping the colony sweeps away from our coordinates, but he's on thin ice over there. The Commander doesn't trust him anymore."

"I don't trust him either," Brynn muttered. The tall, curly-haired woman was standing against the wall opposite the torn sofa, her arms crossed over her chest.

"Me neither," Garrett said brusquely.

Of all the leaders, Garrett was the oldest. He was in his late forties, with a weathered face marred with burn scars. Reese had never been able to pry any details out of him, but someone had told her he'd been badly burned in a fire after an Enforcer unit torched one of his old camps. Garrett's people were now living up north in a bunker they'd stumbled on. Other than Reese's people, they were the most skilled when it came to combat.

"We don't need to trust Dominik," Reese said testily, "because he's not part of this plan." She turned to scowl at Mick. "And the plan isn't to ambush the Enforcer compound. At least not right now."

"Why the hell not?" he argued again. "We have the guns, we have their location—"

"The location doesn't mean shit if they're not all *there*," she interrupted, resisting the urge to rip her hair out. They'd been over this ten times already. "There are only two hundred Enforcers at the base, but there are hundreds more stationed at the outposts all over the colony. We need to target them before we can attack their HQ. Otherwise the base will send an alert and then we'll end up facing off with the re-inforcements. Tell me, how is that a better plan?"

Mick's jaw slammed shut.

Connor spoke up again, sounding as annoyed as Reese felt. "I'm with Reese on this. You're being a fucking idiot, Mick."

The other man glowered at Connor. "Go fuck yourself, Mackenzie. We've been strategizing for almost a year while you've been doing shit all."

"Shit all?" Connor echoed in disbelief. "I'm currently stashing hundreds of stolen weapons and thousands of live rounds at my camp, you asshole."

"Congratu-fucking-lations," Mick shot back. "You *finally* decided to help your people out—doesn't excuse the fact that you joined this party real late, man."

"Because I wasn't invited," Connor said coolly, his gaze flicking toward Reese.

She shrugged. Yeah, she'd taken a long time before deciding to bring Connor on board, but she wasn't about to apologize for it.

"Don't look at me like that," she retorted, her tone equally cold. "You haven't given two shits about your fellow outlaws in the past. All you've ever done is shut everyone out and hide away in your camp. You refused to take other outlaws in, you refused to lead the people who were already following you—why the hell would I ever include you in something this important?"

His hazel eyes flashed. "Well, I'm leading them now. So my opinion means something." Connor shook his head irritably. "And for fuck's sake, we're arguing the same goddamn point right now, Reese. I'm *agreeing* with you."

She drew a breath, forcing her pulse to steady. He

was right. Why was she condemning him for his past actions? Connor was here now, and they needed to look toward the future.

"We're targeting the outposts," she announced, and the finality in her voice finally shut Mick up. "Once we eliminate the threats *outside* the city, we'll turn our attentions to the ones *inside* it. Yea or fucking nay?"

There was a beat of silence, then four low-voiced *yea*s.

From his spot by the door, Sloan met Reese's eyes and offered a smile. Or rather, the tiny quirk of his lips—which, for Sloan, constituted a huge grin.

"Thank you," she muttered. "Now can we go over these maps and make some actual progress?"

The meeting went on for another hour before Reese kicked everyone but Sloan out. Her temples were throbbing, her patience was nonexistent, and she needed sex so bad she could taste it, though the latter was probably the source of the headache and impatience.

She'd been fending off Rylan's advances for two days. If it were up to her, the annoying bastard would be back at his camp already, but that wasn't going to happen anytime soon, not while Connor was in Foxworth. Rylan wouldn't leave until his leader did, which meant Reese's aching body would continue aching, at least for a little while longer.

Give in to him, whispered the seductive devil inside of her.

But nope. Not happening. She wasn't going down that path again. One night with Rylan had turned her into a crazed animal. Even worse, it placed her in an intimate position with Sloan, the one person who meant most to her in this world.

A part of her was still terrified that Sloan would distance himself from her because of it, but so far, he remained by her side. Where he'd always been.

"Do you think they'll be able to handle this?" she asked after everyone piled out the door.

Sloan rubbed his beard. "Garrett's people? Definitely. Same goes for Con's. But Brynn only has a few decent fighters in her camp, and Mick lost most of his after the last southern sweep."

She nodded. "But we're sending each of them ten of our people. Hopefully that balances shit out."

"Hopefully."

Biting her lip, Reese rose from the sofa and walked over to the window. Sloan's cigarette pack was on the ledge, along with a lighter and a cracked glass ashtray. She didn't smoke often, but right now she was too on edge.

Were twenty people enough to send to the other camps? Or should she ask for more volunteers? She knew the teenagers in Foxworth would jump at the chance to join the ragtag army she'd raised, but she didn't feel right putting any of them in the line of fire. Yes, Rylan and Pike had given everyone intensive weapons and hand-to-hand training last month, but that didn't mean she wanted kids like Randy or Sara or Ethan being sent to the front lines. She'd simply wanted them to be prepared.

She lit a cigarette and sucked on it so hard she got a head rush. As she exhaled a cloud of smoke, Sloan came up beside her and rested one forearm on the window ledge.

He stared at the setting sun on the horizon, the burnished orange tint of the sky. Then he asked, "Want me to track down Rylan?"

She took another deep drag and ignored the question.

"Teresa."

Her spine prickled. She hated it when he used her full name. Only Jake had gotten away with calling her that. Before Jake, it had been her mother who'd used it. Now the honor fell to Sloan.

The damned man knew how much it bothered her to be reminded of the woman—no, the girl—she'd once been, but that didn't stop him from calling her Teresa. He usually did it when she was being stubborn.

"Don't give me that Teresa shit right now," she muttered. "I'm not in the mood. And I'm not in the mood for Rylan either. Did I tell you that bastard jerked off in front of me the other day? I turned him down, so he took matters into his own hands. Literally."

Sloan chuckled.

She narrowed her eyes and jabbed her cigarette in the air. "I don't need you laughing at me right now, Sloan."

That got her another chuckle.

"Fuck you," she growled.

"You should've helped him out." Sloan shrugged. "Don't tell me you didn't get off on screwing the guy."

Which was just another source of anger for her. She hated how desperate she'd been that night with Rylan. Hated that she'd been so out of control she'd needed Sloan to be there. To keep her in line. What the hell did it say about her that she couldn't even fuck without needing a chaperone?

"You're losing control again, sweetheart."

"No, I'm not," she answered through clenched teeth.

But he was right—she was. Control wasn't something she'd ever been good at maintaining. Even as a kid she'd had trouble checking her emotions, her temper, her lust. From the moment she was old enough to recognize what a shit show her life was, she'd harbored rage and resentment that threatened to consume her.

Reese still remembered taking the crayons her mother gave her and drawing pictures of dead council members. GC buildings in flames. Enforcers hanging from the power lines running above the city. She'd hated the council for taking her mother away from her, despite her mother's reminders that they should be grateful to the GC. *Grateful.* Ha. Why? Because they'd let Sylvia keep her firstborn daughter? That wasn't exactly a grand gesture on their part. Every breeder was allowed to keep her first baby.

It was all the babies that came afterward that were whisked away.

Reese never let herself think about the fact that she had nine siblings in the city somewhere. Sired by different studs, of course, but they all shared the same mother.

Her mother.

The sight of Sylvia's pregnant belly used to enrage Reese. For the first twelve years of her life, her mom had been pregnant. Always fucking pregnant. It made Reese sick to see it, and not even the nice little house they were given in exchange for Sylvia's "services" had made the situation easier to stomach. She hated that house. Hated being banished to her room every week when the city doctors stopped by to monitor the latest pregnancy. Hated the depression her mom would spiral into after each pregnancy.

Reese had never seen anyone cry more than her mother. Sylvia cried when she found out she was pregnant. She sobbed when the babies were taken away. She was inconsolable the day she was ordered to bring her daughter to the clinic. Reese had been prepared for it, though. She'd been warned what would happen when she became a "woman." The sterilization process was supposed to be painless, and it was. Physically, anyway.

But it left behind the kind of pain that never, ever went away.

Rage and shame and sorrow rose in her throat now, bubbling to the surface along with the memories she usually tried to suppress. She wanted to scream. She wanted to grab her gun and empty the clip into someone's head, but Sloan was the only person in her vicinity, and she couldn't very well shoot *him*.

"Reese."

His eyes had taken on a worried light. He started to reach for her. Maybe he would've made contact this time, actually touched her, caressed her, but she wrenched herself away from him before either of them could find out.

"I'm fine," she mumbled.

"You're not fine." He cursed under his breath. "Fuck. I knew this would happen the closer we got to executing the plan."

He'd known, huh? Would've been nice if he'd given her a heads-up, then. Over the years she'd told Sloan only the barest amount of details about her childhood in the city. He knew she was born there, knew her mother was a breeder. The rest wasn't any of his damn business, but Reese would have been naive if she'd believed he hadn't put some of the other pieces together all by himself.

And goddamn him for always being goddamn right. Getting this close to taking down the people who'd stolen her life from her *was* stirring up all those old memories.

"Plan's not going away," she said. She ground the cigarette into the ashtray in frustration.

"Which is precisely why you should take Rylan up on his offer. You can let off some steam, regain some of your control."

Yeah, but she needed that control with Rylan too. Together they were too wild, burned too fast. Just like it had been with Jake. No, it was worse. She'd been insatiable with Rylan, and she knew the only thing that kept her sane that night was Sloan there as her rock.

But how many times could she ask Sloan to be there with her when she knew his lust rode under a thin layer of skin? It wasn't fair to him, and frankly, she could *not* lose Sloan. She'd rather be celibate than lose him.

So, no, there would be no dipping her toe into the Rylan pool again, even if the mere mention of his name made her core tighten in excited anticipation.

"No," she said firmly.

"I don't understand why you're cutting off your nose here. You couldn't get enough of him—"

"Christ, Sloan!" Reese exploded. "If you're so into Rylan, fuck him yourself." She slapped the pack of cigarettes into his chest and stomped down the hall-way to her bedroom.

Sloan didn't follow. She heard his footsteps at the front door, and a moment later, the door clicked shut.

Sloan dug a crumpled cigarette from the pack and stuck it between his lips before he even exited the building. He lit up and stumbled down the cracked sidewalk toward . . . toward who the hell knew where. He had no idea what he was doing.

Goddamn her.

No other woman had ever gotten under his skin the way Reese did. He'd fallen in love with her from the moment he'd laid eyes on her, but sometimes he wondered if he hated her as much as he loved her.

He hated the way she made his heart pound.

Hated that just the sound of her voice could get him hard.

Hated that she thought she had to be strong for him.

Most of all, he hated that she'd picked Jake. That she'd asked Jake to rule alongside her. That she'd spent her nights tangled up in Jake's bed.

She'd fucking picked *Jake*.

Sloan drew a cloud of nicotine into his lungs, hold-ing it in until his chest ached. The smoke sputtered out on a harsh cough, and he walked even faster, eventually making his way to the redbrick building that housed the town infirmary. Frank, one of their medics, had mentioned that the generator down there was acting up. Sloan had planned on checking it tomorrow morning, but screw it. Might as well do it now. It wasn't like he had anything better to do.

Resentment burned a path up his throat. He *should* have better things to do. In fact, he should be balls deep in someone right now, instead of withering away in self-imposed celibacy.

Three years. He hadn't had his dick in a woman in almost three years. Not since the blade of his knife had sliced a clean line across his best friend's throat—

He pushed the memory aside as hard as he pushed open the door of the building. His boots thudded on the tiled floor as he stalked toward the stairwell.

He couldn't keep doing this to himself. This torturous self-punishment had to end. His uncontrollable desire, his all-consuming love for Reese ... it had to end.

The problem was, there wasn't a single female in this whole town that interested him. When Jake was alive—when Jake was with Reese—Sloan had turned to Cassie for comfort. The quiet brunette had lost her man not long after they'd settled in Foxworth; Ken had died from pneumonia, and Cassie had grieved hard for him.

Sloan knew she was pretending he was Ken when they were in bed together, but that was fine, because he was pretending she was Reese. The arrangement had worked because they were both using each other. But Cassie was off-limits now. He couldn't even look at her without remembering what Jake had done to her.

Besides, he didn't feel right using another woman simply so he could release all the turbulent emotions that Reese instilled in him.

He'd just have to make do with his own hand. Later, when he was in the privacy of his bedroom. And definitely after Reese was asleep, so he wouldn't have to hear her moving around the house they shared. Then again, if she was sleeping, that meant he'd be picturing her lying in bed when he had his hand around his cock. Picturing her long red hair fanned on the pillow, one silky leg hooked around the thin blanket, her bare breasts pressed against—

"Sloan, wait up."

He halted at the bottom of the stairwell, his entire body tightening at the sound of Rylan's voice. Son of a bitch. He hadn't even heard the other man's footsteps.

A blond head appeared at the top of the stairs, and then the man was bounding down to the basement landing.

"What do you need?" Sloan barked.

Rylan's blue eyes narrowed slightly. "What's wrong?" he asked.

Sloan gritted his teeth. Usually he was better at masking his emotions, so either he was doing a shit job of it right now, or Rylan was more perceptive than he'd given him credit for. "Nothing's wrong. What do you need?" he repeated.

There was a pause.

"Spit it out. I've got shit to do."

Rylan ran a hand through his hair. "Was hoping you could help me out with something."

The anger rose again. He wasn't stupid. He knew exactly what kind of *help* Rylan needed. "If this is about Reese, go harass someone else. I've got a genny to fix."

He took a step toward the stairwell door, but Rylan stepped in front of it. "How 'bout this? I'll help you fix the genny, and then you help me by coming to a private party."

He rolled his eyes. "Yeah? Let me guess. It's a party of three." When the other man grinned, Sloan's patience eroded to dust. "Not interested. Now get out of my way."

Rylan's groan of annoyance bounced off the cinder block walls. Under the flickering fluorescent lights, the man's eyes were an even more vivid shade of blue, as vibrant as the cornflowers Reese liked to keep in pots on her windowsill.

"Seriously, what's wrong with you guys?" Rylan asked in exasperation. "I've never met two people who are so against *orgasms*. What, you allergic to them or something?"

Sloan clenched his teeth again.

"We both know you were hard as a rock the other night, Sloan. That filthy show Reese and I put on for you? You loved every second of it. You *loved* holding her down while I pounded into her from behind. I saw your face. I saw *this*"—before Sloan could blink, Rylan's large hand was cupping his groin—"hard as a rock," Rylan repeated. "So why do you keep putting up a fight? What the hell is wrong with you?"

Sloan pushed that large hand away, but not before the other man felt him hardening. When Rylan smirked, a growl tore out of Sloan's throat. "What's wrong with *me*? What the hell is wrong with *you*, jackass?"

Rylan blinked. "Me?"

"Are you addicted to sex, is that it? You got some sort of sickness that prevents you from keeping your cock in your pants?" Sloan curled his hands into fists. "You can't go three goddamn days without getting any action? Jesus, man, you came half a dozen times that night. And then you got your rocks off *again*, jacking yourself in front of Reese—"

A smile flitted across Rylan's lips. "She told you about that?"

The visible amusement only intensified Sloan's anger. Breathing hard, he planted his palms against Rylan's solid chest and backed the other man against the cracked concrete wall, until their faces were inches apart.

"Why is everything a goddamn joke to you?" Sloan hissed.

Those blue eyes locked with his, then lowered to his hands, which were flattened against Rylan's pecs. "What are you doing, brother?" Rylan's voice was low, curious.

"Giving you what you want," Sloan bit out. "Sex, right? Orgasms? Seems like those are the only thoughts your pretty blond head is capable of producing."

"Fuck you." A heavy hand clamped on Sloan's shoulder as Rylan tried to shove him away. "So I like to screw. Big goddamn deal. Not everyone is as uptight about sex as you are—"

Sloan crashed his mouth down on Rylan's before the bastard could finish that sentence.

The kiss was brutal. Merciless. A hard collision of mouths that drew a harsh grunt from Rylan, a hiss from Sloan. He thrust his tongue past Rylan's parted lips and deepened the kiss, grinding his lower body against the erection straining behind Rylan's zipper.

Lust surged through his blood, clouding his senses, fogging his surroundings. It'd been ages since he'd had his tongue in someone's mouth, his dick rubbing up against a warm body.

"This is what you wanted, right?" he rasped against Rylan's lips. "Is this party *private* enough for you?"

Rylan let out a labored breath. "Sloan—"

He cut him off with another kiss, as greedy and punishing as the first. Rylan's answering growl vibrated all the way down to Sloan's aching balls. One of his hands landed on Rylan's waist, curling over it, digging into the waistband of the man's jeans. His tongue slicked over Rylan's, again and again, until finally he broke their mouths apart, breathing hard.

"Is that all you've got?" Rylan's expression shone with humor, glittered with arousal.

Sloan almost slugged him in that pretty face of his. Goddamn it. Everything *was* a joke to this man. Rylan had no idea how close to the edge Sloan was. One push and he'd topple right over it.

"Don't test me, Rylan." He scraped one hand over his beard and stumbled backward. "I'm in a foul mood right now, so unless you feel like bending over and letting me take out all my frustration on that tight ass of yours, I suggest you walk away."

There was a sharp intake of breath. Rylan dragged his knuckles over his mouth, a mouth that was still wet from Sloan's kisses. Then he dropped his hand, turned toward the stairs, and rapidly ascended them without a word or a backward glance.

Sloan chuckled humorlessly as he watched the other man go. "Yeah," he called out, his smug voice echoing in the narrow stairwell. "That's what I thought."

10

Reese swallowed her annoyance when she opened the door to find Hudson behind it. Sloan wasn't back yet from wherever it was he'd stomped off to, though Reese suspected he was staying away on purpose. She didn't blame him. She'd had no right to blow up at him like that.

"Can we talk?" Hudson asked tentatively.

She had to fight from answering with a sharp no. She wasn't in the mood to chitchat with Connor's woman. She didn't know Hudson, and, frankly, she wasn't sure she liked her.

Con might be able to get past the fact that Hudson was the twin sister of an Enforcer, but Reese never forgot it, not for one second.

Still, leadership meant she sometimes had to interact with people she wouldn't normally choose as friends. Besides that, Connor might change his mind about assisting with the outpost attacks if he found out Reese had treated Hudson with anything less than respect.

"Sure," she said, opening the door wider so the blonde could step inside.

Hudson glanced around the apartment as they entered the living area. To anyone else, it might look like she was admiring her surroundings, but Reese didn't miss the shrewd glint in those eyes as they swept the room. The woman wasn't admiring, but assessing.

"You want something to drink?" Reese offered in a reluctant attempt to be a good hostess.

"No, thanks." Hudson gestured to the couch. "May I sit?"

"Knock yourself out."

The other woman settled on the sofa. Reese remained standing, crossing her arms over her chest.

After a beat, Hudson's scrutinizing eyes turned to Reese, who scrutinized right back.

There was no denying that Hudson was stunning. She had big gray eyes, flawless porcelain skin, and golden hair tied up in a messy twist. Reese could see why Connor had such a hard-on for the woman. What she couldn't fathom was how on earth Connor could trust someone who was so closely connected to the GC.

"What do you need?" Reese barked when the silence dragged on.

Hudson met her gaze head on. "I'd like your permission to let Dominik know about our plan to take out the outposts."

Our plan? She managed to stifle a cutting retort by reminding herself that she needed Connor on her side. Which meant playing nice with his woman.

Still, Hudson's request was so absurd it made Reese laugh. "Absolutely not," she replied.

"I urge you to reconsider," Hudson said in a calm, even voice.

"I won't."

"At least let me make my case?"

Another burst of irritation went off inside her. If this woman thought for one moment that Reese was going to include the head Enforcer in her plans to take out his troops, she was out of her mind.

Play nice, warned the soft voice in her head.

She drew a breath and sat down in the armchair opposite the couch. "Fine. Make your case."

Hudson clasped her hands in her lap. "I'm sure Con already told you, but Dominik and I have been communicating over a satellite phone he gave me when he helped me escape the Enforcer compound."

"I'm aware of that, yes."

"Well, Dom's been doing everything in his power to keep the colony sweeps away from Con's camp, and I know for a fact he's working behind the scenes to take Commander Ferris down."

Reese smirked. "I'm sure he is."

"He is," Hudson insisted. "Ferris has been giving the Enforcers a drug cocktail for the past couple years. Some aggression drug that's messing with their heads, making them increasingly violent and short-tempered."

"Uh-huh. *That's* why they're bloodthirsty maniacs— because of drugs." Sarcasm dripped from her tone.

"It's true. The last time I saw my brother, he was a different person. Snapping in and out of rages, confused about where he was and what he was doing. I heard about the drugging from an Enforcer deserter we came across this summer, and after I told Dom about it, he weaned himself off the cocktail. So did some of his men, other Enforcers he trusts with his life. They're all sick about what Ferris is ordering them to do to outlaws."

That triggered another harsh laugh in Reese. "Right. I bet they cry themselves to sleep every night. Sorry, honey, but you're not convincing me of a damn thing here. I don't give a shit that he's your brother— he can't be trusted. He's the enemy."

"Reese—"

She held up her hand to silence the woman, the anger in her gut boiling over. "He kills people, Hudson. He sends troops to hunt us down and kill us!"

Hudson gave a stubborn shake of her head. "That's not Dom. It's *Ferris*. Dominik believed in the Surrender Law. He used to give outlaws a chance to willingly move to West City."

"Willingly?" Reese scoffed. "Bullshit. Anyone who said no would be executed."

"But at least they were given a choice!" Hudson exhaled in a long rush, then inhaled deeply as if trying to calm herself. "Look. I'm not defending the Enforcers, okay? I'm not defending the council or their crazy laws or the way they view and treat everyone in the free land. All I'm saying is that Dominik is *not* like them."

In that moment, Reese realized that it was more than exquisite looks that drew Connor to this woman. Hudson radiated the kind of strength that Reese appreciated, a fiery confidence you didn't usually find in a citizen. Then again, Hudson was no regular citizen. She was born in West City, but raised on the Enforcer compound. Her father had been a council member, and, before his death, the commander of the Enforcers.

"Dom hates what's happening in the city right now," Hudson went on. "He hates Ferris and the council, and he wants to help us. If we tell him ahead of time which outposts we're hitting, he can make it easier for us. Assign certain Enforcers to certain stations . . . Enforcers who buy into Ferris's bullshit. And the ones who are loyal to Dom will work with us to take out the outposts."

Reese leaned forward in her chair. "As tempting as that sounds, I'm gonna have to pass. I don't trust your brother. Period."

Hudson released a tired breath. "Fine. Don't trust him then. It was worth a shot." She slowly made her way to the door, but hesitated before turning the knob. "I have one other request . . . I'm trying to look out for my brother. I don't care if you don't trust him, because *I* trust him, and so does Connor." Her jaw tightened for a moment, and then a puff of breath escaped. "I told Connor I'd follow your orders, so if you don't want me to warn Dominik, I won't. But that means there's a chance Dom might be at one of the outposts, because he stops in on them from time to time. And if he *is* there, and your attack is successful, I'm asking you to spare him. Take him hostage, lock him up, do whatever you want to him, but please, don't kill him."

Reese arched one brow. Damn, Con's woman had some balls.

"At least keep him alive long enough for me to say good-bye to him," Hudson pleaded.

"I'll think about it." With a shrug, she stood up and joined Hudson by the door. "Anything else you want to discuss or are we done here?" she asked with feigned politeness.

"One more thing." Hudson flicked up a brow of her own. "Beckett told me you're screwing Rylan."

A startled chuckle flew out. "Oh, did he?"

"I'm sure Rylan will tell me about it himself, eventually." Hudson's expression hardened with each passing second. "And when he does, I'm going to pat him on the back and congratulate him for finally convincing you to fuck him."

Reese narrowed her eyes. Where the hell was Hudson going with this?

"But I don't understand his obsession with you, and trust me, I'm not thrilled that he's put himself in this position."

"What position?" Reese asked warily.

"In the position to get hurt." Hudson's tone was flat, disappointed even. "You're not a soft woman, Reese. You're not particularly nice either. I get that you have to put on this big, tough act in order to look like a strong, capable leader for your people, but Rylan doesn't need his spirit crushed by some cold, hard bitch—"

Oh, *hell* no. Reese curled both hands into fists to stop herself from pounding the other woman's face in.

"—but that's also an act," Hudson was saying, her expression going thoughtful. "Or at least I think it is. I don't know if you're a bitch, Reese. I don't know if you're as hard as you let on. What I do know is that Rylan isn't as happy-go-lucky as *he* lets on. He pretends he doesn't have feelings, but he does. And if you hurt him, I swear on my mother's life that I'll—"

"You'll what?" she mocked. "Have Connor beat me up?"

"Of course not." Hudson bared her teeth in a humorless smile. "I'll do it myself."

11

"You try to raid an ammo dump by yourself and get torched?" Connor joked as Rylan stomped into Foxworth's cozy corner restaurant the following evening.

Something was getting lit tonight, that was for damn sure, Rylan thought sourly as he threw himself into the seat across from Connor.

His closest friend had gotten in yesterday morning, but Rylan had barely spent ten minutes with Connor since his arrival. Con had been hunkered down with Reese and the other leaders all day yesterday and today, strategizing the outpost attacks. And last night, he and Hudson had disappeared into one of the townhouses on the edge of Main Street, proving that just because Connor had finally chosen to lead his small group of outlaws, he hadn't changed his antisocial ways.

Rylan knew the couple would've welcomed him with open arms if he'd shown up on their doorstep, but he'd been too damn rattled after that unexpected encounter with Sloan. Instead, he'd had dinner with Beckett at the loft that Beck shared with Travis, then ducked into the little apartment he was crashing in and tried to sleep off his frustrations. All of which were of the sexual variety, of course.

Before, he'd only had to contend with Reese busting his balls. Now he had Sloan doing it too? The goddamn bastard had stuck his tongue down Rylan's throat—what the hell was *that* about?

"I need a drink," he muttered. "Scratch that. I need a lot of drinks."

"Probably not a good idea, man. We're taking out outposts in a few days. I need your head in the game." With unexpected concern in his eyes, Connor folded his hands on the table and leaned forward. "If you need to get laid, you know the door to mine and Hudson's bedroom is always open, right?"

"Yeah, okay." Rylan swiveled to see where Bethany was. He was hungry, thirsty, and horny, and felt like only two of his needs were going to be met tonight. Normally, he was an easygoing guy, but everything bothered him right now, making him uncharacteristically short.

Connor leveled a knowing look at him. "So Reese one and done'd you?"

"Something like that."

His friend lounged back in his chair, and while he didn't smile, the air of satisfaction Con had been wearing ever since Hudson laid her claim on him sawed at Rylan's nerves.

He scowled. If Connor's mouth so much as twitched at the corners, Rylan was flying over this table and laying into him. "I'm about two seconds from shoving my fist in your smug face."

Connor merely shrugged. "Hudson wouldn't like it. What she would like is for you to come for a visit tonight. She misses you."

Rylan waited for his cock to harden while he conjured up mental images from all the times he'd joined Connor and Hudson in their bed. But their faces kept being replaced by other people. People who were pissing him off at the moment.

"No?" Connor prompted when Rylan didn't answer. "Well, fuck. Reese really *did* do a number on you." He paused. "So how was she? Lennox says she's a wildcat in bed."

Rylan frowned, surprised by the oddly possessive clench in his chest. He knew Lennox was no stranger to Reese's bed, but it hadn't bothered him until right this very moment. And it bothered him even more knowing that Len had been with her more than once, while Rylan was shunned after one night.

At his prolonged silence, Connor released a low chuckle. "Seriously? You've been running your mouth for more than a year about getting that woman in bed, and now that you have, you're shutting up? The sex didn't do it for you?"

"No, it did. It was hot as hell," he admitted reluctantly. He was even more reluctant as he added, "Sloan was there."

Connor's brows shot up. "Yeah? As an observer or a participant?"

"He just watched." Except when he was holding Reese down while Rylan drilled her hard . . . but he kept that dirty detail to himself.

"Huh," Connor mused.

Bitterness tickled his throat. "Those two are joined at the hip. Are you really surprised to hear that Sloan is around while she screws?"

"Nah, I'm not surprised. Just find it odd that he didn't join in. I mean, hell, we've all seen the way he looks at her—like he wants to feast."

Yeah, Rylan was more than familiar with Sloan's *feasting* eyes. He'd been on the receiving end of them last night. Right before the man kissed the shit out of him.

"Don't even try to make sense of their fucked-up relationship," he said with a sigh. "It's bizarre, Con. Reese won't make a single decision without talking to Sloan first. And I'm not just talking about decisions like *when should we butcher the next cow* or *should we assign two guards to the back gate, or three?* I'm talking sex, brother. She had to ask for his opinion before she spread her legs for me."

Connor choked out a laugh, which Rylan silenced with a dark glare.

"You know what? Let's drop it," he said shortly. He was relieved when Bethany waddled over to take his order. "Hey, gorgeous. Burger, fries, tallest glass of water you've got."

"No problem," she replied, but her smile didn't quite reach her eyes.

The two men watched her leave. "Think she should be up and about still?" Connor asked.

"Yeah, it's fine. If she's moving, that's a good sign for both her and the kid."

Connor rubbed his forehead. "It was easier when we were at the farm. Remember that little acreage down south? Before we settled in the mountains?"

He nodded. "I remember."

"Way fucking easier," his friend muttered. "Fewer people meant fewer problems and fewer worries. We needed a woman, we went and got one. Survived a long time that way. Kade'd probably still be alive if we'd kept it up."

The mild critique of Reese's way of life, her vision for the future, sat wrong in Rylan's gut. He felt compelled to defend the damn woman. "Sure, and we'd still be hiding, rubbing our dicks to porn so old that it should be fossilized, and waiting every day for a troop of Enforcers to come to our door. The Global Council's not going anywhere, man."

"You're right." Connor gave a rueful nod. "Sitting on our asses doesn't cut it anymore. Times are changing. We're gonna have to change with it."

"You wouldn't be saying that if you didn't have Hudson," he pointed out.

"No question, but that's part of what's changing. And so are you."

Rylan only grunted.

"I see. So does this mean you're done with me and my woman?" Amusement crept back into Connor's voice.

"Yes . . . No. Fuck if I know." He sighed with exasperation. Fortunately, Bethany arrived with his food, and he had something other than Reese, Sloan, and sex to focus on.

After a few minutes of companionable silence, he felt sufficiently in control to speak again. Had Connor's invitation been an idle, off-handed one or did Hudson really miss him? "Hudson need something?"

Connor flashed a rare grin. "Nah, we'll survive without you."

"Maybe Pike?" Rylan offered as a replacement.

"Too much of an asshole. He only likes that pup of his." Connor rolled a toothpick between his lips. "If we need a third, I'm thinking Sloan. He's careful and attentive."

Rylan's gut twisted at that. Sloan belonged to him and Reese.

Wait. *What?*

Him and Reese? Was he fucking crazy?

"I need to get drunk," he groaned.

Just like that, Connor's lazy demeanor dropped away, and he leaned forward with serious intent. "Okay, enough with this shit. You're a goddamn mess, Ry. We're attacking Enforcers in a few days and you need to be focused. Which means you need to get whatever it is out of your system before we leave on this mission, otherwise someone's gonna get hurt."

"I know." He scrubbed a weary hand through his hair. "Problem is, only one person is getting my dick hard these days."

Connor rolled his eyes. "Then screw her again."

The dick that hadn't moved an inch when Connor was talking about a threesome with his woman now stood at attention. Thoughts of Reese, her tight pussy and the fierce bite of her nails on his skin had him burning up in the restaurant. Despite the number of times she turned him down, he couldn't stay away, couldn't stop thinking about her. Adding Sloan into the mix wasn't helping him at all.

"She's not interested," he ground out. *They* weren't interested.

That made Connor snort. "Maybe she needs to ask Sloan's permission again."

"Funny."

"Hey, I'm only half joking. Clearly he has influence over her, so why don't you just talk to him and—" He stopped when he saw Rylan's glum face. "Oh shit, you already did that?" Another snort. "Don't know what else to tell you, man. Guess you can't win 'em all."

Fuck that. He wasn't giving up *that* easily.

Rylan drained the rest of his water, then slammed the glass on the tabletop and scraped back his chair.

"Where you going?" Connor asked, his lips noticeably twitching.

"Don't worry about it." He strode with single-minded purpose toward the door, stopping only to call over his shoulder, "Give your woman a kiss for me."

He found Sloan in the rec hall. The man was chatting with Nash and Beckett, but his expression immediately went shuttered at Rylan's approach.

"Got a minute?" Rylan asked lightly.

"Sure." Sloan gave a nod to the other men, grabbed his drink, and motioned for Rylan to lead the way.

He took them to a dark corner of the room. Beckett delivered a beer without asking, while Sloan eyed Rylan as if he were an Enforcer who'd come to make a dirty bargain.

After they'd lowered themselves on opposite ends of a small, tattered couch, Rylan got right to the point. He figured a no-nonsense man like Sloan would appreciate it. "I'm sorry I was an ass last night."

Sloan shrugged.

"That's it? No *I accept your apology*? No *it's all good, bro*?"

Another shrug.

"Look, I'm sure you've seen plenty of men lose their heads over Reese before." Frustration jammed in his throat, so he tried to loosen it with a deep swig of beer. "One taste of her wasn't enough. I . . ." He trailed off, because he wasn't sure what in the hell he wanted from Sloan.

Did he want Sloan to talk Reese into fucking him . . . or to talk her into fucking them *both*?

"I'm sure she appreciates your persistence," was all Sloan said.

"Really," he drawled.

Sloan's lips curved in a reluctant smile. "Okay, maybe I exaggerated a little."

He had to laugh. "You're enjoying this, aren't you? Watching me chase her around with my tongue hanging out and my dick in hand. The entire town must be entertained."

"I don't think anyone's concerned about who's screwing Reese except you."

"And you." He'd be damned if he let Sloan off the hook.

"You want me to acknowledge I'm as miserable as you?" the other man asked.

He nodded. Because, well, knowing that someone else had Reese-induced blue balls would make him feel better.

Sloan snorted. "We're going to need a lot more liquor before I do that."

"I'm down with that." Rylan waved a hand at Beckett. "Beck! Bring over some whiskey. We need to get drunk." He pointed to the big, bearded man beside him. "It's on Sloan."

Beckett laughed, but disengaged himself from his conversation and sauntered over with a bottle of whiskey and two glasses. "What, I'm your fucking servant now?"

"Says the guy who's serving us drinks," Rylan cracked.

"Good point." Grinning, the tattooed man dropped the bottle in Rylan's hand and then headed back to the small group of chatting, laughing men across the room.

"What's your game here?" Sloan asked slowly, his dark eyes tracking Rylan's hands as he poured each of them a shot.

"No game." He shoved a glass in Sloan's hand. "Figured it'd be nice to get to know each other. We've already got one major thing in common."

"Yeah? What's that?"

"Neither of us is getting laid."

The joke got him the desired laugh. It also succeeded in relaxing the tense set of Sloan's shoulders. "Cheers," Sloan said gruffly, before downing his whiskey.

Rylan drank, then poured two more shots. "So, where you from?" he asked in a conversational tone.

Sloan rolled his eyes.

"I'm serious. Where were you born? City or free land?"

"Free land. Grew up in a camp on the coast."

"You have family?"

"Had some. Lost 'em."

When Sloan tipped his head back to swallow another shot, Rylan couldn't look away from the bobbing Adam's apple in Sloan's strong throat. Sloan was big and tough and mean as a son of a bitch. And undeniably attractive. He had a nice mouth.

Knew how to use it too . . .

Fuck. Rylan pushed the memory aside. He hadn't come here to seduce the man—he'd come to win him over.

Then again, who said those were mutually exclusive goals?

"What happened to them?" Rylan asked quietly.

Sloan's expression took on a faraway look. Then he cleared his throat and poured some more whiskey. "Earthquake," he muttered. "Our camp was as close as we could get to the flooded cities. My ma liked the shore, liked the smell of the ocean. But when the quake hit, the whole area went under. Ever seen a building standing there one second and underwater the next?"

Rylan shook his head and drank some more.

"Yeah, me neither. It was kind of beautiful, in a grim sorta way." Sloan didn't even use a glass for his next shot, just wrapped his lips around the bottle and sucked. "There were twenty people in our camp, including my parents. Sixteen drowned. Me and a few other boys managed to swim to safety."

"How old were you?"

"Eight."

Aw shit. Rylan had heard plenty of depressing stories over the years, gruesome tales of violence and hardship. Hell, his own childhood had been—what was the word Sloan had used? Grim. Yeah, it'd been grim and dark and shitty. But something about Sloan's tale tugged at him. The thought of a little boy swimming for his life while everyone he loved was drowning all around him . . . fucking brutal.

"I'm sorry, brother," Rylan murmured.

Sloan's chuckle was low and harsh. "Nothing to be sorry for. You didn't cause that quake."

"I know, but—" He stopped when he noticed Sloan's eyes had gone veiled again. Shit. He was supposed to be winning this man over to his side, not bumming them both out. "So when did you meet Reese?" he asked, hoping to steer the subject somewhere safer.

Those broad shoulders lifted in a shrug. "Four, no, almost five years ago. Ran into her on the road."

"She was alone?"

"Naw, she had people, strays she'd picked up along the way. Bethy and Arch. Nash. Cole."

"Were you alone?"

It was supposed to be another harmless question, but Sloan instantly stiffened. "No. I wasn't."

Rylan snapped into damage control mode. Maybe if he revealed some of his own secrets, Sloan would relax again.

"I wasn't alone either when I first met Con. Pike and I were roaming the colony, screwing around and getting into trouble. Before that, we were at an army camp, training recruits." He grinned. "That's where I got my cock pierced. And here's a tip—"

Sloan chuckled.

The grin widened. "No pun intended. But yeah, a tip—you ever want to get your cock pierced, make sure you're drunk when you do it. Hurts like a motherfucker."

"And the tats? Did those hurt too?"

Rylan blinked, momentarily confused by the question, until he remembered that this man had seen him shirtless. Of course Sloan had noticed the tattoos on his chest. "Nah, I didn't mind the needle. Got me hard, if I'm being honest. I like a side of pain with my pleasure."

"I've noticed," Sloan said dryly.

The air turned thick between them. He wondered if Sloan was remembering the way Rylan had commanded Reese to scratch harder, bite harder, ride him harder.

The glint of heat in Sloan's dark eyes said yes, he was absolutely thinking about that.

Rylan wrenched the bottle from the other man's hand and swallowed several mouthfuls that joined the hot burn already eddying in his stomach. Fuck, he was drunk. But not wasted. He could still think clearly. Still speak without slurring as he said, "Sorry I got in your face that night."

"Sorry I kissed you," came the brusque reply.

"I'm not. Reese keeps turning me down."

A laugh popped out of Sloan's mouth. He had to be drunk himself, because Rylan had never heard such deep, genuine laughter from the guy. "What, so I'm better than nothing?"

"Nah, you're at least two steps up from nothing," Rylan joked, but truthfully, Sloan's kiss had been so damn scorching, he felt like the soles of his feet were still burning.

"You're not so hot in bed either," Sloan mocked.

"The fuck I'm not. I went five times the other night."

"So?"

"So? That's a goddamn superhuman performance."

"If you say so."

Rylan hesitated, wondering if he was taking them down a dangerous path again. But the question had been biting at his tongue for days now, and the whiskey was loosening said tongue. "Why didn't you join in? You afraid to touch my dick?" His groin tightened at the thought of Sloan's big hand wrapped around him.

"Not particularly."

"Are dicks a turnoff for you?" Rylan pushed.

"Haven't been in the past."

"So it's me."

"Never said that."

"I give damn good head." He waggled his eyebrows. "And not just to the ladies."

Sloan smirked. "Sounds like a lot of drunken boasting."

"Sounds like you need a replay."

"You don't have a partner," Sloan pointed out.

"Not true."

"Yeah? How so?"

Their gazes locked for one long moment.

The banked heat looked familiar—Rylan saw it every time Sloan was around Reese—and he knew the same look was mirrored in his own eyes right now.

Shit, they were absolutely going down a dangerous path. Yet even knowing that, he couldn't stop the three words that slipped from his lips.

"I have you."

12

Something perverse was driving Sloan, something hot and twisted and fueled by a primal instinct he didn't usually indulge in. The people of Foxworth relied on him to be dependable and steady. He was Reese's bodyguard, her silent killer, her unshakable support.

Rylan, on the other hand, was good-humored and had a quick and ready smile for everyone. It was that charm that drew Reese to him against her better judgment, and damned if it didn't appeal to Sloan too.

I have you.

The words hung in the air between them, triggering a jolt of heat in Sloan's groin. One he was damn tired of denying. "That right?" he said roughly.

Rylan took a leisurely swallow of his whiskey and stared back in a long, deliberate manner. "Reese isn't the only one who needs a good dicking."

Sloan set down his shot glass. Then he slid off the couch and headed for the door.

He was ducking past the doorway when Rylan's footsteps caught up with him. Wordlessly, the two men exited the building.

This was a bad idea. Sloan knew that. But he was drunk enough not to care, and so turned on he couldn't think straight.

Neither of them spoke as they walked toward the two-story brick building that Sloan called home. The bottom floor used to be a general store, but all the shelves had been raided long before Reese's people had settled in town. Upstairs was the apartment that Sloan shared with Reese.

He didn't know if she was home and didn't care if she was. His dick was rock hard, his vision nothing but a lust-filled haze. He threw open the bedroom door and stalked inside. Rylan had barely crossed the threshold before Sloan pressed the blond man up against the wall.

Screw it. Why should Reese get to have all the fun?

His mouth slanted over Rylan's. The kiss was hungry, angry, brutal. It wasn't like the smooth touch of a woman. Rylan's hands were equally rough, his grip on Sloan's waist punishing.

He didn't have to hold back here, Sloan realized. There wasn't any tender skin he had to worry about marking up. There wasn't any move he could make that Rylan couldn't match. They tore at each other's clothes, ripping the offending items off without a care for the buttons or zippers or snaps.

When Sloan heard a gasp and then a startled curse, he broke away long enough to see Reese in the doorway. Her eyes were wide and confused as she took in the sight of two naked men mauling each other against the wall.

He let out a low, dirty chuckle and then licked a

hot stripe down Rylan's neck, all the while watching Reese.

"So you'll fuck him but not me, is that it?" She directed the puzzled question to Sloan.

"Pot meet kettle," he muttered before placing his mouth at the spot of skin where Rylan's neck curved into his shoulder.

Rylan's hands drifted down to Sloan's ass. Without looking at Reese, he squeezed hard enough to make Sloan groan, then rasped, "You had your chance, gorgeous."

"You two are drunk," she accused.

"Not even a tiny bit," Sloan lied as he ground his lower body against Rylan's. Their erections brushed against each other, and he almost came right then.

"Bullshit. Your eyes are glassy."

Rylan tossed a wicked grin over his shoulder. "Either walk away, or sit down and be quiet. You're distracting us with all your yapping."

Her brown eyes flashed, but neither man paid any more attention to her. Sloan crushed his mouth over Rylan's again, his tongue stealing inside.

They grappled with each other all the way to the bed. They weren't fighting for dominance but struggling against an intense, physical urge toward a climax Sloan had known was coming from the moment he'd kissed this man yesterday.

Rylan's body rubbed against his own as they crashed to the mattress. For once in his life, as another man's muscular chest was pressed tight to his, as hair-roughened legs dragged against his thighs, he wasn't entirely sure which direction to take. Kissing

Rylan was good and hot, but it was a snack when Sloan was hungry for a meal.

After years of restraint, he couldn't make up his mind about what he wanted first. His mouth on Rylan's cock? Rylan's tongue on him? The tight sleeve of Rylan's ass?

The other man made the decision for him by sliding down Sloan's body to kneel at the end of the bed.

"You might want to move over there, gorgeous." Rylan motioned to the chair near the bed. "You'll get a better view of the action."

Without a word, Reese sat down.

Sloan wasn't surprised that she'd stayed to watch them. She was drawn to this type of feral behavior, to the wild recklessness of others that she tried so hard to stifle in herself.

He locked eyes with her as she settled on the chair.

Fuck, he would've liked if she'd settled on his *face*. If she'd taken the choice out of his hands and placed her wet pussy over his mouth. That would've been perfect. Reese's sweetness on his tongue while Rylan sucked him off? Jesus. At the filthy thought, Sloan grew harder than the rods they used to support the town gates.

Rylan grinned as he drew Sloan's long, eager cock in his hands. The throbbing shaft formed a tense arrow of need pointing straight to Rylan's mouth.

The hot wash of breath on his dick had Sloan tightening his hands on the thin mattress. Something dark and aggressive hung in the air as he awaited Rylan's next move.

Rylan gripped Sloan's cock, rubbing it without lubrication even though there was a bead of fluid at the tip. He left it there, like a tease.

The rough gesture had Sloan baring his teeth. "You know what you're doing?" he growled.

A smirk tipped up the corners of Rylan's lips. "Better than you, I'd bet."

"Doubt it." Sloan was choosy about his partners, but there'd definitely been a man in the mix here and there. He usually preferred women, but tonight he needed *this*—the hot male mouth that closed over his cock and nearly swallowed it whole on the first pass.

Everything about women was soft and small, and Rylan was none of those things. No, Rylan was hard and built. His back and shoulder muscles were clearly defined and they flexed and bunched as he bent over Sloan's body. A woman might enjoy his blond hair or wicked grin. Sloan admired Rylan's strength. The purposeful, knowing movement Rylan utilized toward a specific goal, and right now, the man was applying himself to sucking Sloan off with a familiar fierce determination.

The wet suction sent an electric shock down to Sloan's toes. But he wasn't ready. Not yet. He was going to drag this out, because there was no need for restraint here. No worrying about striking the wrong place at the wrong time with too strong of a thrust.

He levered himself up on his elbows and wrapped his hand around the back of Rylan's neck. The other man lurched back as far as Sloan allowed him.

"You thinking about replacing me with Reese?" Rylan's voice had taken on a harsh drawl, a side effect from the throat fucking. Reese had talked like that all day after Rylan had had her. And Sloan's dick had ached for a whole week afterward, thinking about what'd it feel like if it were *his* dick down *her* throat.

But right now? That fantasy hadn't even occurred to him. He looked down at the callused hand wrapped around him, and then into Rylan's eyes.

"Last thing on my mind is replacing you with Reese."

Rylan stroked Sloan's length again, bringing his hand up to close a fist around the cockhead and then slide it down to the root. His mouth provided the lube, but the caress was still on the violent side.

"Yeah?" Rylan gave a knowing smile. "Then that means you're thinking about Reese sitting on your face, fucking herself on your tongue."

Sloan's traitorous cock jumped in the other man's fist.

A strangled sound came from Reese, but he forced himself not to look at her. It was one thing to imagine her whipping off her clothes, throwing a lithe leg over his head and pinning her knees on either side of his head. It was one thing to dream of her pretty pink lips glistening with her need and hear her sigh his name as she ground down on his face. But it was an entirely other thing for it to actually happen.

He took a deep shuddering breath to prevent himself from ordering—no, *begging*—Reese to come and join them.

"No, I'm good," he muttered in response to the taunt.

Rylan's expression transformed into one of evil delight. Still twisting, gripping, and stroking, he spoke casually, as if narrating a scene from a book. "I like your vision of me sucking you off while Reese rides your face, but I think we'd all like it more if we were both inside her. Would you want her pussy or her ass?"

The fantasy of the three of them moving slick and hot against each other roared through Sloan's mind. Jesus. Enough talking. He tightened his grip around Rylan's neck and urged the kneeling man closer. Warm lips opened to take him in again, straight teeth scraping against his sensitive skin. He raised his pelvis and then used the power in his thighs and hips to thrust down Rylan's throat in swift, even strokes.

Reese let out a whimper.

Rylan took every plunge of Sloan's cock with ease. His cheeks hollowed and his throat swelled. His hand cupped Sloan's balls, knowing exactly how brutal he could be when squeezing the tight sac.

Sloan couldn't take it anymore. It was all a blur of wet suction and heat until the light winked out and he shut his eyes. He jerked back but Rylan followed him, taking it all in, swallowing him fully until Sloan was utterly spent.

"Jesus," Reese whispered.

He rolled his head to the side to see her eyes shining bright like coins.

Rylan stood up, his face flushed and lips glossy. He swiped a hand across his mouth, smearing Sloan's come across his cheek. Reese's gasp made him chuckle softly.

"You ready to stop fighting this?" Rylan drawled, stalking toward her like a beast of prey.

She didn't move, pinned to the chair by either Rylan's need or her fevered lust. Both maybe. Then she opened her mouth, but her response—whatever it may have been—was cut short by a knock on the door that startled them all.

Sloan quickly hauled himself off the bed. Whoever

was behind that door had to have heard the husky groans and low growls coming out of this room, which meant there was a good reason for the interruption.

"What is it?" he barked at the closed door.

"Sorry, man." It was Nash and he sounded miserable. "We've got a broken pipe over at the restaurant. We tried to repair it but the damn thing keeps leaking."

Sloan stifled his annoyance. But maybe this was a blessing in disguise. His heart was still pounding uncontrollably, every muscle in his body still coiled tight. And he was already hardening again despite the intense climax that had just rendered him limp and mindless.

He needed to come again.

But . . . if he stayed here, if he came again . . . there was a terrifying chance it might be with Reese.

He cleared his throat and addressed Nash. "I'll be right there."

Reese watched in dazed silence as Sloan picked up his discarded clothing and started to get dressed. Her gaze zeroed in on his bare ass. The tight, perfect ass that made her fingers tingle with the urge to squeeze it.

She'd seen Sloan naked countless of times before. There was no such thing as modesty in the free land— sometimes you had no choice but to take your clothes off in front of another outlaw, especially when you were traveling and there was no privacy to be had.

So yes, she'd seen Sloan naked. She'd admired the hard planes of his body. His long, powerful legs and sculpted arms. His muscular chest and impossibly broad shoulders. His ass . . . God, that ass.

But this was the first time she'd seen him naked in a sexual context. The first time she'd seen him come. A shiver flew up her spine. Christ. She'd just seen him come in another man's mouth.

And she'd never been more turned on in her life.

"Sloan," Rylan started, his voice gruff.

"Gotta go," was the terse reply, and then Sloan slid through the door and latched it shut behind him.

After a beat, Rylan turned his frustrated gaze toward Reese. "You taking off too?" he muttered.

Slowly, she shook her head, causing his blue eyes to narrow as he stared at her face. He searched, studied, probed, for what felt like hours, and Reese saw it the instant that understanding dawned on him.

"Fucking hell." He started to laugh. "It's not just him."

She swallowed hard. "I don't know what you're talking about."

Still chuckling, he sat on the edge of Sloan's bed, laying one hand flat on the tousled sheets. He was completely unbothered by both his nudity and the thick erection rising toward his navel.

"I thought it was one-sided," he said slowly. "I thought it was *his* issue. Wanting you so badly it drives him mad, but not being able to have you. I figured you shot him down." He tipped his head thoughtfully. "But I'm wrong, aren't I? You're as hot for him as he is for you."

She tried to summon a denial, but her mouth stayed stubbornly closed.

"Why won't you fuck him, gorgeous?" Rylan sounded perplexed. "Why won't he touch you?"

Because . . .

She swallowed again. Harder this time.

Because . . .

Damn it, no. She didn't want to think too hard about the answer to that question. She didn't want to slash open all those old wounds that—

Because Jake won't let us.

Fuck. *Fuck.* And there it was, the pathetic truth that both she and Sloan had never, ever spoken out loud.

She'd acknowledged her attraction to Sloan only once—four years ago, when she and Jake had been tangled together in his bed, recovering from a round of hot, sweaty sex that'd left them both breathless. In a low voice, Jake had admitted that Sloan wanted her. Then he'd asked her point-blank if she felt the same way.

Reese had whispered yes.

That was the night she discovered that Jake didn't like to share.

He'd completely lost it. He'd growled that as long as he was alive, no other man would lay a hand on her. His eyes had been wild, his dick harder than stone as he'd proceeded to show her that he was the only man she would ever need, the only man who could ever satisfy her.

Sick as it might have been, Reese couldn't deny that his possessive, feral response had excited her. *Everything* about Jake had excited her. After he'd taken her that night, he'd made her promise that she would never touch Sloan.

And even though Jake had been dead for three

years, it was a promise Reese was still keeping. But for a different reason, this time.

"You know what? It doesn't matter why," Rylan said quietly. "C'mere, baby. I'll give you the answers you need."

His blue eyes warmed as he extended his hand to her, and Reese wondered what he'd seen on her face to make him soften like that. Guilt? Fear? Regret? Whatever it was, she didn't like the thought of Rylan getting such a candid peek behind the carefully constructed mask that she was usually much better at maintaining.

"The answers I need . . . ?" she echoed warily, because what the hell did he mean by that? *He* was the one asking all the questions, poking at old scabs he had no business poking.

Despite her irritation, her confusion, her reluctance, she found herself rising from the chair and approaching the bed. She stopped when they were a foot away, so he reached for the bottom of her oversized sleep shirt and pulled on the fabric to erase the rest of the distance between them.

His fingers slowly dragged the thin material up to her waist and higher. When it snagged on the undersides of her breasts, he murmured, "Take this off."

She obeyed on instinct, slipping the shirt over her head and then letting it drop to the hardwood floor. She liked a bossy man in the bedroom, because in all other aspects of her life, she was in charge. Not having to make decisions when it came to sex was a relief.

She wasn't wearing anything underneath, and one of Rylan's hands immediately moved between her legs, his knuckles grazing her clit. Her aching, very swollen clit, a painful result of the decadent man show she'd witnessed.

Her breathing quickened as she remembered the sight of Sloan's huge cock tunneling in and out of Rylan's mouth. The way Rylan's cheeks had hollowed as he sucked as deep as he could. Sloan's husky grunt of release as he spilled in Rylan's mouth . . . Rylan's hungry moan as he swallowed every drop.

"I'll give you your answers," he said again, those same cryptic words she couldn't decipher. He leaned toward the floor, grabbed one pant leg of his jeans, and dragged the faded denim toward him. Then he slid his hand in the back pocket and emerged with a condom, which he wasted no time rolling onto his very prominent erection.

"You want to know what his lips feel like, don't you?" Rylan prompted.

He tugged her onto his lap so her knees were straddling his broad thighs. His erection rubbed her throbbing core, and when she hissed at the contact, he clutched her ass cheeks and brought her closer. Through the condom she felt the silver barbell at the tip of his cock scraping against her clit with each gentle glide.

"His lips are firm," Rylan whispered, and then he brought his own lips to her neck and sucked on the delicate tendons there. "Hard. Warm."

He kissed her jaw, a gentle brush of heat, before licking his way to her ear. She shuddered when he captured her ear lobe between his lips. "You want to know what his hands feel like?" He tipped his head up, searching her face.

Reese found herself nodding. Helpless.

"His hands are rough." Rylan's palms traveled down to her breasts. "Dominating." He squeezed hard enough to make her gasp, the calluses on his fingertips scratching her hypersensitive nipples. "But maybe with you, those hands would be gentle." Just like that, Rylan loosened his grip and swept his thumbs in a barely-there caress over the tips of her nipples.

Reese whimpered with pleasure. God. She didn't even know what was turning her on more—Rylan's capable hands, or his description of Sloan's.

"You want to know what his dick feels like?"

She gave another wordless nod, and before she could blink, Rylan lifted her hips up, aligned his erection beneath her, and impaled her on it.

Reese cried out, but not in pain. She was soaking wet, so lust-drenched that he slid in with ease. No foreplay necessary, no sweet words. Only his thick shaft filling her, the piercing hitting a spot deep inside. It felt as good as she remembered.

As she grinded slowly against him, his eyes glazed over for a moment before focusing intently. "Where were we?" he rasped. "Right. Sloan's dick."

He gripped his hips to still her, but rotated his own in a circular motion that curled her toes and made her knees wobble even though she was sitting down.

"It's harder than steel," he told her. "Thick. Pulses when it hits your tongue. It tastes . . ." He paused for a moment, and then his lips stretched in a filthy grin. "Here. You can find out for yourself how it tastes."

And then he kissed her, a long, drugging kiss, and

holy hell, she *could* taste it. Her pussy clenched painfully, her clit screaming with excitement as she tasted Sloan's salty essence on Rylan's tongue. It was the hottest thing she'd ever experienced, and for a second she felt like she was tasting Sloan for real. Not through Rylan, but directly from the source as he groaned her name and came in her mouth. It was both exhilarating and terrifying, spurring her hips to move faster, to ride him harder.

He wrapped both arms around her, his palms sliding up and down her sweat-soaked back. "Jesus Christ," he choked out. "You're so tight."

She bore down on him, pushed at his chest so he was falling onto his back, and rode him even harder. Her back arched as pleasure soared through her, the hot waves skating from her fingers to her toes, her clit to her nipples. It felt so good she could hardly see, scarcely breathe.

Rylan gazed up at her with glittering blue eyes. "If you're pretending it's him you're riding, stop," he commanded.

The sharpness of his tone caught her off guard. Reese didn't know if she should apologize, but truth was, she wasn't sure if she was even picturing Sloan. She felt his presence here in this room with them, but not in place of Rylan. *Along* with him.

Her worries faded when Rylan's lips curved in another grin. "You can pretend he's here, baby. As long as you remember that I'm here too. We're both here. My cock is inside you, Reese. It fucking belongs inside you. We can give Sloan your ass, how about that? Keep riding me and pretend Sloan is behind you, drilling your ass."

A moan slipped out.

"You like that?" He chuckled.

She couldn't find the strength to answer, or even to move anymore. She collapsed on his chest and Rylan took over, thrusting upward again and again, hitting that sweet spot, drawing moan after moan from her lips. One strong hand was on her back, the other tangled in her hair. He pulled hard on the long strands, and it was just what she needed—that sting of pain. In her life, there was no pleasure without pain.

The orgasm barreled through her in a violent rush, and Rylan bit her shoulder hard, bringing another jolt of pain and prolonging the blissful sensations. She was a shuddering, sweaty, whimpering mess as she lay on top of him, and he held her through the orgasm, his thrusts never slowing down, not even once.

"Coming," he croaked, then gave one last thrust and trembled beneath her.

Reese opened her eyes to look at him. His cheeks were flushed, lips slightly parted, the muscles in his face taut as he grunted in release. She kissed him again, this time tasting not just Sloan, but Rylan too. His hunger, his need, his recklessness.

Then she closed her eyes again to savor the magic the three of them had made, if only in her mind.

13

Sloan was right about one thing—sex *did* clear her mind. As she sat hunched over maps with the other camp leaders, Reese was grateful she'd eased some tension yesterday, otherwise she might've choked someone by now. After agreeing in the last meeting that they'd attack the outposts, they were now squabbling like toddlers over who was going to take down what.

"We've got fourteen people," Mick argued. "We can take the northeast positions and the one on the upper coast. There's no way you can cover that much ground, Brynn."

"I've got more people. Plus, I know the region better and have contacts with all of the camps along the coast. It makes more sense for me to take those," Brynn said with exasperation.

Garrett sat sharpening his knife on a whetstone. In another man, it would've come off as silly posturing, but the action paired with Garrett's grim expression signaled that it was time for Reese to move along.

She picked up the blue painted bullets Sloan had

slipped her before the meeting started and placed two of them on the map. "Based on the intel we've gathered, there are only two outposts to the northeast. The council maintains a squadron of a couple hundred in the city and combined with the walls, they haven't felt the need to fortify these remote outposts too heavily. Mick, I know you're plenty capable of taking out all of the coastal stations but this is right in your backyard."

She held her breath while she waited for Mick's answer. He still clung to the belief that they should take all the ammunition and make one strong, concentrated push at the city. But the group had voted for Reese's idea, and a year's worth of planning had gone into identifying the outposts, tracking the Enforcers that rotated in and out of the guard towers, quantifying the manpower and weaponry they'd go up against. To assault the council would mean at least another year of planning, and no one was interested in that.

As the silence wore on, Sloan shifted restlessly behind her. Mick's gaze flicked over Reese's shoulder and then back to Reese. "Yeah, we'll be able to handle them."

"Good to have you on board," she replied dryly, then continued as if there hadn't been any hesitation. "If you go before the predawn guard changes, you'll be able to get in and out without alerting the city. The Enforcers will be tired and ready to get the hell out of there."

She pointed to the block east of the city. "Brynn, you'll take the coast. There are three outposts there." Reese set down the red shells at four points along the coast. "This one in the northeast and then two along the bay here and one farther south. You're going to have to split your men up, and I'm sending you two extras from Foxworth in addition to the ten we've already assigned."

Brynn nodded. "I'll split us up into groups of ten. We should be able to take out each tower with little trouble."

"That leaves the south for me," Garrett said quietly. The steady *schnick schnick* of the blade stopped as he set it aside to reach for green painted bullets. He set them in a row south, almost along the old border lines Reese had seen on prewar maps.

He placed them in exactly the positions that Reese would have. Apparently Garrett had done some independent scouting of his own.

She bit back a lick of irritation at his covert activity, because it wasn't as if she showed every card she had to the rest of the leaders. "Nice intel, Garrett."

"Can never have enough," he admitted. "But I've told you everything we know. Don't worry, I'm not dumb enough to hold out on you."

Reese didn't argue. At this point, if she didn't trust him, they'd be fucked.

"That leaves eight in the West. There's no way you and Connor can handle all of those," Mick protested.

"Seven," she corrected. "We're not going to bother with this one right now—" She tapped the southwest corner of the map. "It's just a watchtower, no supplies, nothing that'll make it worth our while. We can deal with it after we take out the bigger stations."

"Fine. Seven. Which is still too much for you and Con."

Connor raised a brow. "You an expert now on what I can and can't handle?"

"These outposts aren't going to be a problem," Reese told Mick. "Each one is fortified the same way. Land mines spaced in a precise square three hundred yards out. The wall security is exactly like the ammo depot we hit earlier. The council isn't very creative."

Granted, lending twenty-two men and women to Brynn and Mick left Reese's squad thin, but Con's men could probably take down half the targets alone and Reese had handpicked the team members that would go with her.

But as confident as she was that they could handle it, the tightness between her shoulders refused to ease. It had nothing to do with the number of enemies she'd face, though, but the friend she'd have to deal with at the end of this meeting. Because she was a chickenshit, she'd put off telling Sloan about who would be on the Foxworth team.

"The council relies heavily on passive defense systems when it comes to these outposts," Connor added when Mick opened his mouth to protest. "Most of them aren't much more than watchtowers used to relay signals and provide a way stop for Enforcers in the field."

"How many men per outpost?" Brynn asked.

"Five to ten," Reese replied, laying down a few kernels of corn next to each bullet. "Maybe more if there's an Enforcer sweep going through, but the council prefers to keep the majority of its troops close to home."

"How reliable is this intel?"

Mick was looking to poke holes wherever he could,

but Reese didn't mind it. She'd rather argue with Mick all day long than face the battle she was going to have with Sloan once this business was concluded.

"We gather it regularly."

"Meaning it's only as good as your last spy run."

"Sure, we could send out another set of runners to scope out each outpost, and by the time they got back, the GC could have changed the configuration. There's no guarantees here. This is the best information we have."

They all waited for Mick to lodge another objection. When it didn't come, Reese figured it was time to bring the meeting to a close.

"Brynn and Garrett should leave first because they have the longest distances to travel. We don't want everyone converging on Con's camp at the same time. So space out the visits. Con and his men will provide you with the ammo you'll need for the attacks."

"How much are we getting?" Mick rubbed his hands together, finally showing some excitement over the plan of action. Or maybe he was anticipating his new toys.

Reese didn't care either way. "Enough to blow up twenty outposts, but hopefully you won't have to use it all. Any leftover ammo will be stockpiled until we're ready to strike against the city."

Brynn and Garrett spoke briefly about their departure plans. When Garrett tucked his knife away, Reese knew the meeting was over. The easy part had been dealt with.

She rose to her feet. "Kiss your loved ones and go screw your partners. This mission is risky as shit, so I'm not going to pretend that we're all coming home."

Brynn gave her a smile. "You always make the best speeches, Reese."

She grinned, then exchanged a quick hug with Brynn and a solemn handshake with Mick. Garrett stepped up to her next, hugging her and whispering, "This is the right thing."

Reese clung to his shoulders a moment longer than she intended before pushing the man away. The three camp leaders filed out the door, heading off to get a drink and maybe some food. Brynn planned to leave that day.

"Connor, a minute," Reese called before he could leave.

Sloan had moved to the doorway, watching for a nonexistent threat, but she knew he could hear every word she said.

Connor drew up. "What is it?"

"I'd like to borrow Rylan."

Reese swore she felt a breeze generated by the speed at which Sloan's head whipped around. She ignored him and focused on Connor, who looked puzzled.

"For what?"

"Between us, we need to take out seven outposts. I can take three and you can take three. I'm going to lead one, and I have Nash and Beckett for the other two. I want Rylan to take point for the seventh one."

Behind them, Sloan made a sound of protest. Reese didn't allow herself to acknowledge it. She'd known it was going to be a fight, but it wasn't one she wanted to have in front of Connor.

Connor rubbed his lips together before replying. "Sure, if that's what you want."

Damn him for phrasing it like that, and in front of Sloan, no less. She blazed with sudden anger. "It is."

"Hope you know what you're doing." He brushed past her and slapped Sloan on the back, then murmured something close to Sloan's ear.

Was he inviting Sloan to be on his team? That was *not* what Reese wanted.

"Sloan will be staying here," she nearly shouted.

The two men startled at the sharpness of her voice.

Fists clenched at her sides, she repeated, "Sloan is staying at Foxworth."

Forgetting Connor's presence, Sloan exploded. "What the *hell*, Reese?"

"I need you to stay here." She forced herself to face his hurt, which was a million times worse than any anger he could direct her way.

"And do what? Fucking knit booties for Bethany's baby?" It was a measure of how upset he was, because Sloan never spoke a word of criticism against her in front of anyone. They always presented a united front. Behind closed doors, he'd tell her she was foolish, her plan was stupid, or that she was making awful decisions, but never in public.

"I'm gonna go now," Connor interjected, but neither of them paid attention to him.

Reese barely registered the click of the latch as Connor shut the door behind him. "It's the best use of our limited resources," she told Sloan, marshaling up the list of excuses she'd formed this morning.

"You're taking one of Con's men, depleting his team, and using Rylan when you have me here? Did I somehow break my trigger finger without knowing?" Sloan shot back.

"This is our town. Someone has to be here to protect them."

"Bull-fucking-shit. There are plenty of men you could leave here. Nash. Travis. Jordan. Vaughn." He rattled off the names of several competent men and women who could, indeed, protect the town.

"None of them are you."

Damn it, didn't he understand why it was crucial that he remain?

Sloan stalked over, stopping barely a whisper away from her. "You do not go anywhere without me."

Her parched mouth grew even drier as she forced out the words that were forming a wedge between them. "You don't get to tell me what I can and cannot do."

"This is about Rylan, isn't it? You fucked him again and now you can't bear to be separated from him for one moment?"

Her own guilt made her snap back. "You really think I'm making decisions with my pussy? Do you realize how insulting you're being right now?"

"Do you realize how foolish you're being right now?" he yelled. "You're letting your emotions dictate your battle plans."

Sloan was so furious, there was a vein pulsing at his temple. His hands were fisted at his sides, and just being near all that barely checked violence flooded Reese's body with inappropriate desire. She wanted him to grab her, tear off her clothes and plunge into her with the same fury until every part of her body that ached and yearned for him was pounded into submission.

Lust was threatening to cave in her brain, erasing

the words she'd cobbled together earlier. "This town is our heart. If anything happens to it, all of our plans are meaningless."

"I don't disagree."

He marched forward and Reese had to back up to keep from being trod upon. She kept moving until her back hit the wall and there wasn't any other place for her to go. No other place to look but at Sloan's heaving chest or his angry, unhappy face.

"There are fifteen men and women who are more than capable of protecting this place," he growled at her. "You need me in the field."

No. She didn't need anything, but, oh hell, did she want. She wanted him in the field. She wanted him in her bed. She was starting to *crave* him.

The sex with Rylan had screwed with her head. She'd never had such intense orgasms, and all she'd done was fantasize about Sloan's touch. This morning she'd woken up bathed in sweat after having the dirtiest dream of her life featuring Sloan, Rylan, and herself tangled up in positions she was positive were not physically possible. She'd caught herself pausing outside of Sloan's door after she'd climbed out of bed, her hand raised as if to knock. And do what? Throw herself inside, take his thick cock into her mouth, and beg him to face-fuck her like he did Rylan? No holds barred, nothing held back?

What then? Reese knew she was a selfish bitch, but she was trying to overcome that. She was trying to put that behind her.

She would *not* kill another decent man.

"When you first came here, you vowed you'd never

challenge my leadership. I took you and Jake in based on that oath."

Sloan's face tightened at the mention of Jake's name coupled with his. She knew what he was thinking— that she could never separate the two of them in her mind. That Jake's sins hadn't gone to the grave with him, but lingered like a radiation cloud around Sloan's broad shoulders.

"Bullshit. You took us in because you wanted to fuck Jake."

She sucked in a swift, hurt breath. That wasn't true at all. She'd liked them both instantly, but it was Jake who'd made the first move. She hadn't even realized that Sloan was interested until it was too late. Far, far too late.

"Talk to me like that one more time and you'll need to pack your bags and leave," she warned.

"Yeah? Then I guess it won't matter if I do *this*."

He slammed a hand on either side of her face and then his lips crashed onto hers.

14

It wasn't a lover's kiss. It wasn't sweet or gentle or at all romantic. It was a feral attack by the animal Sloan kept caged. The one Reese had seen with Rylan. The one that prowled at the edges of what seemed to be his endless control.

He forced her mouth open, ravaging her with his tongue. She stood still for a moment, stunned by the power of his kiss, and then all of her inhibitions crumpled under the heat and pressure of his lust. With a strangled moan, she dug her nails into his shoulders and climbed him like a tree until her legs could wrap around his waist.

Sloan used his lower body strength to pin her to the wall. A commanding palm angled her jaw until he could plunder her mouth mercilessly. She dug her boot heels into his lower back and leveraged his own body against him, while her hands moved to claw his neck, score his scalp, marking him with everything she had.

"Fucking hell," he groaned against her mouth. Then he grabbed her ass and held her while grinding his hips into hers. His cock was hard enough that it felt like iron between her legs.

She'd always worried about losing him. Always relied on his control whenever hers was weak. Except now he'd lost his, and if they were going to survive this, she had to find the will to break away.

But any semblance of rational thought was being pulverized with each invasion of his tongue, each pulse of his steel shaft against her core. The fervid attraction that had simmered between them for so long, that had been pushed back to the dim recesses of their minds, was coming to life. And it would devour them if one of them didn't slam on the brakes.

As always, it was Sloan who found the strength. His lips gentled and the hand on her ass dropped away. He broke contact with her mouth and rested his forehead against hers, his chest bellowing like a thoroughbred's. His heart beat wildly against her chest until he finally straightened and stepped away.

The loss was so acute, she nearly snatched him back. But if he could find his control, so could she.

"Go then and be careful," he said gruffly.

Dry-mouthed and aching at the loss of his touch, she whispered, "Always."

He drew a shaky hand through his hair before spinning on his heel. When he threw open the door, Rylan was behind it, his hand raised and a smile on his face.

One look at Sloan's thunderous face and Rylan's grin faded. "Did I interrupt something?"

Sloan didn't look back at Reese, but she didn't miss the slight slump of his shoulders. He thought he was being replaced, she realized.

But why? Why now? Sloan had never cared whom she slept with in the past. He'd always known that she relied on him more than anyone alive, but in that dip of his broad back, Reese now read fear. Fear that he was being replaced by the man in her bed.

She wasn't sure if she should correct that assumption. If she did, she'd be risking a repeat of what had just happened. Sloan was her heart, even more than this town, and she refused to let her own selfish desires cost her the very last thing in her life that she cared about.

So she licked her lips and said, "No, Rylan, I need you."

The words were like a shot to Sloan's spine—or maybe a knife. He didn't take Rylan by the throat, but he might as well have.

"She comes back with so much as a scratch and I'm peeling the skin from your bones, one painful inch at a time," he hissed at Rylan. "If she dies, you better run, because when I catch you—and I will—you'll wish you'd bled out beside her."

Rylan winced in anticipation of the boom that never came. Instead, the door latched quietly into place, and the muted sound was more terrible than any rage-induced door slam.

"What the hell is going on?" Rylan asked uneasily. "Connor said you wanted to see me."

Reese walked unsteadily into the kitchen. She needed a smoke and a drink. "Did he tell you why?"

"Said you wanted me to lead one of your teams."

"That's right." The glasses clanged against each other as her shaking hand tried to grab one. She closed her eyes and took two deep breaths. *Get it together, woman!*

"I'm guessing Sloan's not one of your team leaders?" Rylan stayed in the living room, as if he knew Reese needed time to collect herself.

She gave up on the liquor for the moment and lit up a cigarette. "That's right."

He let out a whistle. "I'm not gonna pretend to know what's going on in your head, but you do know you're dealing with live dynamite at this point?"

Reese sucked until the smoke was half gone before tapping the ash on a plate and answering him. "Yeah, I know. Anyway, Con and I are giving you your own team and outpost. Happy belated birthday."

She stuck two fingers into shot glasses, grabbed a bottle of whiskey, and walked back to the living room, where Rylan was studying the map.

"Thanks, but my birthday's in three months," he said without glancing up.

"Happy birthday in advance." She slapped the glasses in his hand and took a seat.

"Look, I'm not one to question orders, but I've seen Sloan in action. Keeping him home seems like a mistake." Rylan poured a generous amount of booze in each glass, handed one to her, and took up the seat Connor had used during the meeting. "He's one of the best fighters around."

"And that's why I want him to stay here, so he can protect Foxworth."

"Yeah? You're telling me Sloan's the *only* one who can man the gates?"

"He is."

Rylan laughed. "What's the real reason? Because I know you're not putting me in charge because I fucked you. You're not that kind of leader."

Reese looked sourly into the bottom of her glass. When had she drunk the entire thing? "Nice that someone recognizes that."

"Uh-oh. Trouble in paradise?" He patted his knee. "Why don't you climb on Papa Rylan's lap and tell me all about it?"

She ignored him and poured another healthy splash into her glass.

They drank in silence for the next few minutes. Reese was grateful that he didn't push her. She still felt raw and exposed from her fight with Sloan and wasn't sure what would happen when she cracked. She'd either try to kick Rylan's ass, or rip his clothes off. Neither was the right course of action at this point.

"You think they smoke and drink inside the city?" he asked unexpectedly.

She nodded. "Only surreptitiously. Booze and smokes and recreational drugs are banned by the council, but I know Tamara smuggles shit like that to citizens." She blew out a stream of smoke and watched it dissipate above her head. "Pretty much anything that would make the people happy is banned, unless you're one of the council families or an Enforcer. Then you can do basically anything you want without repercussions."

"What's it like inside?"

Reese hesitated. Her background wasn't a big secret, so confiding in Rylan wasn't giving up anything important. Besides, the liquor was warming her up and his company was nice. Wanting a few moments of relaxed camaraderie wasn't a bad thing, even if she had to buy it with her privacy.

"It's a totalitarian society. Everyone is controlled by the Global Council. Electricity is only allowed at certain times of the day and for limited periods of time. They say it's because they don't have the generator power, but I doubt that's true. The food's good, the accommodations are clean. Everyone is assigned a job or craft at a young age. You're a baker or a mechanic or a technician. You live at home while you train, and when you turn eighteen you're assigned your own living accommodations and put to work. You get a decent amount of free time, though."

"What was your craft?" Rylan stretched his legs out and they were long enough that his boots nearly reached Reese's toes.

"Didn't have one. I was a breeder's first."

He raised an inquiring eyebrow. "What's that?"

"My mother was one of the select few who were chosen to breed. As an incentive to remain a breeder, each woman is allowed to keep her firstborn."

"That's . . . barbaric."

"And they call us outlaws." She gave him a wry smile. "My mother would keep the child until he or she was weaned, and then they'd be taken away."

"How many firstborns are there?"

"I have no idea. Enough of us, I suppose."

She'd never given much thought to the others like her. When she allowed herself to remember, she thought only of her brothers and sisters. Sometimes when the Enforcers came by, she searched their faces for signs of familiarity. She was always afraid one of them might be a child her mom had been forced to give away. Hell, maybe that was why she preferred to make deals with Enforcers instead of killing them outright like other camps tried to do.

But the time to spare their lives had come to an end. Once the outpost mission was underway, there wouldn't be many Enforcers left alive, whether they were related to her by blood or not.

"The population control must be one reason they don't want the outlaws to have babies," Rylan mused. He set down his glass and swiped a bullet off the war map. "If we procreate and they don't, we'll eventually overtake them by sheer numbers. A million people with rocks are eventually gonna defeat a smaller community armed with guns."

"Plus we use up resources. The council controls the Colonies through access to resources."

He tossed the bullet into the air. "None of this really explains why you're punishing Sloan. If anything, it's further justification for why he should be with us. I'm down with leading a team, but we shouldn't hamstring our efforts by leaving one of the most capable fighters at camp."

"I'm not punishing him. Foxworth needs Sloan."

"There are dozens of people inside your gates and enough food, water, and firepower to withstand a siege for several months. You could even leave Randy in charge."

Yeah right. Randy was a sixteen-year-old who'd killed his first Enforcer only two months ago.

"Foxworth is more than a collection of buildings. It's the people who are important, which is why I'd be a fool to leave anyone but Sloan in charge."

Rylan caught the bullet in midair and set it aside. Leaning forward, with his hands clasped loosely between his legs, he looked at her earnestly. "You've always struck me as a straight shooter, gorgeous. You take what you want and make no apologies. It's one of the things I like best about you. But you're different when it comes to Sloan." He hesitated. "If you need to talk it out, I can be a good listener."

"Did you ask Con for his life story before you pledged your gun to him?" Reese muttered, tired of justifying her decisions to the men around her.

"Didn't have to. We knew each other long enough that it wasn't necessary."

"Are you telling me you aren't going to lead a team unless I open my veins and bleed for you?"

He made a tsking note. "Nope. Never said that. You against us getting to know each other better?"

"Right, because you've been so forthcoming with *your* life story," Reese scoffed.

Instead of clamming up, he surprised her. "There's not much there. I grew up on a farm. It was isolated. We struggled for supplies because we were shitty farmers. Dad whored my mom out in exchange for food, equipment, candles and shit. We'd sit on the porch while Mom and Dad's mattress got a workout."

He told the story of his past nonchalantly, but those meager sentences revealed a lot about him. For all his ready smiles, Rylan was as private as Reese was, and she suddenly felt bad for prodding him. She knew what it was like to walk around raw and wounded.

"My story isn't a secret either," she admitted. "If you asked any of the folks around here, they'd tell you. Jake and Sloan came here five years ago. We were smaller then, and my plans weren't really clear to me at that point. I wanted to take down the council but I didn't have the manpower, so I started sending out word through various channels that Foxworth was a community for anyone who wanted to fight the GC. We'd take you, your family, your loved ones—didn't matter how weak you were. I figured there had to be people out there who were turned away from other camps because they were considered a liability. The young, the old, the frail, the sick."

"Sloan and Jake aren't any of those."

"No, but Jake was a hothead. You remind me of him."

"Kinky."

She snorted. "Trust me, if you reminded me *too* much of him, we wouldn't be having sex now."

His gaze sharpened. "Is that why you turned me away in the beginning?"

Damn, he was too perceptive for his own good. "Hardly." The lie rolled easily off her tongue.

"Ah, gotcha. Then it was because you were afraid you'd get addicted to me. I understand. It happens."

Reese noted his cheeky grin was back in place. "Of course. That was totally it."

"So . . ." He took on a thoughtful look. "Why was Jake a liability?"

She took another drag before continuing. "He'd already been kicked out of a number of communities. He was an amazing fighter, but he had a quick-trigger temper, a smart mouth, and he wore out his welcome faster than a bandit in an Enforcer outpost. But as a pair, he and Sloan were irresistible. They gave me solid advice on how to build our defenses. They helped turn this place into a real town. It was my idea, but Sloan was a magician at finding supplies."

"Like that pool table." Rylan shook his head, obviously remembering the new felt Sloan had recently installed on the rec room billiards table.

She laughed. "Yep. He went on a supply raid just to find that damn felt. Jake and Sloan changed things for me. Foxworth grew. Other capable fighters came. And my plans finally had real meat to them."

"No one here talks about Jake," Rylan remarked.

"No. He's a bad memory." She fell silent, trying not to think about that terrible night, and all the other terrible nights she'd turned away from. "Sloan held onto Jake's leash for as long as he could, but Jake was a rabid, sick dog and he eventually had to be put down."

"So . . . what is it, then? You avoid sleeping with Sloan because *he* reminds you too much of Jake?"

"Sloan is nothing like Jake," she said harshly. "He's the man Jake wished he could be."

Rylan threw up his hands. "Then I can't figure it out. Wanna help me out?"

She exhaled in annoyance, but some strange compulsion had her trying to explain it. "Look, you and I . . . we're a lot alike. I don't think either of us believes in love. We can care about someone. We can owe our loyalty to them, but we can't give them more than that."

"Ah, now I get it. You're afraid that if you ever act on the need to bang each other's brains out, he'll want something you can't give and eventually leave you."

Reese sucked hard on her cigarette. Rylan's summary wasn't exactly right, but it was close enough.

Truth was, she'd always wondered if she was somehow responsible for pushing Jake over the edge. She'd done that to her own mother, after all. Been the instrument of her mother's death. Begging her to stop breeding, begging her to run away, begging her to live for her daughter instead of the council. In her selfishness, she'd driven her mom to take her own life.

And Jake . . . she'd driven him into madness. Because she'd wanted too much. Because she always wanted *more*.

She'd never told Sloan what she'd said to Jake to trigger his downward spiral. She wasn't even sure Sloan suspected she was at fault. All she knew was that her selfish wants had resulted in Cassie's assault and Jake's death.

Sometimes, when it was just her and the moon, she acknowledged that her need to crush the council arose from that same selfish desire. To others, she colored it in language of revolution and cloaked her anger with the ideals of freedom. But none of it would exist without that driving need to exact her own vengeance.

Rylan drank the last of his whiskey and rose to his feet. "I'm happy to take point on one of the teams." He leaned down and pressed a light kiss against her forehead. "But I think you're wrong that you don't have enough to give. Worse, you're wrong if you think that a man is gonna be content with the scraps off your table."

As he quietly walked out of the apartment, Reese wondered if he was talking about Sloan . . . or himself.

15

The morning that Reese rolled out, Sloan wasn't there to see her leave. He'd taken himself to the outer edges of Foxworth so he wouldn't be tempted to stand on the street looking like a lovesick calf. He'd walked about three miles, traversing the once carefully plotted community.

Away from the town center, the houses were larger but eerie in their sameness. With the Sheetrock peeling away, the stick-built construction highlighted the similarities—living space attached to a giant kitchen overlooking a backyard that abutted another backyard. Sometimes there were fences. Sloan wondered if those were to keep people in or out.

The Foxworth outlaws had stripped each and every one of these houses of value long ago, leaving skeletons made of wood, moldy carpet, and cement. Someday, he didn't know when, the elements would eventually overtake these structures until they were nothing more than hints of the past—mounds covered by straggly western ground growth.

He wondered if it was a metaphor for his life, if *he*

wasn't much more than an abandoned lot filled with the decayed skeletons of his past. Since Jake's death, Sloan had been in a holding pattern.

From the moment he'd laid eyes on Reese, he'd wanted her. There hadn't been much in the way of women in his life, not since the earthquake that killed all but a few of his people. He'd lost his virginity at the age of twelve to a camp follower, a woman who traded her body for food, shelter, and protection. As he and Jake got older, sometimes they'd turn to each other for comfort. At seventeen, Sloan had formed a crush on a girl in a camp to the south, but she'd died from a fever. Life in the free land was often harsh and short-lived.

He and Jake had rambled from the mountains on the west to the coast on the east and the oceans of the south. An old man had told them that the water in the south was eating away at the land, one tide at a time. They'd laughed at both that and the old man's insistence that there were miles and miles of territory that had simply disappeared.

But later, at night when the stars were winking at him, Sloan remembered the earthquake and how one minute there was dirt under his feet and the next minute the earth split in two.

He'd felt that way when he saw Reese. The earth under his feet fell away. He'd told that to Jake, who'd laughed and said one pretty pussy was as good as another. They'd heard about Reese all the way in the northeast, heard about a camp that was willing to take in anyone so long as they could fight, no matter what kind of baggage they brought to the camp.

Sloan's baggage was Jake. After the quake, the two

boys had become a family. Jake was the risk taker, pushing Sloan beyond his placid existence. And Jake relied on Sloan to be there to pull him back off the edge.

But Sloan hadn't realized his friend's madness was escalating, otherwise he never would've brought Jake to Foxworth.

Ah, or maybe that was bullshit. Maybe he still would've done it. God knew he'd been tired of wandering the free land, constantly looking for a new place to bed down.

After Jake's death, Reese said she'd needed him—and those words were enough to keep him bound by her side, a guard dog for all eternity.

Was he wrong for wanting more? And what was that night with Rylan all about? There was a lot of Jake in Rylan. A certain irrepressible humor. An infectious recklessness. In fact, if Sloan was honest, he'd say that Rylan had all of Jake's best traits and none of the darkness.

The only thing he didn't like about the man was this creeping feeling he had that he was losing Reese to him. But was he really losing her? Or was Rylan the key to winning her?

Fuck, he didn't know anymore. There weren't any answers in the cracked tar or the dirt. None in the still air either. Empty-handed, Sloan returned to town in a foul mood.

"I'm glad you're here." Bethany greeted him cheerfully when he slid into a booth at the restaurant.

He swallowed back a caustic remark about how she was the only one. "Thanks," he muttered.

She clicked her tongue against the roof of her

mouth. "You in a bad mood because you didn't get to play vigilante?"

Bethany was going to make a great mother. She was already adept at making Sloan feel like a stupid kid. "Just worried," he replied. Then he forced himself to stretch out his legs and found a ghost of a smile somewhere, which he pasted onto his face.

She rolled her eyes and yelled over her shoulder. "Graham, we're going to need a cow."

The grizzled chef stuck his head out of the kitchen window and gave Sloan a chin nod.

"Make it extra chewy," Bethany called. "Give him something to work on."

That summoned a more genuine smile from Sloan. "Am I that bad?"

"Your thundercloud of a face is dark enough to blot out the sun," Bethany confirmed. She straightened with some difficulty and reached over to squeeze his shoulder. "Don't worry, sweetie. Everyone's going to come back in one piece."

He wondered how she could say that when her man had gotten shot in the middle of the town square, not more than a few dozen feet from where she was standing now. But as she turned away, he caught a glimpse of her own darkness. Bethany was putting on the best show she could, but she was clearly terrified.

Sloan felt shame crawl over him. Sticking around Foxworth and protecting people like Bethany and Graham and the kids was a worthy task, and he was an ass for griping about it.

He quickly reached up to squeeze Bethany's hand before she could walk off. "You're right. It's going to be fine."

Her expression softened again. "Of course it will." She waddled back to the kitchen a little lighter on her feet.

When she returned a few minutes later, it was with his food. She groaned as she set the plate of burger and potatoes in front of him. The burger was small and the mound of potatoes was huge, but Sloan knew from experience that the starchy vegetable would be spicy and delicious. None of that mattered, though.

"You okay, honey?" He pushed the plate aside and looked up at her in concern.

Bethany placed a hand at the base of her spine and arched as much as her swollen, awkward body would allow. "I'll be better when this baby's out of me. You know," she said, leaning against the booth seat across from him, "Reese told me a while back that in the city they have these machines that tell you what a baby's sex is before you have it."

"That sounds like some voodoo magic bullshit." He grinned. "I can tell you exactly what you're going to have."

"Yeah?" she challenged. "What?"

"You're having a pumpkin."

"Just one? Because I look big enough to be having an entire field of them." She rubbed a hand over her huge belly.

"I don't know about an entire field. Maybe a small patch."

"Whatever it is, I'm ready to give birth to it." With a grin, she took one step toward the kitchen before turning back. "Reese loves you," she said softly.

Sloan stiffened, but either Bethany didn't notice or she didn't care, because she kept talking.

"She might not ever be able to say it, but she'd be lost without you. That's why you're here. Not because she doesn't want you, but because she wants you too much. We want the people we love the most to be the safest. It's why Arch brought me here."

The mention of his dead friend made Sloan wince. "He'd probably be rethinking that decision now."

"No, he wouldn't." Bethany shook her head emphatically. "He's looking down and saying I made the right decision, because there's no safer place for me to have his baby than right here, and you're a big part of that."

As two days went by and no word came from the teams, Sloan became unbearable. People around town stopped talking to him. A lot of the teenagers were actually crossing the street so that they wouldn't accidentally come within speaking distance of him.

By the third day, Bethany grabbed him outside the restaurant and told him to leave.

"And go where?" he demanded.

"I don't know. Anywhere. You're scaring the kids."

Sloan looked at the bent head of Christine, who scurried by him without a word. Fuck. Bethany was right. He *was* scaring the kids.

"Fine. I'll stop in on Scott and Anna," he muttered, and he could swear Bethany almost keeled over with relief.

"That sounds like a fabulous idea," she said cheerfully.

Scott and Anna were the older couple who'd been living on a farm about two miles outside of Foxworth. They'd been there when Reese moved in, and she'd more or less adopted them. In exchange for meat and produce, Scott and Anna were protected by the deals Reese had made with the Enforcers. It was a good arrangement all the way around. Well, for everyone but the cows—the livestock hadn't been able to keep up with the demand, and the herd was down to three.

Twenty minutes later, Sloan killed the engine of his motorcycle and went searching for Scott, finally finding him tilling one of the far fields. Although there was a barn full of machinery fifty yards away, fuel was too precious to use to farm, so Scott did most of the work with a shovel and his own two hands.

"How's it going?" Sloan called out.

The older man pulled a handkerchief out of his breast pocket and wiped his hands before holding one out for a handshake. "It's going well, brother. Any word?"

Reese had come out to warn the couple before the convoy headed out, so Sloan wasn't surprised by the question. "None. I don't know whether to be anxious or happy."

"Hard not to be anxious."

"You two doing okay out here?"

Scott plucked the hat off his head and swiped his forehead with a meaty arm. Years of hard work had kept the sixtysomething farmer trim and fit. "Yup. Anna made a pie the other day. I found some berries in the woods. Come in and have a bite."

No matter what kind of dark mood was riding him, Sloan wasn't dumb enough to turn down a piece of homemade pie. He followed Scott into the house, knocking his boots against a scraper at the door before entering. They both removed their light winter jackets and tossed them on the coat rack in the hall.

They found Anna in the kitchen, looking lovely as always.

Sloan bent down and placed a kiss against her forehead. "You look more beautiful every time I see you."

It was the truth. Her face was lined from the sun, her once yellow hair had all turned gray, and her sturdy frame had thickened as the years wore on, but she never failed to take Sloan's breath away. There was a serenity and contentment that surrounded her, and her home was filled with peace that Sloan couldn't find anywhere else.

With a smile, Anna turned back to the counter. "Scott found berries in the woods. It's still too early for them and they're a little tart, but the honey we had stored from last year sweetened them up good."

She plated a large slice and slid it in front of him. It smelled heavenly.

"When are you going to run away with me, Anna?" he asked as he watched the pastry flake apart under his fork.

"Oh, honey, you know I can't do that. My man would kill you, and we only have so much space on this farm to bury dead bodies."

Sloan choked on his first bite. He'd forgotten how dark her humor was.

"All right then." He winked at her. "I'll just eat this pie and shut up about our illicit plans."

Scott heaved himself into a chair next to him, the pine creaking under his solid frame. His woman had a plate in front of him before his hat could even come off. She laid a weathered hand on his shoulder and Scott gave it a pat before she moved off again.

Meanwhile, Sloan's gaze tracked every small intimacy with barely disguised envy. Even if you didn't know them, you could easily see that they were a couple. That they belonged to each other. They had their own language, all in unspoken gestures, tiny shifts of their bodies, nods of their heads.

It was what Sloan had always wanted.

He dug into his pie so that his attention didn't make Scott and Anna uncomfortable. The three of them chatted about the farm, the town, and Reese's plans, until Sloan had all but licked the plate clean. When he set down his fork, Scott clapped a hand on his shoulder.

"Come on out to the barn. I've got something to show you."

He pushed back his chair and carried his plate over to the sink. "Thanks, Anna. That was delicious. Anytime you want to take me up on the offer to leave Scott, I'm a stone's throw away."

"I'll keep that in mind," she said dryly before shooing him out of the kitchen.

"You're a lucky son of a bitch," Sloan told the older man on the way to the barn.

The corner of Scott's mouth tipped up in a knowing grin. "Damn right I am."

"How'd you convince that fine woman to stick by you?"

"You asking for bedroom tips, boy? You disappoint me."

He shook his head. "Hell, if all it took was being able to give a good orgasm, I'd have a harem."

Scott bent over at the waist and gave a hearty laugh. "You must not be good enough in that department or you wouldn't be asking an old man for tips on how to keep a woman satisfied. You going down on her enough? You gotta take care of her before asking her to take care of you."

"Thanks for the input." Sloan shook his head, not sure if he wanted to know any more details about Scott and Anna's sex life.

Inside the barn, it took a moment to adjust to the dim interior. In the third stall, one of the cows was penned up. Her head was hanging low and she had a wild look in her eyes.

As the two men approached, the cow backed away. Sloan frowned. "What's wrong with her?"

"She's got a calf."

His breath caught. They were down to three cows and everyone had been resigned to running out of beef. A calf could change everything for them. Birth meant growth. Foxworth was growing, which only confirmed what Sloan had already known—everything Reese had done in the past, all her plans for the future . . . it *meant* something. All the deaths mattered if there was another generation to reap the rewards.

After a moment, he managed to work a few words past the lump in his throat. "That's a good sign."

"Yup."

"You have a good life here," he added roughly.

Scott nodded as he dumped a treat into the pregnant cow's bucket before walking toward the door. "I know. And trust me, I don't take a moment of it for granted."

"You and Anna ever wish you had some little ones running around?"

"At one time? Maybe? But this is a harsh land. Babies die. Kids die. It's kind of a miracle that Anna and I are still standing." Scott shrugged. "I don't need kids. As long as I'm with her, I don't need nothing else."

The words rang with a sincerity that no one would dare question, but Sloan did anyway. "Even if she didn't feel the same about you?"

Scott slanted a look that pierced through Sloan's careful nonchalance. "Every man's got to decide what's enough for him. For me? I'd be satisfied if I was just in Anna's orbit. That'd be all I needed to keep going. If she climbed up into a tree and all I got from her were the crumbs from the bread she ate, I'd gobble 'em up because they would've touched her mouth. Even if she didn't love me back, I couldn't stop loving her. That's what I reckon love is. Why it's so painful and so goddamned good at the same time."

"Yeah," was the only dumb thing Sloan could manage to say.

Scott's shoulders suddenly went rigid. "There's someone coming." He pointed to a cloud of dust on the horizon that rapidly turned into Randy on a motorcycle.

When he got within shouting distance, the teenage boy bellowed, "Enforcers headed our way!"

Sloan began to run. "How many?" he demanded when he caught up to the teen.

"One truck," Randy gasped out. He hopped off the bike and held it while Sloan swung a leg over the seat. "Davis thinks it's the ones who were here before."

Sloan sped off without another word.

His mouth was full of dust when he arrived at the back gate five minutes later. Davis opened it immediately to let him in.

"They here yet?" Sloan called out, catching a cloth from Davis and wiping the sweat and dust off his face.

"Yeah, but Cole is with them."

"Are the kids safe? Bethany?"

Davis nodded. "Sent them into the cellar as soon as we saw the dust trails."

The two men raced down the sidewalk toward the opposite end of town. At the main gate, Cole stood with a rifle slung over his shoulder, facing off with six Enforcers.

Sloan gave an inward curse when he recognized Eric. Goddamn it. The senior guard was back.

"Finally," Eric muttered when he spotted Sloan. "Where's Reese?"

"She went to a camp south of here to trade for some spring crop seeds. What do you need?" Sloan asked tightly.

"I'm here to search again."

Eric looked tired and unhappy. The mud splattered on the side of his armored truck looked like it had been baked on, and his men didn't look much better. Their uniforms were wrinkled, as if they'd been left crumpled on the floor of a tent one too many nights in a row. The stench that rolled off their bodies confirmed that Eric and his men had been on the road for many days.

After a beat of reluctance, Sloan stretched out a hand. "Be my guest."

The Enforcers purposefully charged forward, while Sloan trailed behind them.

Shit. He hoped Eric wouldn't notice that the ranks of the Foxworth community were much smaller.

He should've had more faith in his people, though. As he followed the troop of Enforcers through town, Foxworth's thinned ranks streamed into the streets and created a hive of activity to disguise their lowered numbers.

Sloan hid a satisfied grin. Reese had taught everyone well.

Fortunately, Eric didn't ask many questions. He moved quickly through each house, doing only a cursory onceover. Sloan could tell the soldier was exhausted and didn't want to be doing this.

"Alright. Let's go," Eric announced after he and his men had cleared the last building.

"What about the camp leader?" one of the soldiers asked. "Should we be worried that she's not here?"

Eric glanced over at Sloan, then rolled his eyes. "No. Her guard dog is here. She wouldn't take a shit without him holding her hand."

Snorting to himself, Eric took off walking in the direction of the main gates, while Sloan stood there on the sidewalk for a moment, valiantly working to hide his relief.

Son of a bitch. Reese had been right to order him to stay behind. Because if the Enforcers had come to find both Reese *and* Sloan gone? Fuck, they would've instantly suspected something was going down.

He let out a rueful sigh. Yeah. There was a reason Reese was the best possible leader for this town.

He just wished he'd told her that before she'd left.

16

Even with ten miles between Rylan and the Enforcer outpost they'd just destroyed, he could still smell the blood and smoke and gunpowder in the air. Especially the blood. It filled his nostrils and stuck to his throat, but he was in no rush to strip off his blood-stained sweater or throw a coat over it to mask the sharp, coppery scent.

There was no such thing as victory without blood. And they'd spilled a lot of that tonight.

A feral smile twisted his lips as he glanced over his shoulder to peer at the back windshield. There was a second truck behind them, driven by a man named Trace and carrying the four other Foxworth fighters who'd assisted Rylan and Xander on the mission. But Rylan focused his gaze beyond the second vehicle, far in the distance. The thick black plume was hard to make out against the dark backdrop of the night sky, but spiraled wisps of smoke could be seen under the full moon. The acrid odor of soot and ash trailed the trucks as they sped down the cracked pavement away from the scene of their crime.

They'd launched four separate attacks tonight—two earlier in the evening, two in the later hours of the night. Beckett and Nash's teams were already on their way back to Foxworth, their successful missions having left every Enforcer dead and both outposts in flames.

Rylan and Xan had seen the same success and were now speeding toward the rendezvous point where they were supposed to meet Reese's team.

Which still hadn't checked in.

Rylan couldn't fight the worry gnawing on his gut, which only got worse the longer the radio clipped to his belt stayed silent. Finally, he couldn't take it anymore. He clicked the radio on and, using the code names they'd assigned, murmured, "Alpha One, come in."

No answer.

Xander looked over from the driver's seat. "It's only been ten minutes. She'll check in soon."

Rylan wasn't appeased. Ten minutes was a lifetime, damn it. Worst-case scenarios kept flashing through his mind, images of Reese lying in a pool of her own blood, her long red hair fanned around her head, a bullet hole in the center of her proud forehead.

His hands were weaker than a newborn's as he pulled out a cigarette and lit up.

"You're falling in love with her."

Xander's flat remark startled Rylan into dropping his cigarette on the torn passenger seat. "Shit," he swore, hastily fumbling for the smoke before it burned a hole in the leather. Then he shot Xan an aggravated look. "No, I'm not."

"If you say so."

His friend didn't believe him. Well, Xan was wrong.

He wasn't falling in love. Falling deeper in lust, fine, he'd own up to that. But not love. There was no such thing.

He took a drag, then exhaled in a rush. "It's just sex, man."

Xander's gaze stayed on the road. "The first time you fuck someone, sure, it's just sex. Maybe even the second and third times. But like it or not, there always comes a point when the sex turns into something else."

Xan's voice was so bleak that Rylan had to wonder exactly who his friend was talking about. Reese . . . or Kade?

He'd never been able to figure out Xan's relationship with their fallen comrade. Best friends, definitely. They'd shared women. Had each other's backs. In fact, Xan had been as protective of Kade as Sloan was of Reese. And Rylan wasn't stupid—he knew that Sloan loved Reese.

Maybe Xander had loved Kade.

Fuck, there it was again, that word—*love*. It had no meaning. It was just a damn word, and probably the most dangerous word there ever was, because it allowed people to use it as an excuse for unforgiveable actions. That was how his father justified what he'd done to Rylan's mother, breaking her spirit one fuck at a time.

There was nothing wrong with being a whore. In this land, selling your body in exchange for supplies, protection, or a warm bed wasn't any different than selling your gun for the same.

But his mother had been an unwilling whore. She'd had no say in who she spread her legs for, or for what purpose. There were times when it wasn't even about necessities for survival. Rylan's dad ran out of whiskey? He'd send his wife to a nearby outlaw camp where the liquor flowed free. The cigarette stash was whittling down? Rylan's mom would be sucking off the first man who showed up with an extra pack of smokes.

To this day, Rylan couldn't forget the sounds of her sobs. Low and muffled as she tried to hide them in her pillow so her son wouldn't know the pain she was in. But he knew. Of course he knew.

When he was fourteen, he'd confronted his father, demanded to know why his dad kept letting it happen. "Because I love my family," was the curt response.

When he'd asked his mother why *she* let it happen, she'd whispered, "You're going to learn one day, honey, that there isn't anything you wouldn't do for love."

Love. Goddamn love.

Hell, even Reese had agreed with him about the foolishness of that concept.

Except . . . a part of him wished she'd argued, insisted that love *did* exist. Instead, she'd made it clear he was nothing but a lay to her. He wasn't even her friend, not like Sloan, whose friendship mattered so much to her that she refused to ruin it by spreading her legs for him.

Rylan tamped down his rising bitterness and flicked his spent cigarette out the window. He stared at the dark road ahead of them, which was illuminated by the moon rather than their headlights. It was too dangerous to turn the lights on. They couldn't risk drawing attention to their vehicles, not after they'd set fire to one of the council's outposts and killed seven

Enforcers. More than seven, if you counted the soldiers Beckett and Nash had taken out. And who knew how many Reese's team had eliminated.

Reese. Goddamn it. Why wasn't she checking in?

He didn't like feeling like this. Didn't like obsessing over terrifying outcomes that hadn't even happened. And he wasn't obsessing about just Reese either. Ever since they'd left Foxworth, Sloan had been on his mind too, another source of worry for him. He liked the man, and not just because he'd had Sloan's cock in his mouth.

Rylan knew Sloan could handle himself, but it bothered him that they hadn't left him with sufficient backup. All of Foxworth's most capable fighters had been assigned to the outpost mission, which meant Sloan was the only line of defense between the town gates and the dangers beyond it.

As if a higher power had decided to spare him any further panic, Rylan's radio crackled to life. "On our way to the rendezvous," came Reese's soft voice. "Should be there in an hour."

Rylan pushed the button. "Everything okay?" he asked, hoping she couldn't hear the relief in his voice.

"All good. Just hit a bit of a snag."

Suspicion tightened his chest. "What kind of snag?"

"Our intel was wrong. The guards weren't stationed where they were supposed to be and we lost the element of surprise. Had to go in guns blazing."

"Any casualties?" he said sharply.

"None."

Another wave of relief washed over him, until he

remembered what an evasive bitch Reese could be. He quickly rephrased himself. "Anyone hurt?"

There was a slight pause, then, "No, we're all good."

Just like that, his panic returned. "Goddamn it, baby, are you hurt?"

"I'm fine." She sounded annoyed, and a second later the radio fell silent. She'd cut off the feed.

"What?" he snapped when he noticed Xander's knowing look.

"You don't care about her, huh?" his friend mocked.

"Shut up. I'd be worried if any one of you was hurt."

Xander cocked a brow. "And would you call every one of us *baby*?"

Rylan scowled. But Xan was right. No, he wouldn't call anyone other than Reese that.

Bone-deep worry ate at him for the rest of the drive. It was the longest thirty minutes of his life, followed by another thirty of waiting for Reese's crew to arrive at the clearing where they'd arranged to meet. Xander would be taking whatever supplies Reese's team had stolen from the outpost back to Connor's wilderness camp. And while Rylan should probably go back to Con's too, he intended on returning to Foxworth, a plan that hadn't made sense to either Con or Xan, or, frankly, to Rylan himself.

If he wanted sex, he had plenty of willing partners at the other camp. Hudson and Connor. Layla and Piper, the two young women under Lennox and Jamie's protection. But he wasn't sure his reasons for going back to Foxworth had anything to do with sex. There was unfinished business between him and

Reese . . . and Sloan . . . although he had no fucking clue what it was.

The rumble of an engine jerked his gaze toward the edge of the clearing. Relief hit him square in the chest when a Jeep covered in rust and mud appeared on the overgrown path. A black SUV followed, and then both vehicles came to a stop.

Rylan saw the "snag" the moment Reese slid out of the Jeep. She wasn't wearing a coat, so he could clearly see the bloodstained piece of fabric tied around her upper arm as she gestured something to the driver. Her men quickly began unloading the stolen supplies and carting them from one convoy of vehicles to the other.

Her expression was all business as she walked over to Rylan. "Everything went as planned?"

He nodded, reaching for her arm. "What happened?" he asked grimly.

She shifted away before his hand could land on her. "It's nothing." Her sharp brown eyes surveyed the clearing. "We need to do this fast. Load everything and then get the hell out of here."

He went for her arm again. "Let me see it."

"Later." Dismissing him from her gaze, she strode off to exchange a few words with Xander.

Ten minutes later, the two convoys were back on the road. This time, Rylan was in the back of the Jeep next to Reese, who cursed in protest when he snapped open the medic kit he'd grabbed from the trunk.

"I'm fine," she insisted.

"Humor me."

He untied the bloody fabric binding her arm. It was someone's shirt sleeve, he realized, and soaked crimson. To his relief, the wound he found underneath wasn't as serious as he'd thought. Just a surface gash that was no longer bleeding.

"You'll live," he declared as he reached for a small bottle of antiseptic.

"No shit," she muttered irritably. "I told you I was fine."

He kept his touch gentle as he cleaned the wound, but although he knew the rubbing alcohol must sting like a bitch, Reese didn't even flinch. "What happened?" he pushed.

She made a grumbling sound. "Got grazed by a bullet."

His heart flipped in concern. "You serious? Those bastards shot you?"

"No, they *grazed* me." She sounded annoyed again. "There were three Enforcers posted at the back gate. Our intel said there was only supposed to be one, so that's what we based our assignments on. I was handling it alone."

His pulse sped up in alarm. "You took on three Enforcers by yourself?"

"I didn't have anyone to provide cover fire." A pained look crossed her eyes. "That's usually Sloan's job. Or rather, that's my job and Sloan is usually the one throwing himself in front of the bullets."

Of course. Because that was what Sloan did: protect Reese at all costs.

"You regretting asking him to stay behind?" Rylan adopted a careless tone, but tension filled his gut as he waited for her answer.

Which never came. She simply pressed her lips together and said nothing. But her silence was as clear as the full moon overhead.

He tossed the pink-tinged gauze on the floor of the Jeep and silently bandaged up her arm, wishing like hell that she would confide in him. He didn't even care if she wanted to sit there for the entire eight-hour drive and talk about nothing but Sloan. Hell, he'd listen to her talk about the weather as long as it meant being included in her thoughts, as long as she recognized his fucking presence.

But she wasn't even looking at him, damn it. Her gaze was fixed out the window, and her silence . . . it grated. It really grated, so much that he found himself clapping one hand around her chin to wrench her face toward his.

"What are—"

He didn't let her finish. His mouth crashed over hers in a hard kiss, all his frustration coming out in the greedy thrust of his tongue, the curl of his fingers around her slender throat. Reese gasped against his lips, but she didn't push him away. She kissed him back with fervor, her hands pressing against his chest, stroking him over his shirt.

When they finally pulled apart, they were both breathing hard and the back windows of the Jeep had fogged up. Reese's men, Trace and Daniel, sat quietly in the front seat. Neither commented on the display of passion and aggression that had just filled the car.

"Rylan," she started, her expression holding a hint of reluctance.

"You should get some sleep," he said gruffly, then tugged her toward him. When she tried to squirm away, he forcibly moved her head against his shoulder. "Sleep, Reese. We've got a long drive ahead of us."

After a few seconds, she relaxed, her steady, even breathing warming the side of his neck.

He, on the other hand, was the farthest thing from relaxed. The tension refused to leave him. So did the worry, which gnawed harder at him each time his gaze lowered to Reese's bandaged arm.

She could've died tonight. That bullet could've done more than graze her flesh. It could've pumped a hole in her head, burned into her abdomen and made her bleed out, punctured a lung and she would've drowned in her own blood. And then what the hell would he have said to Sloan? *Sorry, brother, but our woman got iced by an Enforcer. My bad.*

Fuck.

Fuck.

In a moment of clarity, Rylan suddenly understood Connor's longing for the old farm. For the days when it had been him, Con, and Pike. The days before Xander, before Kade, before Hudson and Reese and Sloan and all the other outlaws they'd met and formed connections with since then.

Connor was right. Life was so much easier when there was nobody around for you to give a damn about.

17

It was morning when the convoy drove through Fox-worth's gates. Reese expected to find Sloan waiting in the courtyard for them, but to her chagrin, he was nowhere in sight.

He must still be angry with her, then.

And he had every right to be.

She slid out of the Jeep and issued a few orders before stalking over to Vaughn and Davis, who, unlike Sloan, *were* there to greet her on arrival. She felt Rylan's blue eyes boring a hole into her back as she spoke with the men, but she didn't turn around. Nor did she go to him once she dismissed her people. Instead, she took off in a swift walk toward the building she shared with Sloan.

Their apartment was empty.

Fuck. Where *was* he? She hoped he didn't plan on avoiding her all day, because she had important things to say, and damned if he was going to deny her the opportunity to say them.

In her room, she stripped out of her dusty jeans and let them drop to the floor. She was just removing her shirt when she heard the muffled thud of footsteps outside her door.

Sloan entered the room without knocking. His dark eyes rested briefly on her breasts, covered only by a snug black bra, before shifting to the bandage on her upper arm.

"You okay?" he asked.

She nodded. "It was just a graze."

"Let me have a look."

Reese didn't voice an objection as he led her to the bed and gently forced her to sit. Then he settled beside her and peeled off the bandage. He examined the wound, his fingertips skimming the outside edges of the long, red scrape.

Maybe with you, those hands would be gentle.

Unwittingly, Rylan's words floated through her head. Right now, Sloan's touch *was* gentle. Infinitely gentle. But it hadn't been gentle before she'd left on the outpost mission. His hands had been rough and unforgiving then, gripping her ass tight enough to leave marks on her flesh.

She shivered at the memory, but Sloan mistook the response for one of pain rather than remembered pleasure.

"I'll be right back," he announced, then left the room in purposeful strides.

Reese heard his footsteps in the hall, in the living area, in the small kitchen they shared. When he returned, he held a plastic pill bottle in his hands.

"No," she said immediately. "We're not wasting our antibiotics on one silly cut."

"That cut is as prone to infection as any other, silly

or not," he replied in a stern voice. He shook two pills out of the vial and onto his palm. "Open your mouth."

Her chin jutted out in a stubborn pose.

"Teresa."

"Goddamn it, Sloan, it's a waste of resources—"

He took advantage of the parting of her lips by pressing the pills on her tongue. The coarse pad of his finger slid across her tongue on its way out of her mouth, and then he pinched her lips together and said, "Swallow."

Reese made a disgruntled sound, but since his fingers were keeping her mouth closed, she had no choice but to swallow the meds. Without water to ease their way down, the pills scraped the back of her throat and brought a sour taste to her mouth. "Asshole," she accused.

He chuckled.

Sighing, she leaned toward the night table and grabbed the half-empty bottle of water sitting atop it. After she'd gulped down a few mouthfuls, she twisted the cap back on. "You weren't at the gate when we drove in," she said softly.

"I was dealing with the pipe in the kitchen. It's leaking again."

She shifted awkwardly. "Oh. Did you fix it?"

"Yeah."

"Okay, good. Thanks."

He acknowledged that with a nod.

Silence fell, long and agonizing, as they sat there staring straight ahead.

There were so many things she wanted to say to him, but she was having trouble making her vocal cords work. Talking to Sloan didn't used to be this hard. She could always tell him whatever was on her mind. The good, the bad, the terrifying. Sloan was the only person who'd seen her at her most vulnerable, the only person in this messed-up world who she was able to show that side of herself to.

Fuck, why had he kissed her? Why had he opened that door? They'd kept it under lock and key for a good reason, damn it.

She took a breath, forcing herself to say something.

"I was wrong—"

"You were right—"

Their startled gazes collided as they both spoke and halted at the same time.

"What?" she said stupidly.

"You were right," Sloan repeated.

"Right about what?"

He rubbed his beard, and Reese shivered again, remembering how those sexy bristles had abraded her skin when his mouth had devoured hers the other day. His blistering kisses had left red marks on her cheeks, her neck, her collarbone.

"I needed to stay behind," Sloan told her, his tone rueful.

"No. I was wrong. You needed to be with me." She gestured to her arm. "This wouldn't have happened if you'd been there watching my back. And yes, it's only a silly cut, but . . . it didn't feel right being out in the field without you."

He gave a steadfast shake of his head. "I needed to be here in Foxworth. Goddamn Enforcers showed up, sweetheart."

Her breath hitched. "Shit."

"They searched the town again. Nobody else

would've been able to handle that, Reese. And they wouldn't have believed the story we fed them if it had come from anyone other than me. They've been monitoring us for years. They know I'm your shadow, that if you were planning an attack, you'd make sure I was by your side." Grudgingly, he said, "It was a smart move on your part, going without me."

"It didn't feel smart when we were at that outpost. It felt . . . unbalanced. Like I was missing a limb." She sighed. "You're my right hand."

"And you're mine."

Her heart sped up when Sloan took her hand and threaded their fingers together.

"But sometimes hands need to work independently of each other," he went on. "And that's okay. They can each be doing their own thing, as long as they recognize that they're stronger together."

She laughed. "Well, aren't you poetic this morning."

"What can I say? You bring out that side in me."

Reese lowered her gaze to their joined hands. His fingers were long and masculine, his hand so much stronger than hers. Her fingers looked downright fragile laced through his.

"We need to talk about the kiss," she whispered.

"We don't have to."

"Yes, we do." She squeezed his knuckles. "We don't avoid things, you and I. Well, except for . . . that one thing."

He snorted. "Yeah. That one thing."

Silence fell between them.

"I shouldn't have kissed you," he finally said, his voice thick with remorse. "You didn't want it."

"I . . . I *did* want it. Fuck, Sloan . . . I've always wanted you. You had to have known that."

There was a sharp intake of breath.

"It's true," she said quietly. "When I first met you and Jake on the road, I honestly can't say which one of you I thought was more attractive. Jake, with his lopsided smile and all that golden hair. Or you, so big and powerful, with that intense stare that saw right through me." Her hand lifted to his face to stroke his beard. When she rubbed her thumb over his lower lip, he inhaled again. "But Jake made the first move."

Sloan nodded. "I know. That's why I backed off." He swept his fingers over her knuckles in a tender caress. "I set aside my lust and disappointment and tried to be the best friend I could be for you. I wasn't mad that you picked him, sweetheart. Jake's star shone bright."

"But I wanted both of you. Not just him."

The sadness in his expression was unmistakable. "You never said anything."

"I did."

His eyes narrowed.

"I said something to Jake," she clarified. Pain sliced through her. "The night before Cassie was attacked."

"Before he attacked Cassie," Sloan corrected flatly.

"Right." She swallowed the massive lump in her throat.

She wasn't sure why she'd phrased it that way, as if an unseen, outside force had been the one to attack Cassie, when in reality that dark force had been Jake.

"He asked me if I was attracted to you, and I said yes." Reese tightened her grip on Sloan's hand. "I told him I wanted you and he lost it. He said he'd kill any man who touched me, that only he had the right to do that. He was so out of control that night. He fucked me harder than he'd ever done before." Shame bubbled in her throat, causing her to turn away from Sloan's serious eyes. "And I loved it."

She jerked when he wrenched her face toward him so she had no choice but to look at him. "It's okay to like it rough, sweetheart. It's okay to like what he did to you."

"But what he did to Cassie . . ." The lump in her throat grew impossibly bigger. "That *wasn't* okay. God, Sloan, you should've heard the things he was screaming at her. How it was his right to touch whoever he wanted, to take whoever he wanted. Cassie was lying there on *our* bed, bleeding from all the places he'd beat her. Crying, begging for me to help her."

"You did help her."

"I helped her too late." She bit her lip. "I drove him to that. I told him I wanted you, and he had to go and show me that I wasn't allowed to touch another man, but that *he* was allowed to touch whoever he wanted even if it was against her will. *I* did that."

"No, you didn't," Sloan said firmly, but then his resolve crumbled and a ragged breath shuddered out of his throat. "If anything, it was my fault."

She blinked in surprise. "What are you talking about?"

"I said something to Jake too," he confessed.

Her heartbeat took off in an erratic gallop. "You did?"

"After he laid his claim, I tried so hard to keep my feelings for you in check. But it wasn't easy." Guilt clung to his tone. "The more time I spent in this town, the more I admired you. And the more I admired you, the harder it was to keep my cock under control. I wanted you so badly I couldn't stand to be around you."

His voice, so deep and gruff and laced with regret, brought the sting of tears to her eyes.

"I managed to keep my dick in my pants. I managed to keep my mouth shut. But then . . ." He swallowed visibly. "Jake's eye was beginning to wander."

Reese's teeth clamped onto her lower lip again. Yeah, she'd always suspected.

"So I asked him if there was room in the bedroom for one more. We'd shared women before, so it didn't seem like an outrageous request at the time. But . . . Christ, he didn't like that. He told me that he'd slit your throat before he let another man touch you."

Her eyes widened.

"That's when my allegiance shifted from Jake to you," Sloan admitted. "From that day on, I was your man. When I got up in the morning, it was to make sure that your day ran smoothly. When I lay down at night, I would think about all the ways I needed to protect you so that you could protect everyone else. And most of all, I kept an eye on Jake."

Reese blinked rapidly to try to stop the tears from spilling over. She'd always known Sloan was loyal to her, but . . . she hadn't expected to hear this. Any of it.

"But it wasn't a close enough eye," he muttered darkly. "I didn't see what he was doing. All those women he'd been with while he was fucking you weren't willing bed mates. I should've known that, damn it. I should've known that the women in this town loved you. *You*, Reese, and they wouldn't, not for a second, let Jake in their beds behind your back."

When he touched her cheek again, Reese sagged into the warmth of his palm. The nausea grew stronger, swirling in her stomach. She'd known that Jake was getting out of control. She'd seen him forcing the women to serve him his food and drinks. Dishing out punishment for any minor transgression committed in the camp. He'd even set up a whipping pole in the town square, where men and women alike were belted for whatever crime he believed they'd committed.

But the rapes . . . taking the women and even some of the men against their will . . . that was a whole other level of savagery. He'd told them it was their duty to serve him, but even Jake must've known that what he was doing was wrong, otherwise he wouldn't have sworn his people to secrecy. He told them it was their duty, but really it was his own twisted perversions, his own distorted ideas of what it meant to be a leader.

Jake had been sick.

"I didn't know," she whispered. "I really didn't know."

"I know you didn't," Sloan assured her. "Neither did I. If I had, I would've put him down long before that, spared everyone all that pain and terror."

"I don't know if you could've done it by yourself. I don't think I would've been able to," she admitted. "You loved him."

"Yeah, I loved him . . . until I hated him."

A sad smile touched her lips. That was what it boiled down to, wasn't it? They'd loved Jake until they'd hated him.

"Do you regret it?" Sloan asked in a hoarse voice. "Killing him?"

She shook her head. "Do you?"

He shook his head.

A humorless laugh slipped out of her mouth. "But it doesn't feel like he's dead, does it? We killed him three years ago, but he's still here. A ghost in this town. Watching us. Judging us."

"Then let him watch," Sloan said fiercely. "Jake was my only family, he was my best friend, but he was *not* a good man. It wasn't anything you or I did, sweetheart. He was sick and he got addicted to the power. You didn't make him do what he did. Neither did I. So if he wants to be here with us?" Sloan gestured to the empty space around them. "Let him. Let him watch. But you and I? We're not giving him another second's thought."

The heat in his eyes made it hard to breathe. She'd seen it when he'd kissed her, when he'd let Rylan suck him off. That kind of passion wasn't supposed to be restrained. It should be allowed to flow free, and Reese found herself cursing Jake harder than she ever had, for keeping Sloan on a leash he didn't belong on.

When he kissed her, she welcomed him with an eagerness that was almost embarrassing. His tongue slid into her mouth, and Reese gasped because he tasted like . . . Sloan. Like whiskey and man and something so heady it fogged up her mind.

She clung to his broad chest, digging her fingers into his pecs. When her thumbnail brushed his nipple through his shirt, he hissed out a breath. His big body was trembling, but she knew he wasn't scared or nervous. He was fighting the same loss of control that she always fought.

"Sloan," she started, but she had no idea what she wanted to say.

It didn't matter. Sloan kissed her again, long and deep and drugging, making her dizzy with the hungry swirl of his tongue, the greedy clasp of his lips. He pushed her back onto the mattress and slid the top of her bra down. One breast popped free and instantly he had his mouth around it, sucking deep enough to make her cry out.

"Reese," he groaned against her aching flesh. But he didn't finish his sentence either. He simply flicked his tongue over her nipple while freeing her other breast.

God. Her entire body was on fire. Everything about him called to something hot and carnal inside her. His wicked tongue. His cropped hair sliding beneath her palm as she ran her fingers through it. His beard on the swell of her breast, scratching her sensitive skin. His impossibly hard cock pressing against her thigh.

She wanted to free it from his jeans, take him inside her mouth, inside her body. The need to have him was so overpowering it turned her into a crazed woman. Suddenly she was clawing at his zipper, growling when it snagged halfway.

Sloan chuckled and reached down to help her out. "You want my cock?" he rasped.

Reese couldn't even form the word *yes*. Raw, unchecked lust had clogged her throat, and all she could do was give him a desperate nod.

Anticipation swelled between her legs as he slowly dragged his zipper down. He reached inside and gripped what she was craving more than her next breath, but before he could release his erection, a knock sounded on the door.

They both hissed in displeasure.

"Reese, we need you." It was Nash, who must have

drawn the short straw again, because he always seemed to be the one interrupting them.

"What is it?" she ground out. She knew both Sloan and Nash could hear the throatiness of her voice, thick with desire.

"Uh . . . we need you," Nash repeated, sounding like he'd rather be anywhere but outside her door at the moment.

Sloan's expression flashed with annoyance as he hurled a question at the closed door. "You feel like telling us why? Or are you just gonna keep repeating yourself?"

There was a brief pause. "Bethany's gone into labor."

18

Bethany looked terrible.

For a moment, Reese was tempted to spin on her heel and let someone else handle this, but she forced herself to stay put. The panting, red-faced woman thrashing on the bed was one of her people. She couldn't turn away from someone she'd sworn to protect.

"She was walking home from the restaurant and suddenly bent over. Something like . . . piss, I guess, poured out of her and she started crying. We carried her up here and then . . ." Nash grimaced helplessly, making that face men wore when someone was hurting but they couldn't do a damn thing to help them. "Then *that* started happening. We didn't know what to do."

He gave Reese a pleading look. *Fix this*, it said.

Reese glanced back at Bethany, whose body bowed off the bed from a wracking pain that left her visibly drained and weeping.

Sloan had followed Reese into the bedroom but backed away almost immediately, his normally stoic face full of horror. But at least he was still here. Travis and Beckett were hiding downstairs—hell, they may have even left, those cowards—and Nash was already inching away.

Bethany stared at the ceiling as tears streamed from the corners of her eyes. "I can't do this," she cried. "Where's Arch? Why isn't Arch here?"

Reese's heart broke into a million pieces. Arch wasn't here because he'd taken a bullet in his chest to protect Reese. Fuck. *She* shouldn't even be here. She wanted to run out of the room behind Nash and take Sloan with her. Facing a thousand Enforcers seemed less terrifying than trying to bring a baby into the world without a lick of medical assistance.

"Reese?" Bethany's plaintive sob echoed in the room.

"I'm here, honey."

Sloan gave her a push forward.

Reese shot him a dirty look over her shoulder. Sure, send her over to the tormented woman.

"Is this right? Should I be feeling this?" Bethany struggled to raise up to her elbows, but fell back immediately because even that required too much effort.

Reese thought frantically back to all of her mother's deliveries. Those events had been attended to by three doctors in white coats. They'd marched into Sylvia's bedroom and came out hours later with a newborn. There was no sound, no cries of terror and anguish. By the time Reese was allowed to see her mother, sometimes an entire day later, Sylvia was glowing with happiness.

She carefully approached the bed. "Of course it's normal," she assured the sobbing woman. But she had no fucking idea what constituted "normal" during childbirth. "I think you should start to push soon?"

"Push? That's it? That's all you have for me?" Bethany demanded, and the force of her anger brought her upright.

"I . . ." Reese's feet had taken her too close to the bed, and Bethany snatched at her wrist.

"I've got a watermelon in my stomach and you're telling me to push it out my vagina! Where are the drugs? I need some drugs!"

Reese knew there had to be drugs for this sort of thing, but in all the pharmacies and clinics they'd raided over the years, nothing had ever been marked USE IN THE CASE OF BIRTHS. The proper meds were probably only stocked in the city hospital.

Shit, and they'd used the last of the painkillers on Kade, first on trying to save him and then to give him a mercy killing.

"Okay, here's what we're going to do." She tugged at the hold on her wrist, but Bethany's grip was stronger than a steel vise. "I'm going to sit beside you, and you tell me where it hurts. I'll rub while you push."

Bethany, sweet, mild, wonderful Bethany, bared her teeth. "Where it fucking hurts? You're asking me where it fu—"

The rest of that sentence was cut off by another long scream, accompanied by Bethany's nails tunneling their way through Reese's wrist. Holy *hell* did that hurt, but apparently it was nothing compared to what was going on inside of Bethany.

"Get Rylan," Sloan said.

"Why?" Reese grumbled.

"He grew up on a farm. He told me he knows about delivering babies."

"Get him. Get him. Get him," Bethany scream-chanted.

Sloan rushed to the door and called for Nash. "We need Rylan. Now." Another scream punctuated the air and the two burly men flinched. "Yesterday."

Nash took off at a sprint.

"Good thing Arch is gone," Bethany snarled, "'Cause I would've killed him for putting me through this."

Again, Reese's mind turned toward her mother. Had Sylvia endured this agony for each baby? And her reward had been to *lose* them? No wonder she went mad. No wonder she killed herself.

Bethany endured two more rounds of intense birthing pains, each one seemingly more horrible than the last, before Rylan finally—blessedly—showed up.

He stepped over the threshold, clapped his hands together and started barking out orders.

"Clean hot water. Three bottles of whiskey."

"Three of them?" Sloan asked warily.

"Two to disinfect my hands and one for you two to share so you don't pass out." Rylan turned to Bethany. "Did your water break?"

Her head jerked in a nod.

Rylan nodded back. "Good. That means the baby will be ready to come out soon." He patted the end of the mattress. "You two help her down here so her legs dangle off."

Reese and Sloan jumped up and did as Rylan asked. He knelt between Bethany's legs, took a long look, and then had Bethany lie back. He placed his hands on her belly, pushing harder than Reese thought was safe or necessary, but Bethany's cry was almost one of relief.

"Feels good. Head's down. All you gotta do is push. Might be easier if you stand up."

"Are you crazy?" Reese exclaimed. "She can't sit up by herself. What if the baby falls? What if—"

Rylan shrugged, cutting off her litany of bad outcomes. "Things fall. I'll catch it."

Bethany struggled to sit up. "Help me up."

Reese settled on Bethany's right side, while a pale-faced Sloan took up position on the left. As the young woman hung between them, they all stared at Rylan, who remained kneeling.

"Pretend like you're taking the biggest dump ever," he said with a grin.

"You're an awful midwife," Reese accused.

He didn't even bother to respond. Bethany bore down, screaming and holding onto Reese and Sloan as if she were trying to withstand hurricane-level winds. Bethany was a tiny woman, but her grip rivaled the strength of ten men. Reese genuinely feared her hand might come off.

Rylan, however, was the picture of calm. He encouraged Bethany, telling her that she was doing a good job. That everything was going to be fine. That this was all normal. He alternated between rubbing her back and then her belly before returning to his knees again.

He didn't let up, hour after hour, speaking until he was hoarse. It was a side of Rylan that Reese had never seen. A side that Jake had never possessed. And under Rylan's steady eyes and calm voice, Reese finally found her footing.

A quick glance at Sloan revealed that he was responding to it too. Rylan was soothing all of them. The man with a ready smile and a propensity for snarky wisecracks was coaxing them into a calm that Reese would have sworn couldn't exist in this room.

This Rylan was a revelation, and the fissure that Sloan had created inside of her earlier opened even wider.

Bethany was a wreck. A vein had burst in her right eye, turning the white of her eyeball completely red. Her hair was drenched in sweat and she was flushed like a lobster from head to foot.

She hadn't ever looked more beautiful.

Both Rylan and Sloan stared at her with awe and a newly formed devotion.

Reese . . . well, she couldn't take her eyes off the baby.

Rylan had caught the infant, as he'd promised he would, with his whiskey-cleaned hands. He'd tied off the umbilical cord, urged Bethany to make one last push to rid her body of the afterbirth, and then handed the baby to Reese so he and Sloan could clean up the bed and get Bethany situated. Sloan had cradled Bethany while Rylan stripped the bed of its sweat-stained sheets. Someone produced clean ones and then Bethany was placed back onto the mattress, exhausted and sleepy.

Reese knew she should give the baby to his mother, but she didn't want to. She was in love with Bethany's baby. She wanted to run off with Bethany's baby. Wanted to climb into the helicopter and take off. She'd find one of those islands Tamara was always talking about and get lost with this newborn.

She stared into his blue eyes and ran a hand over the tuft of red hair that he'd obviously inherited from his father. A wrinkled hand clutched at her breast as his tiny mouth opened and closed, looking for something to latch on to. Reese lifted the baby to her nose and breathed in the scent of life.

She wanted this so badly and she'd never be able to have it.

"Reese . . ."

She looked up to see Rylan standing at her side. Her grip tightened and she turned her shoulder, shielding the baby from Rylan's grasp.

"Reese, sweetheart." This time it was Sloan calling her name.

The two men looked at her expectantly. So did Bethany.

Rylan held out his hands for the baby and Reese reluctantly handed him over. She forced herself not to snatch the bundle of love back.

Sloan bent over Bethany, stroking her forehead. "Your baby is so gorgeous, Bethy. Arch has gotta be wearing the biggest smile."

The new mother tucked herself under Sloan's big arm and laid her head against his chest, as Rylan stopped on the other side of the bed and placed the baby into her waiting arms. Bethany pulled open one side of her shirt, and the little one turned his perfect lips toward her breast. Sounds of suckling were mixed with Sloan and Rylan's low-pitched voices praising Bethany and exclaiming over the perfection that was little Archer.

Reese burned with jealousy. She'd never be able to give Sloan that. Or Rylan, for that matter. She'd never be able to put that awe into their faces. She bit back a hundred bitter, stupid words and spun on her heel. She had to get out of there.

Downstairs, she found nearly a dozen people waiting for her. "She had a boy," Reese announced. "Everyone's doing well."

Clapping and cheering broke out. People hugged each other. Some cried. None noticed that Reese had left.

She thought she'd be able to breathe once she was outside, but even the fresh air couldn't drive away the choking fog of jealousy.

She ran to her building, not even bothering to shut the door behind her. She made for the kitchen, wrenching open the cabinet that housed the liquor. With shaking hands, she pulled the bottle down, but it caught on the edge of the shelf, flipped out of her slippery hands and crashed to the floor. The sharp smell of booze filled the air as Reese cried out in frustration. She couldn't even pour herself a damn glass of whiskey.

Cursing wildly, she grabbed the remaining bottle and managed to tear off the cap and gulp down a healthy swallow before giving in to the tears. Salty drops rained down her face and the wracking sobs shook her body with such force that she couldn't stand up. She sank to the floor, not even feeling the sharp bite of glass in the palm she flattened in an effort to keep herself from face-planting into the booze-covered tile.

"Reese, sweetheart, what's wrong?"

She glanced up to find Sloan in the doorway. "Get out," she growled.

Worry creased his handsome face. Behind him, she could see Rylan. They were both looking at her like she was nuts.

She hated that. Hated that they were seeing her like this. She was the strong one, damn it. She was the one with the vision and the plan. She did *not* fall apart because she couldn't have a damn baby. Yet here she was, sitting on the floor with a whiskey bottle dangling between her fingers.

A sudden burst of anger coursed through her. She threw the bottle at Sloan's head.

He ducked, and it hit the wall with an explosion of glass and liquid. "What the hell was that for?"

"I can't give you that!" she yelled.

"Give me what? A cracked skull?"

"A baby! I can't give you a goddamned baby!"

Sloan turned around to seek help from Rylan, who raised both shoulders in wordless confusion. Then he turned back to Reese and softened his voice. "Come away from there, sweetheart."

She looked at the wreckage—the broken glass, the spilled whiskey, her fucking life—and gave a mutinous shake of her head. What would either of these two men, these two gorgeous, capable, amazing men, want with her?

She was defective—part woman, part nothing. She was a good lay, but when it came down to it, she wasn't worth keeping. A flawed vessel. Pour all the shit you wanted into her and she'd be empty by morning.

"I told you to get out." The command sounded more like a plea. She kept her gaze fixed on the bottle, teetering between hating herself for this uncharacteristic act of self-pity and anger toward them for witnessing it.

Glass crunched under someone's feet. "Heard you the first time." It was Sloan who picked her up, and she didn't have the energy to fight him.

"The whole town probably heard you." Rylan, cracking a joke as usual.

"You coming?" Sloan asked the other man.

"Yes."

She should have protested. She should have reminded them that she was an utter waste of their time. She should have. But she didn't.

And without another word, Sloan carried her into her bedroom, and Rylan was right behind him.

19

Reese was hurting, and it broke Sloan's heart to see it. Years ago, he'd vowed to be this woman's shield, to stop anyone and anything from hurting her, but there was no outside threat to battle right now, only an internal demon that Sloan feared he couldn't reach.

He brushed the tears from her eyes as he kicked open the bathroom door. "Rylan, start the shower," he ordered without turning around.

While the other man cranked the hot water, Sloan quickly and methodically stripped off Reese's clothes. She stared straight ahead, but when his fingers slid under the waistband of her panties, she started to protest.

"I'm fine."

They all heard the shakiness of her voice. "You're not fine," he said quietly. "You're ice-cold, sweetheart. Let's warm you up, okay?" He nudged her toward Rylan and began removing his own clothes.

Once he was naked, he gently lifted Reese into the tub and under the shower spray. As the water coursed over their bodies, Sloan wrapped both arms around her from behind so his chest was supporting her trembling back.

From the corner of his eye he saw Rylan undressing too. A moment later, the big blond man stepped into the shower. Sloan twisted Reese around while Rylan came up behind her, and she seemed to sag in defeat when she found herself sandwiched between the two men.

Not a word was spoken as Rylan grabbed a bar of soap and lathered it up in both hands. He soaped up Reese's back, her shoulders, her arms, before kneeling down to get her legs. Then he rose to his feet and handed the soap to Sloan, who wasted no time running it over the front of Reese's body.

He ignored the slippery curves and smooth wet flesh gliding beneath his fingers. He ignored his hardening dick and the sudden quickness of his pulse. As much as he wanted to get inside her, he couldn't erase the image of her grief-stricken face, her wild eyes as she'd hurled that bottle at his head, her anguished words—"I can't give you a goddamned baby!"

He knew Reese had been raised in the city, but some mental malfunction had prevented him from recognizing the implications of that. If a female citizen wasn't chosen to breed, then she was sterilized. He *knew* that. But he'd never thought about it in relation to Reese.

And it didn't matter to him, damn it. His heart ached because *she* ached, not because he harbored silly fantasies about being a father. He didn't want a baby. Never had, probably never would. Holding Bethany's tiny newborn had flooded his chest with warmth and affection, but not because he wanted a kid of his own. He was happy for Bethy, that was all.

He didn't ever want Reese to think that she was lacking. That there was something, *anything*, she couldn't give him. Because he already had everything he'd ever wanted.

Her.

His hand brushed Rylan's as they both caressed Reese's hip, and Sloan faltered for a moment. He had *more* than he'd ever wanted, he realized. He hadn't exactly sat around dreaming about sharing Reese with another man, but he couldn't deny that having Rylan here felt . . . right.

"What do you need, sweetheart?" Sloan's gruff question was muffled by the rush of water, but he knew Reese heard him, because she stiffened slightly.

"I don't know," she mumbled.

"You want to talk?" he pushed.

She slowly shook her head, causing damp strands of dark red hair to slither over her full breasts.

He gently cupped her tits and rubbed her nipples with his thumbs. "You want us to make you feel good?"

After a long beat, her head dipped in a weak nod.

Sloan met Rylan's eyes over Reese's shoulder, and he tipped his head in an unspoken question. Rylan nodded as if to say he was up to the task, then slipped his hands to Reese's thighs and gently spread them apart.

As his heart hammered erratically, Sloan sank to his knees in front of her. Something akin to wonder floated through him. This was the first time he was going down on her. He wanted to memorize the sight of her, the taste of her, but Reese needed a swift, powerful release that would extinguish her sorrow and replace it with something sweeter. Something hotter.

His lips tingled as he brought them to the glistening pussy he'd fantasized about for years. Reese's entire body jerked hard when his tongue made contact with her clit. Sloan glanced up briefly to see Rylan wrap one strong arm around Reese's waist. His other hand was cupping one breast, squeezing and fondling as he rested his chin on her shoulder.

"I've got you, baby," Rylan murmured. "Close your eyes and let him taste you."

Sloan didn't wait to see if she obeyed. He was already dragging his tongue down her slit toward her opening, groaning roughly as he lapped at the moisture pooled there.

Damn, he wanted to savor this. He really, really, *really* wanted to go slow. But he'd save that tantalizing option for later. Right now, he would help Reese release all the tension coiled up inside her. He licked his way back up, wrapped his lips around her clit, and sucked hard enough to make her cry out.

"That's it, just let go. We'll take care of you."

Sloan was barely aware of Rylan's soft words of encouragement. He finally had his face buried between Reese's shaking legs, and it was making his head spin with desire. He slid two fingers inside her wet channel, glorying in the way she clenched and squeezed him in return.

Her moans bounced off the tiled walls, fueling Sloan's own urgency. His cock was heavy between his legs, leaking from the throaty sounds escaping Reese's throat. He curled his fingers and stroked her as he lashed her clit with his tongue, over and over again until she began to convulse.

"There you go," Rylan rumbled. "That's a good girl. Come all over our man's face."

Sloan relentlessly stroked and licked her hot flesh, filling himself with her flavor until she spiraled out of control. He stood up only when Reese's body finally stilled. The taste of her was imprinted on his tongue, the sweet evidence of her orgasm coating his fingers.

Rylan's look of approval when their gazes met triggered something hot and primal inside of Sloan. Without a word, he brought his fingers to the other man's mouth. Reese gasped, and the heat blazing in Rylan's eyes as he sucked on Sloan's fingers sent a bolt of electricity right to Sloan's dick.

Jesus.

The water had grown cold. Sloan lifted Reese into his arms, and she looped her hands around his neck as he carried her out of the bathroom. The faucet creaked as Rylan turned the shower off and joined them in the bedroom a moment later.

Neither man said a word as Sloan deposited Reese's wet, naked body on the rumpled bedspread. He and Rylan didn't need to speak, because they both had the same agenda. They also had massive erections that throbbed in need as the two men stretched out on either side of Reese.

"I'm sorry I lost it." Her shamed voice broke the silence.

"Nothing to be sorry for," Sloan murmured before flicking his tongue over a pink puckered nipple.

"Nothing at all," Rylan concurred, then captured her other breast with his mouth and sucked hard.

Her hips shot off the bed. "Fuck," she moaned. "That's . . . oh God, don't stop. Keep doing that . . ."

Rylan gave a husky chuckle, and Sloan felt the vibrations of it against his mouth. "We don't stop until you tell us to stop," Rylan promised.

Sloan wholeheartedly agreed. He worked that perfect nipple in his mouth, licking and suckling while his palm drifted down her flat stomach toward the juncture of her thighs. When his hand bumped Rylan's, it was his turn to laugh. Looked like they both had the same idea.

In perfect synchronicity, they toyed with their woman, Rylan spreading her delicate lips open so Sloan could rub her clit. After a few teasing strokes, Sloan covered Rylan's knuckles with his palm and slid both their hands lower, pushing their fingers inside her tight sheath.

She made a low, desperate sound. Sloan lifted his mouth from her breast to find that her brown eyes had completely glazed over. She was mindless with lust, squirming on the bed, rocking against his and Rylan's fingers as if she couldn't get enough.

"Christ, baby, you're so wet," Rylan groaned, pushing deeper inside.

Sloan was well aware of how wet she was. She soaked their fingers and tested his restraint each time her inner muscles clutched them tighter. He couldn't stop the urge to rub his aching cock against her leg.

A strangled laugh flew out when he noticed Rylan doing the same. This woman got both of them so hot they were liable to shoot their loads before either of them even entered her. But not yet. First, he wanted to make her come again.

"Eat her pussy," he told Rylan. "I want to see the look on her face when you make her come."

The other man didn't need to be asked twice. With a wicked smile, he crawled between Reese's legs and started tonguing her clit. Sloan's fingers stayed lodged inside her, and Rylan's eager tongue grazed his knuckles with every long, lazy lick.

Sloan shivered with arousal. He knew firsthand how good Rylan was with that tongue.

So good, in fact, that Reese began trembling almost immediately. She clamped tightly on Sloan's fingers as she moaned with abandon. "Coming," she gasped, and holy hell, was she ever.

He watched as raw ecstasy filled her eyes, making them hazy and heavy-lidded. His heart beat faster as he felt her orgasm rippling around his hand. There was nothing hotter than watching—no, *feeling*—this woman lose control. Reese was . . . fire. A fire that ran so hot it turned men into mindless, panting savages who existed only to serve her. To please her. To love her.

And that was fine by him. As long as he had Reese in his arms, shuddering and coming and sobbing his name, he was happy to let her fire consume him.

More.

That was the only thought that beat in her blood. She wanted more. More of Rylan's tongue tracing her clit. More of Sloan's harsh-voiced commands. More orgasms. More releases. Just . . . more.

Reese sat up and watched in anticipation as the two men knelt on the mattress. She knew what was next. How the two of them would possess her at the same time.

She could not *wait*.

"Tell us what you want first," Sloan ordered.

Her body sang with delight at the word *first*. This was merely the beginning.

"I want this." She grasped Sloan's hard shaft and circled it with her fingers. Then she reached for Rylan's. "And this."

Rylan flashed a quick grin at her. He moved beside Sloan and positioned himself close to her face, holding his cock in one hand. She tongued the tip of it, enjoying his masculine taste, the velvety feel inside her mouth. Her other hand continued to pump Sloan, who watched for a few seconds before taking over for her, handling his cock more roughly than Reese would've ever dreamed of doing.

Sloan stroked himself as Reese flicked her tongue along the underside of Rylan's tip. Just when Rylan released a husky growl and tried pushing deeper into her mouth, she released him and turned her attention to Sloan.

He groaned the moment she swallowed him up, his fingers tangling in her hair, gripping the damp strands to the point of pain. It was Rylan's turn to pump himself, his eyes greedily taking in the sight of her sucking Sloan.

As tension began to build again in her core, Reese dropped a hand between her legs to rub the ache away. Before she could make contact, Sloan's hand shot out.

"No." He gripped her wrist. "That belongs to us tonight. No touching." He pressed her hand back on his hip and then slid his fingers back in her hair. He jerked her head up. "Now suck."

She sucked hard. First on Sloan, then Rylan,

alternating between each man, summoning deep, desperate noises from both of their throats.

Her pulse sped up when Rylan grabbed Sloan around the neck and kissed him. Sloan's hand tightened in her hair as he returned the kiss.

Fuck, that was the hottest thing she'd ever seen. Or maybe it wasn't—the memory of Sloan's cock in Rylan's mouth was even hotter. She was so turned on she felt like she might self-combust. And if she couldn't touch herself, then she was going to torture these two men. She took one shaft in each hand and stroked faster.

When Sloan backed away, Reese voiced her disapproval. "No. Come back."

"Too close to coming," he grunted. His chest heaved as if he'd run all the way out to the farm and back at top speeds, his lips glossy from his kiss with Rylan.

Rylan wasn't in much better shape. He licked his lips and gave her a hungry look. "My dick needs to be in someone right now," he growled.

Sloan gave an abrupt nod and slid in behind Reese. He stretched out his legs and placed her knees on the outside of his hips.

It was an awkward position for her. Her center of gravity was off and she had to rely on Sloan's broad back to support her. He lightly ran his hands down her sides. Ghost touches under her arms, fingers marking each separate rib while Rylan waited impatiently for his order.

"C'mere." Sloan gestured for Rylan, then cupped Reese's breasts, thumbing her tightly-peaked nipples before holding them out for Rylan's mouth. "Suck until she comes again."

"That's not going to take long," she said ruefully.

"Look how hot you are, sweetheart," Sloan whispered in her ear as Rylan bent forward. "Do you like this? My hands squeezing your tits while Rylan sucks those pretty nipples into his mouth?"

"*Yes.*" It was incredibly decadent.

Sloan's cock sat at the base of her spine, big and ready. "I'm going to fuck your ass while our man gets your pussy." He licked a line of heat up her exposed neck. "It's gonna be a tight fit. You're gonna be sore tomorrow. Every time you take a step, you'll feel it and you'll remember what it felt like to have both of us taking you at once."

She shuddered.

He tipped her forward, one hand at the center of her back. Rylan caught her around her waist and held her over Sloan's dick, and Reese moaned when she felt the blunt head nudge at her opening.

"Take a deep breath, sweetheart," Sloan instructed, running a hand down her spine. He curled an arm over her thigh to catch her clit between his thumb and forefinger.

She closed her eyes and concentrated on that sweet touch as the invasion of her body began in tiny, slow increments.

Rylan held her flush against his body as he looked over her shoulder. "Christ, baby, your ass is tight. Sloan's barely got the head in. Ease up, baby."

His encouraging words were accompanied by long sweeps of his hands along the tops of her thighs. Between Sloan and Rylan's petting, she stretched enough for Sloan to slide in completely. They both hissed—him from the tight fit, her from the burn.

Her body felt like one exposed nerve. Everything was turning her on. The scratch of Sloan's wiry chest hair against her shoulder blades. The muscles of Rylan's chest flexing against her sensitive nipples. The harsh sounds of their breathing.

"Feels good, doesn't it?" Rylan murmured.

She couldn't even nod. Her mind was a swirling vortex of pain, need, and pleasure.

Sloan suddenly surged to his feet, driving hard into her tight passage, and Reese cried out as the swift stroke triggered an orgasm. His arm clamped around her waist while the other lifted one of her legs and draped it along Rylan's hip.

Rylan pushed her head to the side and held her chin in place so Sloan could kiss her.

Holy fucking hell. She'd asked for more, and boy, were they giving it to her.

Sloan's tongue slid into her mouth as Rylan reached between her legs to palm her core. "Fuck, I need another taste," he mumbled, and then he dropped to his knees and slung both her legs over his shoulders. His mouth between her legs while Sloan pulsed in her ass was the most incredible feeling in the world.

And clearly she wasn't the only one on the edge, because Sloan abruptly broke away from her mouth. "Get up here, you asshole. I'm going to shoot my load if you keep tonguing me."

Reese choked on a laugh.

Rylan slowly rose to his feet. That feral smile was back—the one that promised a dose of heaven and hell at the same time.

"Ease out," he ordered.

Sloan backed away, and Reese moaned at the loss.

"Don't worry, gorgeous," Rylan reassured her. "We're gonna fill you up again." Then he bent his legs and fit the broad tip of his cock against what felt like an impossibly tiny entrance.

He pushed, and it was painful at first, making her whimper.

"Keep going," Sloan ordered.

And Rylan, who'd held back for so long, couldn't anymore. Sloan's command jerked his hips forward and he powered into her so hard, she would've been thrown on the bed if Sloan hadn't been at her back.

The three of them stood there, quivering with emotion and lust and *feeling* until Sloan began to move. He dipped his legs, shifted Reese slightly and then powered in.

Her grasp on reality thinned. The room, her worries, the victories behind her, the battles to come . . . it all became a blur as the two men worked her in hard, relentless strokes. Her body opened as if she'd been made for two men. Not any two, though. *These* two.

The intense sensations were exhilarating and frightening, like the time she'd walked to the edge of the earth and looked down a jagged cliff to see the ocean eat away at the land. For an infinitesimal moment she'd allowed her toes to hang over the edge, while bits of soil and tiny rocks skipped down to land soundlessly on the shore where they were immediately gobbled up by the water.

She had felt weightless and insignificant but so alive. She'd been tempted to throw herself off the cliff for the sheer exhilaration of it. She hadn't, of course. That was madness.

But wasn't this some kind of madness too? Reese

felt like she was on the verge of something that would engulf her. That would change her completely.

Their cocks shuttled in and out of her, separated by only the tiniest membrane. She knew they could feel each other. She heard their heightened lust in their raspy breaths, the concaves of their chests as they gulped for air.

Pleasure thudded inside her skull.

More.

"There is nothing we won't give you," Sloan said softly. "Nothing you could want that we can't deliver."

Their bodies thrust and hammered against hers to enforce his vow. The rough pads of Rylan's fingers scraped along her thighs. Sloan had an arm around her middle and his other hand splayed right under her neck, his thumb pressed against the pulse point.

The thump of Sloan's heart at her back and Rylan's at her chest drove through the center of her body to meet at hers, until the three of them moved as one, breathed as one, beat as one.

Reese gave into it. She hung on to her men as they drove her over the edge, knowing that she couldn't fall with the two of them holding her up.

Sloan, the one with the iron control, broke first. He broadened his stance and jacked into her with quick, uncoordinated movements. Rylan followed close behind. Fingers dug into her skin hard enough to bruise. Teeth bit into her shoulder.

Rylan threw his head back and cursed up a blue streak as he came. Sloan laughed in her ear, and that unexpected sound shattered her. The orgasm seized her body, wave after wave of sensation surging through her, leaving her shaking and weak.

Good thing she didn't need to stand.

She felt her body being pressed forward as Sloan slowly withdrew. Then Rylan slipped free, and Sloan laid her on the bed and covered her with a blanket.

She closed her eyes, still feeling the echoes of that intense orgasm. Beyond the bed, she heard sounds of water splashing and the deep murmur of satisfied male voices. Footsteps neared the bed and a washcloth was pressed gently between her legs. Sloan's hand, she thought dimly. And that was Rylan's in her hair, brushing the strands away from her sweaty forehead.

"That was fucking amazing," Rylan said as he curled his body around hers.

Sloan's footsteps took him away from the bed. Was he leaving? Dismayed, Reese stretched out an arm.

Rylan grabbed it and tucked it back under the covers. "He's not going anywhere, baby. Just putting the washcloth away."

A moment later, Sloan returned to take up his place on the other side of her.

Wait. *His* place?

They had places in her bed now?

"Stop thinking," Sloan ordered.

"I can't," she admitted. She'd always wanted more, but she hadn't realized that *more* existed in Sloan and Rylan. In the perfect rhythm of their bodies. In the press between the hard slabs of their chests. In the thick penetration of their cocks.

For the first time in her life, she felt completely and totally satisfied. She felt . . . whole.

And that scared her to death.

20

"This mattress sucks."

Reese rolled her eyes when Rylan shifted his ass for the millionth time in ten minutes.

"You got better at Con's camp?" Sloan challenged.

"Nah, but this is Foxworth, man. You've got the best of everything. You couldn't find one of those plump white things on one of your raids?"

"This is the best there is. And if it's good enough for Reese, it's good enough for your hard ass."

"Reese is fierce, though. I'm just a good ol' boy. I came to Foxworth for the finer things in life."

"And the fighting," Reese interjected wryly, grateful for Rylan's lighthearted postcoital talk. There was a heavier one coming and she wasn't ready for it.

"That's a given." She felt, rather than saw, Rylan's cheeks move as he broke out in a large smile. "And the fucking. No better fucking on earth than at Foxworth."

Sloan's big hand crossed over Reese's head to slap the side of Rylan's skull. A love tap, really, because she knew he was too spent from the sex to put any power behind it.

They all were. Like little children at naptime, they all lay in a sweaty, happy row staring at the ceiling.

"Baby, get your hunter to find us a better mattress," Rylan told her. "We're going to destroy this thing in a week."

Her heart leapt in excitement before the fear inside her grabbed her and pulled her back to earth. She felt Sloan's eyes fix on her, and when she turned her head slightly, she saw the unspoken questions. *Are you all right? Was this good for you?*

She and Sloan had crossed a line tonight. As good as it had been, and as much as she wanted to do it again and again and again, there was as much apprehension as there was satisfaction swirling in her blood.

Sloan's arm was still extended, and Rylan tipped his head into Sloan's palm as if neither of them wanted to lose the connection they'd built tonight. Reese, meanwhile, lay cocooned between their two big bodies. If she turned her head to the right or left, she could place a kiss on the side of either man's broad chest.

The mattress might not be thick or white, but it was big. Sloan had hauled it back with him shortly after Jake died. Her old one had been covered in a pool of blood, and Sloan had removed it immediately after killing Jake. He'd taken the body, the mattress, the clothes, and burned it all outside of Foxworth. And the next night, he'd left. Gone for more than a day, and when he'd returned, he'd had this futon frame in the back of his truck.

But even though Sloan had done his best to erase Jake from Foxworth, the ghost of the dead man still haunted Reese.

Some things couldn't be burned away.

Rylan must've felt the growing tenseness of her body, because the good ol' boy, the one with the ready smile and equally ready erection, rolled his head to the side and frowned deeply. "You thinking about Bethany?" he asked cautiously.

She didn't know why she turned to Sloan for direction. She just did.

Sloan searched her face and murmured, "Tell us what happened back there."

She blinked, surprised he was encouraging her to talk in front of Rylan. It felt almost like . . . an invitation to something even more intimate than sex.

One of the best things about fighting and fucking, as she was sure Rylan would attest to, was that those were straightforward activities with straightforward rewards. Fuck and fight and get a burst of adrenaline that carried you to the next round of physical exertions.

Lying in bed and cozying up to a partner wasn't something Reese was used to, at least not since Jake. Even with Sloan, her trusted advisor, the one who knew all of her secrets, she kept part of herself closed off.

Now they both wanted to flay her open, and Reese felt suffocated. She felt—

"It's okay, sweetheart. If you don't want to talk about it, don't." Sloan's free hand came over to stroke down her arm as if she was a child in need of comfort.

That raised her hackles. With thin lips and a glare at Sloan, she said, "I want one. A baby. But I can't have one."

She waited for their pity with fisted hands. When

both men continued to stare at the ceiling, as if her admission was no big deal, some of her tension began to fade.

Reese forced her fingers open. "The council never allows the firstborns to breed. They don't want any of the commoners to have a strong lineage." She took a deep breath, and added, "They sterilized me."

"That sucks," Rylan said.

Those two simple words leeched away the last of her anger. She wasn't sure why she'd expected some sort of judgment, but the fact that Rylan didn't think less of her for wanting a kid or falling apart brought a rush of warmth to her chest. Like Sloan, this man just . . . accepted her.

"I never thought about having kids," he admitted.

"Me neither," Sloan spoke up.

"You already had one. You were practically Jake's parent." The thought popped in Reese's head and out her mouth before she realized it.

"Yeah, and look how good that turned out. I don't want that responsibility again." Sloan rolled on his side and placed a hand on her hip.

The meaningful pressure from that touch told her he didn't want to bring Jake into this bed or this room, and sure enough, he was quick to change the subject.

"Rylan, you were pretty good back there," he said gruffly. "With Bethany."

"I told you, I grew up on a farm. We didn't have a lot of animals, but I witnessed a birth or four." Rylan caught the edge of his lower lip in his mouth and shifted closer to Reese. "The council sucks, no doubt, but people outside of it aren't so great either."

Sloan reached out and stroked Rylan's hair away from his forehead. "Evil's evil. It doesn't need to be ugly or wear a council robe."

Reese was pretty sure it was Sloan's touch that kept Rylan talking.

"Bandits killed my parents," he confessed. "Raped my mom and my dad and then killed them. Or hell, they could've killed them and then raped them. I only got there in time to bury the bodies after those bastards took off."

Reese swallowed the words of sympathy that she would've been pissed if Rylan had expressed before. She knew he wasn't sharing these things because he wanted them to feel sorry for him. He was sharing for the same reason Reese had just admitted to her desperate desire to have a child. Because the explosive connection forming between the three of them was somehow summoning these confessions.

"Hard to say," Sloan agreed.

"I wasn't too broken up about it," Rylan went on. "Mom probably welcomed death, and Dad? Well, in a few years, I would've put a knife in his belly anyway."

"He mistreat your mom?" Sloan asked.

"Is whoring her out mistreating her? Is making his son do it too so that we could eat and have clean water all that bad?" Sarcasm colored Rylan's words.

"Yeah, that's pretty bad." Sloan tugged on Rylan's head, turning it so the man could see the same thing he'd offered Reese earlier—acceptance with no judgment.

Rylan closed his eyes briefly and shook his head. "First thing I remember thinking when I came back and saw the two of them dead was *Good. Now she's not hurting anymore.*"

"You get those bandits?" Sloan asked in a low voice.

Rylan's face took on a savage expression. "Took three years of tracking, but yeah, I did."

Silence fell over the bedroom. Reese ran her hand over Rylan's bare chest, and then, for the first time since she'd met him, she actually took the time to study the tattoos inked on his golden skin. She traced her finger over one name in particular.

"Is this your mother's name? Julia?" It was the only woman's name she saw, unless there were female versions of Connor and Pike she didn't know about.

"Yeah," he said sadly.

"I guess your dad's name isn't anywhere on here."

"Nope."

A wry smile touched her lips as she continued to read the random lines of black text. "What do all these things mean?"

He shrugged. "Just words of wisdom I picked up over the years. Names of people who saved my butt at one point or another. Some poetry I heard."

Sloan leaned over Reese's body and dragged his thumb along Rylan's left side. "I know this one. My ma read it to me once when I was a kid."

Reese peered in to take a closer look.

Do not go gentle into that good night, it read.

She laughed softly. "Suits you," she told Rylan. "Nothing you do is gentle."

"I can be gentle when I want to be," he protested.

Then he rolled all the way over until the two men formed a wall on either side of her. He placed a fingertip at the hollow of her neck and began a slow trek down the center of her chest, stopping at the splayed fingers Sloan still rested on Reese's pelvis.

"I'm done with this talking but I'm not sleepy," Rylan drawled. "Anyone got any ideas?"

Sloan's hand drifted between Reese's legs. "I've got a few."

Reese couldn't get out of bed fast enough the next morning.

She slipped out from underneath Sloan's heavy arm and quickly pulled on a pair of stretchy pants and a long-sleeve T-shirt. Sloan's eyes tracked her every move, but thankfully he stayed silent. Rylan, meanwhile, slept on, shifting restlessly as if he missed Reese's body next to his. When Sloan reached over and placed a hand on Rylan's shoulder, the blond man immediately settled.

The two of them looking lazy and sated in her bed simultaneously made her want to break out in hives and rip her clothes off and go for round three. Or would it be round four? She'd lost track of all the orgasms they'd given each other last night.

The memory of their hot touch rendered her clothes tight and uncomfortable. Her body urged her to return to the bed and crawl between the two men, but her racing mind wouldn't let her.

What was she actually doing?

Why had she slept with both of them?

How could she ever go back to the ordinary practice of sleeping with one man?

How could she ever go back to her ordinary practice of sleeping with men she didn't care about?

She'd known Rylan was trouble from the very start. It was why she'd resisted his charms for so long. And she'd known keeping Sloan at a distance, physically anyway, was vitally important in order to keep up the pretense that despite everything they'd shared, he wasn't necessary to her well-being.

So why had she let them both in?

Reese exhaled in a rush, and she was running almost before she shut the bedroom door behind her. Sloan undoubtedly heard her rapidly retreating footsteps, and she could almost hear him sigh heavily in her ear.

Sweetheart, he'd say, *this changes nothing. I'm still the sword at your back. You have a mess, I'm there to clean it up. Plan your attacks. Inspire your people. Let the rest of us work out the details.*

She ran harder, hoping the physical effort would drive out his voice and ease her tension. Scott was up doing chores when she ran past the farm. She raised an arm in greeting but didn't pause. Despite the cool winter morning, sweat began to drip down the sides of her face as she pushed forward toward a cluster of trees and a torn-up cement trail that snaked for miles around the more wooded and scenic areas at the outskirts of town.

Even as her feet ate up the miles and her shirt became soaked with perspiration, none of the tension abated. By the sixth mile, she wasn't even sure what she was worked up about, only that she was.

But why? The outpost attacks had been successful. Between her and Connor, there was only one station left in the southwest. There'd been no word of casualties or defeat from the other camp leaders, and in this case, no word was a good sign. Enforcers had already come and gone twice, which meant that Foxworth wouldn't be due for another visit anytime soon. The town was safer than ever.

So what if she'd slept with Rylan and Sloan? Any woman would jump to be the center of that man-sandwich. So what if Bethany had a baby and Reese couldn't? Having a baby in the free land with Enforcers sniffing around was dangerous and stupid—neither trait anyone would associate with Reese.

But the itch in the middle of her back wouldn't go away. The headache in her temples pounded in time with her feet. With each stride, she should have been shedding her stress and anxiety, but Reese had a feeling she could run all the way to the coast and still not get rid of her unease.

It was that remaining outpost, she decided. And the fact that there were still Foxworth soldiers lent out to Brynn and Mick. She wanted all her people back behind the gates. And she wanted the Global Council destroyed.

What she needed was to take down the remaining outpost. It'd be stocked with only a few men. Ten at the very most. She'd taken out three men by herself the other night. Sure, she'd gotten winged, but she'd be more careful next time. And she'd have Sloan.

Once the final outpost was gone, the next step would be to aim for the council.

Yes. Her footsteps grew slower, but firmer. That was what she needed to do—a full and complete destruction of the watchtowers. Enforcers touring the colony wouldn't have those stations to refuel, and the lack of backup would either force them to make deals with Reese again or it would tire them out and make them sloppy.

Reese finally gave up on her run. Any other morning, the crisp air and the burn in her lungs, the monotony of her feet slapping at the dirt, would have left her energized and ready to face the day. But no amount of sweat was going to fix what was ailing her today.

She had an idea of what would, though. Her internal check system wasn't allowing her to relax and enjoy herself because the job wasn't done.

It had nothing to do with Rylan or Sloan or the intimacy that had been stirred up in her bedroom.

Nope, nothing to do with that.

Back at Foxworth, the town was starting to wake up. She hoped the men were up and gone, because she really needed to shower but wasn't in the mood to have a post-sex talk with either one of them.

She was halfway inside her doorway when she heard a soft voice say her name.

"Reese."

Christine ambled up, and she seemed . . . different. Her shoulders were back and her head wasn't bowed like it usually was. She still looked as sweet and shy as ever, but there was a new confidence about her that made Reese hide a wry smile. Yeah, getting your period would do that to a girl. Obviously Christine had overcome her embarrassment and decided she was a woman.

"How are you feeling?" Reese asked the teenager.

Christine scuffed a toe in the dirt. "Better. I wanted to apologize for being such a baby the other day."

"You weren't. First time I got my period, I cried my eyes out. I couldn't figure out why my body suddenly decided to torture me."

Christine giggled, and the two of them shared a look of understanding that filled Reese with a confusing amount of warmth.

She quickly tried to shake it off by asking, "Why are you up so early?"

"I want to see Bethany and the baby. Wanna come with me?"

Dread churned in her stomach, but Christine looked so excited that Reese didn't have the heart to make up an excuse. The girl was even holding out her hand, when in the past she'd always avoided physical contact.

Drawing a breath, she took the girl's hand and allowed Christine to drag her toward Bethany's.

Inside the house, the new mother was sitting up by the front windows.

"You should be in bed," Reese reprimanded from the open doorway. "You just had a baby."

Bethany lifted the newborn from her breast and grimaced. "All he's done so far is eat and sleep and poop. I wanted to look out the window." Her chin jutted out. "Besides, Rylan told me to get up and move around if I felt like it."

"Oh my gosh! He's so little," Christine breathed in awe, taking a hesitant step closer to the couch.

"Want to hold him?" Bethany offered with a smile.

Christine had her arms out before Bethany was done asking the question. A moment later, the young girl was cuddling the baby to her chest, and the two

of them made a picture of such heartrending innocence that Reese struggled to control her jealousy.

In the city, a girl's first period meant a visit from
the medics. It marked the first and last time she'd be
fertile. But for Christine, the promise of motherhood
was very real. It should've made Reese fiercely glad,
because wasn't this the whole purpose behind Foxworth? To build a community that would have the
freedom and peace to grow?

Instead, she was practically choking on envy and
hating herself for it.

"You eaten breakfast yet?" Bethany asked.

Reese jerked her head away from Christine. "No.
Haven't had time."

Bethany started to rise, but Reese shook a hand in
the woman's direction, gesturing for her to sit her
just-delivered-a-baby ass back in the chair.

"I'll make it myself," Reese said firmly.

"All right." Bethany grinned. "Go cook something
for me too, then. Because I'm famished."

"Yes, sir." Rolling her eyes, Reese headed for the
kitchen. "Is everyone doing okay after the Enforcer
visit?" she asked as she pulled a bowl of farm fresh
eggs and a jar of milk from the refrigerator.

"Yeah, but the bunker's getting crowded," Bethany replied.

"Some of the older boys and girls can stay up top
next time." The Enforcers might wonder why they
had so many young people, but their orders were to
snuff out the babies. As long as the older kids could
pass as adults, hopefully they'd be left alone.

"You think there's going to be a next time?"

"Yes."

Christine squeaked.

Reese shot a glance over her shoulder and fought a jolt of anger at the fear she glimpsed on Christine's face. The anger wasn't directed at the girl, but the council. Sure, Christine and Bethany were able to have babies, but none of them were truly free. As long as the Global Council existed, Reese's people would never be free.

She swallowed her bitterness and turned back to the stove. "Want meat in your eggs?"

"Yes, please." Bethany paused. "Oh. Hey. Did Sloan tell you that one of Scott and Anna's cows is pregnant?"

Reese slammed the skillet down harder than necessary. Was everyone on the fucking planet pregnant these days? She wondered briefly whether Connor's woman was sterile. Hudson wasn't a designated breeder, but she came from a wealthy and powerful family. The rules didn't always apply to those folks.

"Need help over there?" Bethany called out.

"Nope. I'm good."

Reese whipped the eggs and decided she was done chatting for the morning. When she emerged from the kitchen, she was carrying plates of toast, potatoes, and eggs for Bethany, Christine, and herself. Bethany's dish also had a small side of steak.

Reese settled into a chair and watched as Bethany managed to fork food into her mouth with one hand and hold the baby with the other. Then she turned to Christine and asked, "How's your training going?"

As per Reese's orders, everyone in town was learning self-defense and how to shoot a gun, but she considered the training even more important for the females. Men outnumbered women in the free land, and Reese would be damned if her girls didn't learn to protect themselves. There were men out there, bandits mostly, who would have no qualms taking a pretty girl like Christine against her will.

Christine smiled. "Pretty good—I've been practicing with the bow and arrow. I'm sad Jamie is gone because I really wanted to show her how my aim has improved." She blushed guiltily, and Reese realized she was probably remembering the fight Jamie and Reese had gotten into during the onset of training.

What had that fight even been over? Reese scanned her brain for a second, then grinned in memory. Right. It'd been about how Reese was never to touch Lennox again.

"Don't worry, I'm sure Jamie will be by one of these days. Nash radioed her about Bethy's baby, so I bet she's already making plans to get here."

Christine looked confused, as if she didn't understand how you could beat the shit out of someone one day and welcome them into your home the next, but Jamie had been fighting for her man that day, and fighting for what you wanted was something Reese wholly believed in.

"Have you heard from the other camps?" Bethany asked.

"No, but that's a good thing. That means they're focused on the mission and executing it. If we'd already heard back from them, that'd mean someone broke away from the outpost attacks and had to flee for safety." Reese set down her fork and washed the breakfast down with a gulp of water. "Anyway, thanks for breakfast, but I've gotta go."

"Want to hold Archer before you leave?" Bethany tipped her head to the infant.

"No, thanks." The refusal came out brusquer than Reese intended.

"He won't bite," Bethany said with a laugh.

"You gotta hold him, Reese. He smells *so* good. Like an angel," Christine cooed.

"You know you want to." Bethany clearly meant to tease, but the expectant look in both her and Christine's eyes stung Reese.

She stared at them coldly until the light faded in Bethany's eyes and the woman shifted uncomfortably. Even Christine got the hint, sliding back in her chair as if to make herself a smaller target.

Fuck. Reese hated that she'd brought a chill into Bethany's room. Hated that there was distance growing between herself and her friend. But she was helpless to stop it, and she knew it ran so much deeper than envy over the baby. Reese wasn't sure if she'd ever be able to look at Bethany again without the guilt of Arch's death breathing down her neck.

She took a breath and pushed the rising guilt aside. Feeling too much was what had pushed Jake over the edge. She needed control, needed to forget about emotions, because emotions would only get everyone killed, from old Anna and Scott to the newborn in Bethany's arms.

So, no. She wasn't allowed to *feel*. She was only allowed to *act*. And there was only one way to make sure the people under her care remained safe.

The total annihilation of the council.

21

Rylan opened his eyes to find a heavily muscled arm flung over his chest. Shit, no wonder he'd been dreaming about suffocating. Sloan's arm was like an iron beam. And his callused hand was curled so protectively around Rylan's left pec that it brought a choked laugh to his lips. Even in slumber Sloan wanted to protect the people he cared about.

Rylan had never thought he'd be welcomed into that very exclusive circle.

"Sloan," he wheezed softly. "Can't breathe."

The man beside him stirred, head lifting as his dark eyes slitted open. "Pussy."

He swallowed another laugh. "Not my fault you weigh a million pounds."

"You calling me fat?"

The rumble of indignation had him running a hand through Sloan's short hair. "Nah. You're just big-boned."

"Fucker." And then a pair of sharp teeth dug into Rylan's shoulder.

Okay, this was messed up. Who woulda thought

he'd be cuddling in bed with *Sloan*, of all people? Not to mention joking around with the man. The man who Rylan had always believed was allergic to humor. It felt really fucking nice waking up this way, though. Only thing that would've made it better was if Reese were still snuggled up between them.

He craned his neck and peered around the bedroom. "Where's Reese?" He'd been sleeping so soundly he hadn't even felt her slide out of bed.

Sloan, of course, proved yet again that he was always aware of Reese's movements. "Snuck out around dawn," Sloan said in a sleepy voice. "She's an early riser."

"And you didn't go with her?"

"She likes to go for a run after she wakes up. Not my workout of choice."

Rylan snickered. "Let me guess, you prefer your exercise routine to involve your dick."

Sloan didn't take the bait. "Naw. I do push-ups."

Before he could stop himself, Rylan skimmed his hand down Sloan's arm, tracing the defined muscles of his biceps and forearms. Damn, those pushups were doing their job.

"Speaking of dicks," Sloan murmured.

Rylan groaned when a warm hand encircled his morning wood. Sloan gave a slow, languid pump, and the bolt of excitement that whipped up Rylan's spine would've knocked him on his ass if he hadn't been lying down. His body's swift, lusty response floored him. His cock had gotten so much action last night it was a miracle it could still function.

"You're a sex addict," he muttered, but he didn't swat Sloan's hand away.

"Three years of celibacy," Sloan muttered back. "That kind of torture turns a man into an animal." And then the self-proclaimed animal slid down and took Rylan's erection in his mouth.

The tight suction and the greedy swirl of Sloan's tongue was enough to shut down Rylan's brain altogether. His eyes snapped closed as he lost himself in the wicked sensations, rocking his hips to push deeper into Sloan's mouth. When he came, it was with a weak croak, because his throat was too sore from all the groaning he'd done last night.

Sloan swallowed up his release, then wiped his mouth with the back of his hand and sat up. He winked at Rylan before hopping off the bed, naked as the day he was born. Another surprise—Sloan was cheerful in the morning. Rylan never would've guessed.

"You just gonna lie there all day, you lazy asshole?" Sloan taunted as he slipped on a pair of jeans.

Rylan could barely find the energy to sit up. "You kidding me, brother? You think I can actually *move* after that blow job?"

"I suck a mean cock, huh?" Sloan was chuckling as he disappeared into the bathroom.

As the sound of running water wafted out of the open doorway, Rylan forced himself to climb out of bed and search for his clothes. Where . . . ? Right, they were on the bathroom floor, tangled up with Reese and Sloan's clothing.

Reese and Sloan. Jesus. How had those two gotten to him like this? They were in his blood, the mere thought of them making his entire body feel warm and achy and tight with anticipation. Rylan had run into a few triads over the years, committed relationships with two men and one woman, or two women and one man. Hell, there was even a trio of females living in Garrett's camp who'd decided they didn't want or need any dicks to complete them.

But he'd never envisioned himself involved in that kind of relationship. He'd never envisioned himself in a relationship, period. He didn't do commitment, and he didn't believe in love. Whenever anyone got too close, he walked away.

So why did the idea of walking away from Reese and Sloan fill him with such crushing anxiety?

"You have time to check in on Bethy and the baby today?" Sloan asked, meeting Rylan's gaze in the small mirror over the sink. "I'm planning on tackling that goddamn pipe in the restaurant this morning. Swear to God, I'm fixing this motherfucker once and for all."

Rylan managed a chuckle, but inside he was still worrying about the repercussions of last night. Sloan had completely lowered his guard around him. These past few weeks had cemented not just a friendship between them, but something deeper. Something that made Rylan's pulse speed up every time he thought about it.

And Reese . . . Christ, he couldn't get enough of the woman. Everything about her excited him—her strength, her stubbornness, her fire.

He'd told them about his past, damn it. He'd confessed to hunting down the bandits that had brutally murdered his parents. He'd revealed that his mother hadn't been the only whore in their household, that his father had expected the same of him. He'd never told anyone about that before, and he ought to be running hard and fast after placing himself in such a vulnerable position.

Instead, he'd let Sloan suck him off and now they were standing around planning their day.

The back of his neck suddenly began to itch.

"Yeah, I can drop in on Bethany," he answered. "And if you need help with that broken pipe, I might be able to—" He stopped when footsteps sounded in the hall.

When Reese appeared in the doorway, Rylan instantly knew something was up. The soft, rosy-cheeked woman who'd been in bed with them last night was gone. Her hair was no longer sex-tousled, but pulled back in a tight, low ponytail. Her brown eyes were no longer blazing with passion, but damn near vacant.

Sloan noticed the difference too, because his expression flickered with unease. "Morning," he said carefully.

"Morning." Even her voice was different. Cooler, more reserved. "I need both of you downstairs."

Rylan and Sloan exchanged a wary look. "What for?" Sloan asked.

"Got something important to discuss," was all she supplied. "I'll wait for you guys down there."

With that, she turned on her heel and stalked off, leaving them alone in the bathroom to wonder what the hell was going on.

They dressed in silence and then went downstairs to the small meeting room. Reese had her maps out and was placing a painted bullet on one section, a sight that made Sloan stiffen. Rylan didn't know what that represented, but it was clear that Sloan didn't like it.

"What's going on?" the man asked brusquely.

Gone was the hazy-eyed seductress of last night. A steely-eyed military leader looked back at them. "There's one outpost in the southwest that still needs to be taken out. Here." She jabbed her finger on the map.

"Reese . . ." Sloan warned.

She was having none of it. "We strike now and we strike fast."

"We have no good intel on this outpost. All we know is that it doesn't contain any supplies and it's supposedly lightly guarded, but they could've made changes to it since the last time we took a look. Which was . . . six, seven months ago? Plus, we haven't heard back from any of the other leaders," Sloan argued.

She waved a careless hand. "We're not going to hear back from them for a while—they're busy with their own missions. But the council has to be reeling. This is the perfect time."

Rylan knew Sloan wouldn't like what he had to say, but he said it anyway. "I agree. Let's strike now. Garrett's definitely taken out his outposts by now, and the council's got to be scrambling for answers. Being hit at these different outposts will thin their ranks. They'll be rushing to the four corners trying to figure out who's behind the attacks." He paused. "How many men are supposed to be at this outpost?"

"Five to ten." Reese was eyeing him in approval.

Rylan tried not to preen like an idiot, but damn, he craved that approval. And Sloan's too. For some fucked-up reason, he wanted to show them both that he had more going for him than what hung between his legs. He could be Reese's left hand while Sloan was the right.

Last night, Sloan had looked to him for support. They'd acted as a team. A solid, cohesive unit that had taken care of and pleasured their woman—and each other.

And it had filled him with more satisfaction and contentment than he'd ever thought possible. He couldn't get enough of either one of them. With Reese, he was drawn to the fight in her. The woman wouldn't do a damn thing that she didn't want to. She certainly wouldn't have spread her legs for some dirty traveler in exchange for a sack of potatoes if her man ordered her to. Reese would never allow herself to be used like that.

And Sloan . . . he was as steady as a rock. He wouldn't use a person for his own benefit. Hell, the man would cut off his own arm before he'd let anyone hurt the people he cared about.

So yeah, maybe Rylan wanted to be a part of that. And . . . since he was being so damn honest with himself, he couldn't deny he was excited about torching another Enforcer station. There were only two things worth doing in life: fucking and fighting.

Well, he'd already fucked last night, and now Reese was asking him to fight. This was a no-brainer for him.

"Five to ten men," he echoed thoughtfully. "That's it?"

Reese pointed to the map. "Maybe not even half as staffed. It's got no supplies, and it's nowhere near the city. It's protecting nothing."

"Not nothing," Sloan reminded her. "Hudson said

the council is establishing a colony out there. There could be more soldiers there than anywhere if it's being considered as the location for a new city."

Sloan made a good point, but up until now, Reese's instincts hadn't steered them wrong. "I'm with Reese on this," Rylan said quietly. "She was right about launching the outpost attacks and she was right to keep you here in case Enforcers showed up."

Sloan ran a ragged hand through his hair. "This is a low value target. We've got tired fighters and our ranks are depleted. We haven't even gotten our men back from Mick or Brynn."

"Mick's probably finishing up his attacks and sending them our way. I bet they'll be here in a couple of days," Reese said, sounding impatient.

"Who are you going to leave to protect Foxworth?" Sloan challenged.

Now she looked annoyed. "Last time I was leaving, you said I could put anyone in charge. Even Randy, remember?"

Sloan's expression darkened. "And I was wrong. I was wrong then, but I'm not now. Look, let's send some runners out first, gather some intel, and then figure out what to do next."

"If we send a scout, we might alert the Enforcers. Let's use the element of surprise." She turned to Rylan, expectant.

Again, he backed her up. "Agreed. I'm still not seeing the point of waiting."

"This is a bad idea," Sloan said flatly.

Reese smiled. It wasn't a full-fledged grin, but a fierce one, full of teeth and a lot of anger. "If you don't want to come, then stay here," she told Sloan. "We don't need you."

Sloan froze. Beside him, Rylan sucked in a breath as if he'd been the target of the blow Reese had delivered, but it was Sloan's gut that took the punch. He nearly staggered backward from the force of it. For a second, even Reese looked stricken.

But then her features hardened and she bent over the map, brushing away the bullets and rolling the papers into a tight tube.

It was a sight Sloan was used to. Sometimes Reese coped by shutting down. She wrapped her defenses around her and there was no penetrating them. No amount of cajoling or even sex would bring her out of it. She raged and fought and then when it all got to be too much for her, she turned off. Jake had found that out early on, and he'd complained bitterly about it to Sloan on more than one occasion.

Well, fine. She could shut down all she wanted right now. But Sloan knew that her and Rylan's assessment about this mission was dead wrong. Something bad was out there. He could feel it in his bones, but he also knew he wouldn't stay behind.

"I'm coming with you," he said grimly. "I don't fucking like it, but I'm coming."

Reese's eyes flared with relief, but it was Rylan who clapped him on the back. "You'll see, brother. This fight will be so easy, you'll wonder why we even bothered arguing about it."

Sloan looked at Reese. "When do we leave?" he asked with resignation.

She dumped the rolled-up map on the desk across the room. "First thing in the morning. I'll tell the rest of the crew."

"Fine. I'll get the supplies. Rylan, you handle the vehicles," Sloan ordered. "Gas 'em all up and make sure they're ready to roll out."

As Reese and Rylan discussed the transportation they'd need, Sloan stood there with his fists clenched and his throat aching from the agony of keeping his fear locked down. He knew that throwing a temper tantrum wouldn't succeed in changing Reese's mind. She was stubborn as fuck, and she'd made up her mind.

What bothered him, though, even more than this reckless plan of hers, was the crushing sense that she was drifting away from him. He'd dreaded this moment, and he didn't even blame Rylan for it, because Reese's distance had always been inevitable.

Ever since Jake's death, Sloan had watched her brush aside more than one lover whenever shit got too real for her. He'd thought all their years of friendship made him immune to that, but he should've known better. The moment he'd unzipped his pants, he'd become a threat to her carefully composed armor, whether she admitted it or not.

"Sloan."

He lifted his head and met Reese's big brown eyes. "Yeah?"

"We're going to need to get some sleep tonight, but . . . I don't see why we can't enjoy some after dinner entertainment. You down?"

Sloan knew perfectly well she was trying to distract him with sex, but the hot look in her eyes, coupled with the wicked groan that Rylan let loose, had something warm curling south of his stomach.

He licked his dry lips. "We'll see."

Those words sounded as weak as three-day-old coffee. Reese gave a slight smile, Rylan winked, and Sloan went over to the rec hall to count guns, cursing himself the entire time.

Morning rolled around fast. Sloan had intended for them to get at least *some* sleep, but the sex had been fueled by anticipation of the fight and no one had wanted to rest, not when there was a hard cock to suck or a hot sleeve to fuck.

Still, he felt weighed down by fatigue as the three of them started out in the truck barely past dawn. Nash, Davis, and Sam tailed behind them in the other truck, while Beckett rode ahead on his motorcycle.

"Sloan . . . you know I appreciate your caution, right?" Reese's quiet voice drifted over from the passenger's seat. "Just because I don't choose to follow all your advice doesn't mean I don't value it."

"I know." And he did know. He was done sulking. There wasn't much point to it when they were on their way to attack another outpost.

He'd just have to make the best of it. The important thing was that they were all together. And he was doubly glad that Rylan was with them, resting in the backseat in anticipation of taking the next round of driving. They would be on the road all day and night.

Reese, meanwhile, was fidgeting beside him. She tapped her fingers against her knee, shifted every other second, fiddled with the radio dials even though they were listening to dead air. "I saw you coming out of Bethany's house before we left," she said after a beat of silence. "How'd she look?"

"Sleepy. Apparently the baby kept her up most of the night. She needs full-time help, I think."

"Maybe we could ask Christine to move in with her," Reese suggested.

"That's a good idea."

"One of my few?" she asked tartly.

He slid a surprised glance in her direction, wondering why she was bitching when she'd already gotten her way.

"Sorry," she muttered. Her cheeks turned pink and Sloan knew it wasn't from the morning chill. "Oh, hell, Bethany's baby still bothers me, all right?"

"Gosh, sweetheart, I had no idea you were having problems with that," he said wryly.

She sighed and let her head loll back against the seat. "Christine told me yesterday that she wanted to have a baby, and I stood there full of a weird kind of jealousy over a fourteen-year-old. It was damn embarrassing."

He tightened his grip on the wheel. "I'd have kicked Bethany out a long time ago if I knew it was going to affect you like this."

"You would not."

"Would too. I'd let the whole town burn down if it meant keeping you happy." Sloan's gaze flicked to the rearview mirror. "I'd keep the one in the back, but the rest of them can go to hell."

"Thanks a lot," came the sleepy reply.

Reese studied him curiously, as if she didn't quite believe what he was saying. But Sloan was dead serious. Yesterday, as he'd counted the guns for the third time because he wasn't paying close enough attention the first two times around, he'd come to a conclusion: he was perfectly willing to take whatever scraps Reese threw his way.

He knew she was a complicated woman. Only a person who felt as deeply as she did would've ever thought to shake her small fist at the council and believe she could take it down. And he loved her for it. He loved her enough that anything she gave him would *be* enough.

"I love Foxworth, so no, please don't set it on fire when we get back," she retorted, but her twinkling eyes belied her indignant tone.

"Nah, you don't love Foxworth," Rylan spoke up, leaning forward to fill the open space between the two front seats. "You love the people. And you need to stop obsessing over Bethy's baby—you already have a town full of kids, gorgeous. Maybe it doesn't register for you since you're so used to it, but those kids look to you for guidance and comfort and support. You're their mama in every way that counts."

Reese frowned.

"Hey, it's true. We both know passing a kid through your legs doesn't give you some kind of special status. It's what you do with the kid afterward that makes you a parent."

"Well, then that makes Foxworth all the more important, doesn't it?" Reese replied with a faint smile.

Sloan looked up to meet Rylan's eyes in the rear-view mirror. *Thank you*, he silently conveyed, and Rylan tipped his head in response.

"You promised to keep Foxworth safe," Reese said softly, reaching out to touch Sloan's arm. "I hope you haven't forgotten that."

"Sweetheart, I haven't forgotten a single promise I've ever made to you."

"What about all the promises you made me?" Rylan piped up, his blue eyes dancing playfully.

Sloan lifted a brow. "And what promises would those be?"

"You know," Rylan gave the careless wave of his hand, "how you'll suck me off whenever I ask, how you'll let me fuck your ass, all that fun stuff."

Sloan snorted loud enough to drown out the engine.

Yeah, he'd definitely take the man in the back along with Reese. And a part of him suddenly felt like pulling over, hauling Reese out of the truck, and laying her on the hood. Rylan could fuck her mouth while Sloan ate her out, all of them heated by the engine and the sex.

They were a unit now, whether Reese liked it or not.

22

As Reese had expected, the outpost was nearly deserted. There were two Enforcers stationed out front, two in the back, and, she assumed, four more inside. That was the configuration they'd found at the other stations, though she supposed the Enforcers could've boosted security to protect the interior.

Only, there was nothing to protect. All of Reese's scouting had shown that this outpost didn't contain any provisions; it was used only as a watch station. Which was the reason it hadn't been included on their initial attack list, though they planned to take it out eventually.

But the thought of eight Enforcers right there within her reach was too tempting to ignore. She needed to spill more blood. She needed to release the aggression that had been coiled tight in her gut ever since last night.

She knew Sloan was still mad at her, but at least Rylan had her back. He fully agreed that they should take out this last western outpost, and he and Beckett were currently watching the front of the building.

During these past three hours of watching and waiting, Rylan had been cracking jokes over the radio.

Sloan, on the other hand, hadn't said much. He'd spent most of those three hours sharpening his knife on a stone, which was pointless because he wouldn't be using the blade. He and Reese were both armed with assault rifles, along with the handguns strapped to their hips and hidden in their boots.

The guards they were watching were oblivious to the fact that Reese and Sloan were hunkered down a hundred yards away in the wooded area bordering the outpost. Reese's binoculars allowed her to keep a close eye on the Enforcers, who'd been smoking cigarettes and chatting since Reese's group had begun their covert surveillance. Both Enforcers were in tactical gear, but the taller one also wore a winter coat with a ridiculous fur hood.

Every time she saw the man's coat, she was reminded that it was indeed winter, and yet it didn't feel like it. Reese was wearing only a thin coat, a pair of leather gloves, and a wool hat to cover her red hair. Her knee-high snow boots were unnecessary because there wasn't a snowflake to be seen.

This was the mildest winter she'd ever experienced. Actually, it seemed like every winter in West Colony was getting warmer and warmer, not to mention shorter. Reese's mother had once told her stories about melting ice caps in the north and the rising of the oceans, but Reese hadn't paid much attention. She'd never cared about the geography of the planet— her only goal in life had been, and still was, to destroy the council.

Now, as she and Sloan hid in a forest that didn't

have so much as a dusting of snow in the middle of February, she wondered if maybe the world had more serious problems than the Global Council.

"I don't like this."

Her head jerked in Sloan's direction. "What don't you like?" she asked. "The plan, or spending this quality time with me?" She couldn't keep the bite out of her voice. She'd hoped that the peace they'd experienced during the drive would carry through to this mission, but it hadn't.

"The plan," he said irritably, visibly clenching his teeth. "It's too quiet. Too few guards."

"It's exactly the amount of guards we accounted for. We might encounter a few extra ones inside, but I can't see the Enforcers wasting manpower to guard one measly watchtower."

"They might," he countered.

"A waste of manpower," she repeated, shaking her head. "They won't be expecting us to hit it."

"They would if they were smart. You should always expect your enemy to do the opposite." He cast her a worried look. "Let's turn around. Right now, sweetheart. We don't need this outpost. Six, seven dead men? Is it really worth it?"

"I can't believe you'd even ask me that." If it were up to her, there'd be no Enforcer left alive in West Colony. Or any of the colonies, for that matter. Those bastards didn't deserve to live.

The radio crackled as Rylan checked in. "There are only two guards out here," he murmured. "Nash and Davis scouted the perimeter—no other Enforcers lurking in the trees."

Reese glanced at the small one-story building. Ten

yards away from it stood a brick tower manned by one guard. Sam was positioned in the trees with a clear vantage point to the tower, ready with her own rifle to take out the sniper. All Reese had to do was give Sam the word.

Fuck. This was the same situation she'd been in during the raid on the munitions depot last month. Everyone waiting for her command, and her questioning whether it was a good idea. Only this time it was Sloan questioning, Sloan urging her to reconsider.

She didn't know if the itchiness of her spine was her instincts' way of telling her to abort, or if it was discomfort from being this close to Sloan. She wanted so badly to reach out and stroke her fingers through his beard. Grip his chin and tug his mouth toward hers for a kiss.

She fought the urge, though. Avoiding his gaze, she clicked the radio on. "When I give the word, take out the sniper," she told Sam.

"Got it," was the quiet response.

"Rylan, after Sam neutralizes the sniper, you and Beck, and me and Sloan will take out the front and back guards simultaneously. Once we've secured the front and rear doors, wait for my word and then we go in."

"Yes, sir," came Rylan's playful voice.

Sloan didn't look nearly as amused as Rylan sounded. He adjusted his rifle and gave her a look that said he was unhappy with this course of action, but Reese knew he wouldn't argue with her. Sloan always followed her lead. Which was part of why she felt so guilty. He'd followed her for so many years and she knew he would continue to do so, but . . . she was terrified of where she might be leading him.

To a childless existence? To a relationship with her and another man, because one cock apparently wasn't enough for her?

She couldn't choose between the two of them. They both made her feel such different things. Sloan was her rock. Rylan was her sunshine. She didn't want to choose, damn it.

They didn't ask you to choose, a little voice reminded her.

No, they hadn't. But eventually they would. Wouldn't they?

This perfect little triad wasn't going to work out. It *couldn't* work. Sloan and Rylan didn't deserve someone so broken, a woman so driven by revenge that she'd leave the warmth of their bed in order to fire bullets at men she didn't even know.

Reese swallowed her dismay and focused on the task at hand. "Sam," she murmured into the radio. "Now."

She and Sloan didn't even flinch when the sharp report of a rifle cracked through the air. Reese smiled grimly as she watched the tower guard jerk from the hit. Rather than fall inside the platform, he lurched forward, half-draped over the window as his rifle dangled over the edge by its strap.

The guards in the back snapped to attention and raised their guns toward the trees.

Adrenaline sizzled in Reese's blood as she clicked the radio and hissed, "*Now*. Rylan, Beck. *Go*."

A moment later, she and Sloan tore out of the

woods and opened fire. Their aim was spot on—both Enforcers dropped like stones, blood pouring out of newly created bullet holes. The gunfire from the front of the outpost died just as fast, but before Reese could bask in the triumph of such an easy takedown, Rylan's voice burst out of the radio.

"Sloan! I need you. Beck's been hit."

Reese's heart sank to the pit of her stomach. *Shit.* So much for easy.

She peered at the side of the building, waiting for Rylan to appear, but there was no sign of him. "How bad is it?" she barked.

"Not sure, but he was hit in the leg and can't put any weight on it. And I can't man the door and carry him at the same time." Rylan cursed. "Sloan, get your ass over here."

Reese glanced urgently at Sloan. "Go. I'll stay here, Rylan can handle the front. You take Beck back to the trucks. Sam can cover me if I need it."

"I'm not leaving you," he said instantly.

"You have to. Go take care of Beckett, damn it. We can't have him bleeding out or slowing us down. The interior guards are going to rush out any second." Already she could hear footsteps beyond the metal door. Her team had used the communication jammer Xander had given them to distort any signals going in or out of the outpost. The Enforcers inside were trapped, and soon they would burst out to make their last stand.

"Go," she begged him.

His reluctance was etched into his face, but then he spun around and ran toward the side of the building.

Reese kept her rifle trained on the door, her heart

pounding as she waited for another report from Rylan. "It's a flesh wound," he finally said. "But he's bleeding a helluva lot."

"Sloan's coming," she assured him.

Half a second later, he said, "Yup, he's here. Hold on."

Reese held her breath, then released it in a shaky gust of relief when Rylan checked in again.

"Sloan's taking him to the truck. Looks like it's just you and me, gorgeous. Ready to storm the castle?"

She checked her ammo situation and nodded to herself. She was ready to go. All that was left to do was kill the bastards inside, scavenge for supplies—though she didn't expect to find any—and call it another successful victory.

"On my count," she told Rylan. "One. Two—"

The back door swung open, and the number *three* died on Reese's lips.

When she saw Eric's face, his smug smile stretched from ear to ear, she immediately recognized the grave mistake she'd made.

As her pulse shrieked in her ears, she had only a split second to scream into the radio. "*Rylan—abort. Now. Run.*"

She didn't hear his response because someone had yanked the radio from her hand. The two guards she'd expected to find charged out the door, except they were followed by two more, and two more, and two more, until she finally lost count of the number of armed uniform-clad men streaming out to surround her.

Eric, meanwhile, stood there with his gun pointed at her forehead, still smiling like this was the happiest night of his life. "Evening, Reese," he said warmly. "I've been waiting for you."

Her gaze darted to the side of the building, her ears ringing from the gunshots blasting through the air. She prayed that Rylan had made it to the woods, that he was throwing his big body over the back of the motorcycle stashed there and speeding away. The alternative—that he was lying in a pool of his own blood on the other side of the building—was too terrifying to contemplate.

"Drop the weapon," Eric ordered.

She obeyed, because she had no choice. There were a dozen Enforcers pointing guns at her. Even if she managed to kill one, or six, or eight, one of them would blow her brains out.

"That's a good girl," Eric said as he kicked her discarded rifle away.

Another wave of gunfire drowned out his next words. Reese's heart pounded in fear. Fuck. Why were there still gunshots? Where was Rylan? And Sam?

Eric stepped closer and fingered a strand of hair that had fallen out of her hat. He tucked it underneath the black wool, then rubbed his thumb over her bottom lip. Reese almost bit that thumb right off, but even she was able to recognize when she was beaten.

"What now?" she asked tiredly.

"Now we go for a little ride." Eric's smile widened. "Excited?"

She pressed her lips together and didn't answer.

"Aw, not feeling talkative? Don't worry, that'll change."

He took her arm and forcibly dragged her to the truck near the gate, while his sharp-eyed men continued to aim their weapons at her as if they were afraid she'd somehow manage to escape.

"Get in," Eric said cheerfully. "We've got a long drive ahead of us." With a chivalrous bow, he opened the back door for her. "The commander is dying to meet you."

23

Sloan dropped Beckett beyond the ridge, shouldered his rifle, and readied himself to run back to cover Rylan—only to watch the man grind to a halt. Instead of blasting open the gate as they'd planned, Rylan dropped to the ground and rolled left. That instinctive action—born out of his years of training with the People's Army—saved his life. The front gate flew open and a hail of bullets came with it, trying to mow down any and all resistance.

Sloan jumped up, firing and moving before he'd given his body a conscious command to do so. An Enforcer truck was speeding away from the courtyard. Sloan shot twice at the driver's side, and when the truck swerved, he aimed for the front tires. A crack to his right took out the passenger, courtesy of Sam.

"Cover me." He tossed the rifle at Beckett, who rolled over on his stomach and laid down suppressive fire while Sloan raced toward Rylan, gun in one hand, knife in the other.

"We need to get to the back gate!" Rylan shouted.

He scrambled to his feet and started tearing through the middle of the encampment, his gun at the ready.

Sloan followed, leaving the disabled truck and whatever Enforcers were left inside it to Beck, Sam, and the others.

Reese was at the rear—alone. They needed to get to her.

Behind them and beyond them, they heard engines and gunshots. Then came the roar of a motorcycle. Nash sped by with Davis riding bitch and shooting at an unseen target ahead. That there was something to shoot at gave Sloan an injection of hope, spurring him to sprint forward.

The back gates were open and a cloud of dust billowed from the retreating wheels of a multi-truck convoy speeding away from the gate.

Fear kept Sloan moving. He shot at the tires, the back doors, at anything and everything. The magazine emptied and he slammed another one into place without breaking stride.

Gunfire rained in their direction, but Sloan still didn't stop. Neither did Rylan, until the last truck in the convoy swerved erratically and then stopped. A stream of Enforcers flowed out of the back.

"Cover me," Rylan shouted as he ran.

Without hesitation, Sloan blasted every black-clad target. The Enforcers returned fire, but there weren't as many of them as Sloan had first thought and they weren't burning with the fire of fear and vengeance like Rylan and Sloan. Within seconds, the only firepower in the air came from the outlaws. Rylan arrived at the truck first and was hauling an Enforcer upright when Sloan reached them.

"Where are they taking her?" he heard Rylan demand.

The Enforcer smiled. The blood around his lips made the movement of his mouth obscene. "West City. They should be at the extraction point in fifteen minutes."

West City was hours away. Extraction point no doubt meant they had a chopper. Shit. Foxworth had a chopper too, but Foxworth was hours away, and the dust cloud from the Enforcer trucks was already getting smaller.

Rylan bared his teeth and plugged the Enforcer between the eyes. Then he leaned down, swiped the guns, extra ammo, and radio, and headed for the driver's door that was hanging open. "Come on. Let's go. They're getting away."

Nash idled on the motorcycle and shook his head regretfully. No way the Harley was catching up with those trucks, and even if it did, one man against an Enforcer troop with that many trucks would be suicide.

There was gunfire behind them as Sam and Beck exchanged shots with the truck that had come out the front gate. Sloan jerked his head toward the commotion, and Nash started the bike up immediately.

"Hey, wait—" Rylan bit off his words with a tiny shake of the head. "Right, we don't need him. We'll take the truck."

Sloan looked past Rylan to the vehicles that were taking Reese away from them. He clung to the hope that the council would want to make an example out of her. That they'd plan some big event that would mark their power over all the land. That they'd keep her in some cell that Sloan and Rylan and whoever they had to strong-arm into helping them would break into and free her.

You promised to keep Foxworth safe.

Sweetheart, I haven't forgotten a single promise I've ever made to you.

"We're not going after her," Sloan said flatly, crushing all those feelings of fear and helplessness under a single purpose: save Foxworth.

He and Davis would get Sam and Beck and they'd drive these two trucks back to Foxworth; they were going to need the extra vehicles in order to transport everyone in town. He eyed the flat tires. Hopefully there were spares in the bed of the truck or inside the now abandoned station.

"What the hell do you mean we're not going after her?" Rylan demanded.

Sloan ignored him and moved to the back of the truck. He grabbed a latch and pulled the floor up to find two skinny spares. Good enough.

A rough hand grabbed Sloan's shoulder. "I'm talking to you!"

His heart thudded against his breastbone. He wanted to tear after Reese too. He wanted to be reckless and stupid and hopeful. But he was none of those things. So he braced himself to face Rylan's disappointment, his utter disgust. "We're heading back to Foxworth."

"You goddamn coward," Rylan raged as Sloan lifted out one spare and then the other. "You gutless shit. Do you hear me? Where are your fucking balls? Did they shrivel up after you got your rocks off on her?"

Sloan dropped to one knee and slid the jack behind the truck's rear axle.

"I didn't realize that fucking me would mean you stopped giving a shit about her safety. If you're not going in, then I am."

Sloan thought of the tattoo on Rylan's side, the one about not going gently into the night. Yeah, this wasn't a man who did anything gently. It was one of Rylan's best traits.

It was also one of his worst.

Rylan spun around and headed for the driver's seat, but before he could climb in, Davis appeared and slammed the butt of his gun against the back of Rylan's head.

The blond man dropped to the ground like a brick.

"Thanks," Sloan mumbled.

Davis gave him a grim nod. "How's Beck?"

"Surface wound but lots of blood." Sloan jerked on the tough lug nut with so much force he was nearly knocked back on his ass when the metal started spinning free. He reapplied himself to the task, knowing that each extra second he took meant Reese was getting farther away from him. "How many do you think there were?"

Davis squinted in the distance. "There were eight in the truck. Six here. Three trucks got away, so thirty or more," he calculated.

Thirty or more Enforcers with an armory of guns, radio equipment, and a chopper at the ready? It would've been a suicide mission. One that Rylan would've gladly died trying to attempt.

Ignoring the self-loathing that was threatening to swallow him whole, Sloan concentrated on the tasks at hand. Change the tire. Get in the truck. Wave to Sam, who'd gotten the other truck moving. Order Davis to attend to Beck. Wrestle Rylan into the passenger seat. Gesture for Nash to lead the way back to Foxworth on the motorcycle.

Forget that the woman he loved was in the hands of a vicious, heartless enemy.

Rylan came to an hour into the drive, a flurry of bared teeth and accusations. Sloan let the man rant at him for the next hundred miles. Saving Foxworth instead of Reese ate at him, and his devotion to her wishes never felt—or looked—as ugly as it did under Rylan's inspection. But he'd made her a promise, damn it. He'd sworn to protect their town.

Every Enforcer in the colony knew who Reese was. There was no doubt in Sloan's mind that the council would send troops to burn Foxworth to the ground. Hell, they might already be there, for all he knew. He and the others might be walking into another ambush. But it didn't matter. If there was even the slightest chance of saving Reese's people, Sloan was taking it.

He thought he'd be grateful when Rylan stopped raging, but the silent condemnation was almost worse. They'd been on the road all night. Nash had nearly wiped out a couple of hours ago from fatigue, so they'd had to stop to load the bike onto the bed of the truck.

Fuck. He couldn't take this silence anymore. He just couldn't.

Sloan cleared his throat and glanced at the passenger seat. "Foxworth needs to be evacuated." But that reason didn't sound any stronger now than it had when he'd offered it earlier, so he added a few details in the hopes that it would appease Rylan. "Beck is injured. Sam got winged. Davis may have broken his foot, and your ear just stopped bleeding a few miles back." Their team was a bloody, damaged mess.

"We were fine," Rylan said stubbornly.

Sloan stifled a sigh. Obviously there was no explanation he could provide that would convince Rylan he'd made the right decision, so he decided to stop talking and save his strength. They'd be coming to Foxworth soon—if there was a Foxworth left—and Sloan knew he wouldn't be able to lay his head down for another ten hours, at least.

"Connor would've never left Hudson behind. He indebted himself to Reese, flew directly into enemy territory, and was prepared to storm the entire fucking city until he saved Hudson." Rylan flicked the safety of his gun on and off, as if trying to wrestle down the instinct to shoot Sloan in the head, commandeer the truck, and go after Reese. "Goddamn you, Sloan. You said you'd let the town burn if it meant saving Reese."

His stomach clenched as Rylan threw his own words back in his face. "We both know Reese would castrate me the minute she got back if every member of that town wasn't completely intact." He tipped his head toward Rylan. "Is Connor gonna take us in?"

"He owes Reese, doesn't he?" was Rylan's stiff answer.

"Yeah. He does."

They made it back to Foxworth in one piece. The minute that Travis saw their faces, he sounded the alarm.

"We have to leave, don't we?" he said sharply.

"Yup." Sloan didn't have time to explain, so he barked out orders instead. "We're going to Connor Mackenzie's camp. Rylan, there's a sat phone in Reese's war room. Let him know we're coming. Sam and Davis, you two go door to door. Trav, grab Randy and get all the trucks, cars, and bikes gassed up and ready to go. We're gonna roll out in thirty minutes."

He didn't wait to see if everyone obeyed him. He had stuff to do.

A minute later, he was on Nash's motorcycle, speeding out to Scott and Anna's homestead.

Scott met him on the porch. "What's going on?" the older man asked in concern.

"There was an ambush at the Enforcer station," Sloan explained. "They took Reese, and soon they'll be sending Enforcers to wipe out the town."

Dressed in a heavy barn coat thrown over a long pajama gown, Anna appeared in the doorway with a mug of something steaming and hot in her hands. Sloan accepted it gratefully and chugged the coffee down, not caring that it burned his tongue or his tonsils. He needed the energy kick.

"We're not leaving," Scott informed him.

He closed his eyes for a moment, searching for patience and finding none. "Goddamn it, Scott. We leave in thirty minutes. Grab a chicken and some clothes and let's go."

Scott's only response was to wrap an arm around his wife. "This is our home. Let the Enforcers come. We've got the cellar under the barn and thirty days' worth of food. I'd invite you to stay but I suspect you'd be insulted by that."

He dragged a hand over his forehead. If Reese and

Rylan were standing here with him, he'd probably trample the older couple on his way to that cellar. But Reese *wasn't* here, and he was going after her the moment he made sure her people were safe.

"They took her," he choked out.

Anna's eyes flared with sympathy. "I'm so sorry, Sloan."

"We're getting her back." He stared stonily at them, daring them to contradict him with reason and facts.

Nearly eighteen hours had passed since Reese was taken.

The Foxworth force wasn't at full capacity.

Even if it was, the chopper would only be able to take a team of ten or so to the city.

The only reason Hudson had been saved this summer was because of someone on the inside—her brother Dominik. Connor had admitted there was no way they could've rescued her without Dominik's help.

"If anyone could bring her back, it'd be you," Scott agreed.

Safe room or no, Sloan didn't like leaving these two behind. When Reese had asked him to make sure Foxworth was secure, she'd meant *all* of their people. Not all of their people minus Scott and Anna.

"They'll come for you," he warned.

"Let them." Scott's voice rang with confidence.

"We don't want you to die out here." He kept saying *we* like Reese was standing right beside him, and it killed him each time he remembered that she wasn't.

"We're together," Anna said, leaning against her man. "This is our farm and we want to stay. You don't need to save us. Go save the others—it's what Reese would want."

He didn't have time to argue with them anymore. He handed the mug back to Anna and drew her against him so he could press a kiss against her forehead. "Be safe, then."

"You're making the right decisions," she called after him as he turned to go.

He looked over his shoulder. "You don't even know what those are."

"They're the right ones, Sloan. You trust in that big heart of yours. It hasn't led you astray before and it won't now," she said with a conviction that Sloan didn't feel.

With one last look at the older couple, he climbed on the motorcycle and then sped back to town, where he found that all of vehicles were loaded and ready to go. Some had already left under Nash's tired direction, Randy told him when he reached the courtyard.

Sloan clapped the teenage boy on the shoulder. "All the kids out?"

Randy nodded. "All of them. Christine and Bethany are taking charge. We put them all in the same truck and it left about ten minutes ago with Trav in the driver's seat and Cole protecting them."

"Good man. You've got everything?"

"Yep. We're just waiting for you to get your things . . . and Reese's."

Sloan had to wait a beat for his throat to accommodate the sudden lump. "Give me five and I'll be ready."

Randy lowered his voice. "Con's man is up there."

"Rylan?" Sloan glanced up at the second story of

his and Reese's building, but Reese's bedroom was in the back.

"Bethany asked him to gather Reese's stuff," Randy said awkwardly. "I hope that was okay."

"It's all good, kid." He squeezed the boy's shoulder in reassurance, then headed inside the building and took the stairs two at a time.

When he passed Reese's room, he noticed all the drawers of her dresser gaping open, but he kept walking until he reached the bathroom. He grabbed a towel and shoved all of Reese's stuff onto it—her soap, shampoo, razors, a bottle of lotion that Tamara had brought back from the south. Then he reached a hand behind the toilet seat and jerked down a brick wrapped in cellophane and duct tape. It was a stash of emergency coin along with a gun and ammo. He tossed that onto the pile, secured the ends of the towel into a sack, and slung it over his shoulder.

When he stepped into the hallway, Rylan was waiting there for him. "You got all your shit?" the man muttered.

"Almost. I need a sec."

Rylan's face was rigid, each line filled with anger and betrayal. It was nothing like the good-natured expression that he usually wore, and it pained Sloan to see such a drastic change. Rylan's first instinct was usually to smile, but Sloan had killed that.

The loss of Rylan's admiration and affection was carving what was left of Sloan's heart into thin, brittle pieces.

He ducked into his room and packed up his meager possessions as the other man watched from the doorway in silent but obvious disapproval. Fuck, he wished Rylan would yell at him or something, because at least that would mean he still believed Sloan was worth the effort.

He zipped up his duffel and headed back to the door. "Ready."

Rylan gave a tiny chin lift, the barest of acknowledgments, and then clambered down the stairs without a word.

There was one truck left in the courtyard. The two men climbed into the back, while Randy slammed the door behind them and jogged to the front. The truck heaved a little as the teenager hoisted his body into the driver's seat, then jolted forward as he gassed the engine.

Sloan leaned his head against the metal wall of the truck and closed his eyes, but all he could see was Rylan's devastated face and Reese's terrified one.

There would be no rest for him until Reese was safe.

24

The interrogation room was small, no bigger than ten by ten feet. A metal table and two chairs sat in its center. Against the far wall was a narrow cot with a thin wool blanket. The bed was . . . alarming. Since Reese highly doubted they were going to let her take naps between torture sessions, this could only mean that the cot would play a part *in* the torture sessions.

She wasn't sure how much time had passed since Eric and his men had captured her at the outpost. There was no clock or windows in the room, no indicators to help her figure out what time it was. She didn't even know if it was day or night.

Instead of the long drive that Eric had taunted her about, they'd traveled only ten minutes to a nearby airfield, where a military chopper was waiting for them. The bird had taken them not to West City, but to the Enforcer compound east of it.

Reese had strained to get a good look of the compound, but all she'd seen was a flurry of soldiers on the tarmac. They'd ushered her into this room too fast for her to gather much useful intel, though she did have some previous knowledge of the compound: Hudson had provided a detailed sketch of it to Connor, who in turn passed a copy along to Reese.

She knew there were about two hundred soldiers living there. That there were barracks in the west building and training facilities in the main one. That it was heavily guarded and surrounded by a twelve-foot electric fence.

As she stared at the cinder block walls, Reese forced herself not to give in to the fear and worry gnawing at her insides. She desperately hoped that Rylan and the others had gotten away. And she hoped to *hell* they weren't planning a rescue for her. Even Connor knew that was suicide—he'd had to make a deal with Dominik in order to free Hudson from this same compound. Security here was tighter than at any other Enforcer station in the Colonies.

It felt like at least another hour passed before the door finally opened and a stocky, balding man entered the room. He had harsh features, a heavy brow and a square jaw, and wasn't much taller than Reese's five-eight. His lips were so thin it almost looked like he didn't have any—until he smirked and the hint of a curve appeared.

"Hello, Reese," he said briskly. "I'm Commander Anthony Ferris." One bushy black eyebrow flicked up. "You don't know how long I've been waiting for a face-to-face with you."

She crossed her arms and leaned back in her chair in an insolent pose. She didn't give him the satisfaction of an answer.

Frowning, Ferris strode up to the table and pulled out the second chair. Metal scraped against concrete, a grating sound that lingered in the air. As he sat down, two more men entered the room.

Dominik was one of them.

Reese worked hard to mask her reaction. She knew he and Hudson were twins, but the man's resemblance to his sister was downright eerie. Dominik's features were more masculine, his hair a slightly darker shade of blond, and he was a good head taller and far more muscular than Hudson. But those eyes . . . those vivid gray eyes were damn near identical. It was uncanny.

Reese shifted her gaze to the other man, but he wasn't anyone she recognized. He looked like every other Enforcer, with his black uniform and a gun holstered to his hip.

Dominik closed the door and then both men stood on either side of it, their attention fixed intently on her.

"Shall we begin?" Ferris spoke pleasantly, but there was nothing kind about his expression.

He didn't pull out a pen or notepad, a recorder or camera. He didn't need to—cameras were mounted on all four corners of the ceiling, their blinking red lights indicating everything was already being taped. Reese had no doubt the room was bugged for sound too. Oh yeah. Every word was definitely being recorded.

"You're not doing yourself any favors by remaining silent," Ferris told her. "I already know who you are and everything you've been up to."

She chuckled, speaking for the first time since she'd been hauled into this room. "If you . . ." After hours of silence and not a drop of water, her voice was hoarse, so she had to clear her throat before she continued. "If you already know everything about me, then what's the point of this interview? Why don't you kill me now and be done with it?"

He clasped both hands on the metal tabletop. "That's not how we operate."

She snorted.

He ignored the derisive noise. "We're not savages like you and your people. We don't go around murdering innocent citizens, imposing our ideas of freedom and right or wrong on people and killing those who disagree."

She couldn't stop the burst of laughter that flew out of her mouth. Her response brought a cloud of annoyance to Ferris's face, but fucking hell, was he joking right now? That was *exactly* what the Enforcers did. What the Global Council did. If you didn't agree with their ideals, if you didn't give them the control they demanded under the guise of preserving resources and preventing another war, they killed you without batting an eye.

Either Ferris was choosing to ignore that, or he genuinely didn't recognize the irony.

"You've been living outside the city walls for so long you've forgotten what civilization is," he said coldly. "The government exists to protect its citizens."

She arched a brow. "Did the government protect the world all those decades ago? Did it stop all those countries from dropping bombs on each other and destroying our planet?"

"That system was flawed because there wasn't one government. Nations implemented their own regimes—dictatorships, democracies, monarchies . . . so many conflicting systems. It didn't work. But what we have now, it *does* work. One government. A global rule."

Reese faked a yawn. "So I'm here for a politics lesson, is that it? Because that's even less interesting than the interrogation I was expecting."

"Fine. You want to be interrogated? Let's interrogate you." An ominous look darkened his eyes. "Who else is responsible for the outpost attacks?"

She smiled innocently "What outpost attacks?"

His fingers curled into fists on the table. "Don't test me, you stupid bitch. You were caught red-handed on the scene, armed with weapons and explosives—weapons and explosives that were stolen from an ammunitions depot a few weeks back. There were others with you. You and your people engaged my men."

Reese shrugged. "What people? I was acting alone."

"So you admit to being part of the attack?"

"Hey, asshole, you just said I was caught red-handed. This isn't exactly surprising news."

His nostrils flared. Clearly he didn't like being talked back to. "I want the names and locations of everyone else involved. And not just in the west. Outposts in the north, south, and east have also been targeted."

Satisfaction surged through her. Brynn, Garrett, and Mick had done their parts, then. They were smarter than her, though. They hadn't gotten greedy.

Guilt arrowed into her gut, so deep and acute that it made her feel like throwing up. She really hoped Sloan wasn't looking for her right now. He'd promised that if anything ever happened to her, his first priority would be to take care of Foxworth.

Reese would kill him if he broke that promise.

"We already know all about your town," Ferris said. "My men are on their way there as we speak."

Her stomach twisted harder. Fuck.

"One of my men informed me that he heard there were children living there. That's a clear violation of our population laws." Ferris sneered. "In fact, everything you do is a violation. You've broken every law in the book, and now you're going to face the consequences."

She rolled her eyes. "You're doing a lot of talking, *Commander*, but it doesn't seem like you're saying anything important."

"How's this for important? I'm going to set your little town on fire. If you don't tell me the names of the people involved in the attacks, I'm going to assume they all helped you. I'll line them all up and shoot them in the head, one by one. I'll make sure one of my men records it and then I'll sit beside you while we play the tape so you can watch your people die."

She said nothing. Foxworth had protocols in place. Escape plans. Rylan and the others knew she'd been captured—as long as one of them made it back to Foxworth, they would instantly implement a plan and take the others to safety.

"You're not going to let those people die," Ferris said with a harsh chuckle. "I know you."

She smiled again. "You don't know a damn thing about me."

"Oh, I beg to differ." He nodded at the blond-haired Enforcer behind him. "Dominik."

Hudson's twin stepped forward, bending over

Ferris's shoulder as he placed a blue file folder on the table. When he straightened up, Reese met his gray eyes and said, "Your sister says hello."

Dominik flinched. It was barely noticeable, but she'd been looking for it, waiting for it.

Then he set his broad shoulders in a rigid line, his lips curling in a sneer. "My sister is a wanted fugitive and an enemy of the Colonies. If you know where she is, you need to tell us her location."

So that's how they were playing it? Reese suddenly had to wonder—was Dominik playing both sides, or did his loyalty really belong to his sister? Hudson seemed to think it did, but Reese was having a tough time reading the man.

Ferris flipped open the folder and said, "I don't know you, huh? Trust me, I know everything about you, Teresa."

She didn't even blink at his use of her full name, and when he didn't get the reaction he'd desired, he began spouting off details from the file.

"Teresa Robertson, daughter of Sylvia Robertson." He tapped one of the pages. "We ran your fingerprints when we brought you here—imagine my surprise when I discovered you were a firstborn. That the most feared outlaw woman in West Colony is not even a real outlaw, but spent the first thirteen years of her life in the city. I wonder if your people would feel the same way about you, offer the same undying loyalty, if they knew the truth. That you haven't struggled the way they have. That you didn't spend your childhood running and hiding and starving in the 'free land.'" He used air quotes at the end.

Again, she didn't answer. The people she trusted knew she was from the city. It made no difference to them.

Ferris kept reading. "Last seen the day of her mother's burning . . ."

Reese's stomach churned at the word. Her mother's *burning*, not burial. That was how the city disposed of bodies, because the council was too worried about disease. They couldn't have corpses rotting underground and people breathing that air, so they burned the bodies and held a ceremony that was attended by anyone who cared to attend.

Not many people had been at her mother's burning. As a breeder, Sylvia hadn't spent much time with the general population. She was given her own house, had her own kitchen so she didn't have to eat in the dining halls. Her only contact had been with her daughter, the doctors, the studs, and the babies she got to keep until they were weaned and stolen away from her.

"Who helped you out of the city?"

Ferris's question brought another smile to Reese's lips. "Who says I had help?"

"You're telling me a thirteen-year-old *girl* snuck past the city gates? There's no way you could have done it alone."

Actually, she had. But she wasn't surprised he didn't believe her. From what she'd heard about him, Ferris didn't have much faith in women.

The previous commander—Hudson and Dominik's father—had made it possible for women to train as Enforcers if they chose to. Most didn't, but at least the option had been available to them. When Ferris took over, he dismissed every female Enforcer and recruited only men. And if Hudson was right, he was drugging those men and turning them into blood-thirsty maniacs.

Reese hadn't believed it before, but now that she was sitting across from Ferris, staring into his cold face, into eyes that didn't contain a trace of human-ity . . . Hudson's claims didn't sound so outlandish.

Ferris closed the file and released an annoyed breath. "You won't talk, will you?"

She leaned back in her chair again.

"I could torture you for days, weeks. I could kill everyone you know right in front of you, and you still wouldn't give up the names of your accomplices."

Reese wasn't as confident about that. She couldn't imagine idly standing by while this monster held a gun to Sloan's head, or Rylan's, *anyone's*. She wouldn't let him kill one of her people . . . she wouldn't . . .

Would she?

She swallowed hard as she second-guessed her-self. The vengeance she'd craved her whole life—*that* was what drove her. She didn't believe in love. She didn't believe in anything but her own need to de-stroy the Global Council.

Would she let them rip Bethany's baby from her arms if it meant continuing forward with her plans to crush the GC? Would she let them kill Bethany? Kill Christine?

Reese desperately wanted to believe she wouldn't. That she'd save the people she cared about. But . . . she couldn't be sure.

Ferris saw her dark side, her ruthlessness, and that was the side he chose to believe.

"No, you're not going to give anything up," he said, making a tsking noise with his tongue. "You're a coldhearted bitch." He glanced over his shoulder at Dominik. "Unless you think torture could work in this case?"

Dominik shook his head. "Coldhearted bitch," he agreed.

Something inside of Reese fractured. She wasn't always cold. She burned so hot when she was with Sloan and Rylan. But maybe Ferris and Dominik saw the real her. Maybe she *was* coldhearted.

"All right then." Ferris nodded. "This interrogation is over. Let's skip to judgment."

"Judgment?" Reese echoed.

"I'm going to recommend to the council that they sentence you to death."

She wasn't surprised. These bastards' agenda was always murder.

"I want it to be public," he continued. "The method of death will be firing squad. We can make an event of it. Have the citizens come out and see the enemy that they're facing beyond the gates."

His expression was bright, the first trace of emotion she'd glimpsed in his eyes. It looked like actual pleasure. Arousal, even. This man was a sick bastard.

"We'll paint the streets red with your blood, and the people will cheer." Ferris turned to the Enforcer who wasn't Dominik. "Tablet, please."

The man handed him a computing tablet. Ferris's fingers moved over the screen, typing rapidly while Reese sat there with her gaze locked on Dominik, whose face revealed nothing.

Ferris finished up and handed the tablet back to

the guard. "Send this execution order to the council. Secure the appropriate signatures."

"Yes, Commander." The Enforcer ducked out of the room, and Dominik followed suit without a backward glance.

Ferris looked at Reese and smiled. "I'd offer you food or water or other comforts, but . . . I'm not that kind of man. And you're not the kind of woman who needs comforts, are you?" He scraped back his chair and stood up, tucking the folder under his arm. "It won't take long for the execution order to be approved. No more than twenty-four hours. You can spend your last hours in this room, thinking about what you've done."

Chuckling, he sauntered out and closed the door behind him.

A moment later, she heard a lock click into place.

25

Rylan's eyes felt like they were composed of glue and sand by the time the tired group reached Connor's camp. He tumbled out of the truck without acknowledging Sloan, who looked like death had kissed him. The entire ride over, Rylan had been telling himself that Sloan could rot in hell, but that did nothing to erase the disturbing image of Sloan's face, creased with pain. The man had aged ten years in the last ten hours.

Rylan ached all over, inside and out. The physical pains would resolve by themselves. The internal pain was something he didn't understand and wasn't sure how to ease other than to get Reese back. It wasn't right, leaving her behind. It had nothing to do with the fact that he'd slept with her. When he'd been part of the People's Army, training for a rebellion that never happened, they'd drummed into him that a good soldier never left his brother behind.

He'd not only left Reese behind, but he'd all but abandoned her.

There had been no discussion about saving her,

only Foxworth. And as much as Rylan enjoyed the town and its people, they only existed because of Reese. The whole damn town should have been riding toward West City, rattling the cages and demanding that the council release her. Instead, they'd come here to Connor's camp with their tails tucked between their legs.

It pissed him off. He'd save her even if he had to trade himself to do it. All he needed was some intel. He needed to know where she'd been taken and who was going to pilot the Foxworth helicopter that was currently sitting in the north pasture field at Con's camp.

The camp leader was standing on the porch of the main lodge when Rylan walked up. "Have you made any contact?" Rylan asked his friend.

Connor shook his head. "Not yet." He frowned as he took in Rylan's appearance. "Jesus. You look two inches from death's doorstep. Go get some shut-eye, man. I'll let you know as soon as anything comes through."

"No. Let's call again," Rylan insisted, refusing to believe he'd come all this way to get nothing. He slapped the sidearm at his waist to signal he was ready.

Connor placed his hand on Rylan's shoulder and pushed gently. "You couldn't rescue a mouse in your condition. Get some sleep."

Rylan hated that the man was right, but he gave a weary nod. He was so tired, a child could do him in.

As he turned to go, he saw Sloan approaching.

"Thank you for taking us in." The bearded man held out his hand. And Connor, that bastard, shook it.

Rylan seethed at the unknowing betrayal. Con shouldn't be shaking this shithead's hand. Con had rescued his woman. He hadn't left Hudson in the council's clutches. If Connor knew how faithless and gutless Sloan was, he'd kick the man to the curb.

"We're going to help you get Reese out," Connor said. "But for now, you need to get some rest too. In the condition you're in, neither of you are any good to her."

Sloan nodded. "Point me in the direction of the nearest horizontal surface. I'm sure I could sleep anywhere."

"All the cabins are filling up fast," Connor admitted.

Shit. Rylan began to inch away from the porch, but his leader held up a hand.

"Ry, why doesn't Sloan crash in your—"

Oh no. He was not letting Sloan into his cabin. No way in fucking hell. He opened his mouth to say just that when Hudson appeared at the door.

"I've got something," she announced.

It was hard not to run her over on the way into the lodge. Sloan charged forward too, and Rylan attempted to shove him, but the man was having none of it. They reached the meeting room at the same time and then stood shoulder to shoulder while Hudson bent over the table. She tapped on a tiny satellite phone.

"Dom? Are you still there?"

Rylan couldn't help but glance at Sloan, whose eyes flared with hope.

"Still here, sis. I've only got a couple more minutes before I have to go, but here's what I know—they brought the outlaw leader here to the Enforcer base. She's being held in an interrogation room in the main building, underground. It's about five feet of reinforced concrete and there's only one entrance, guarded by a rotation of handpicked Enforcers. Most of them are related to council members—Ferris assigned them because they're considered highly loyal."

"Any form of communication?" Hudson asked.

"Negative. Hard to maintain a signal because of the concrete. Even the radios don't work past the second step. I tried it out earlier today."

"How is she, Dom?"

"She's alive," he said flatly.

Rylan closed his eyes. *Alive* meant a hundred different things. Was she beaten? How many bones had they broken? Had they taken turns raping her?

Beside him, Sloan remained utterly silent. As if he didn't give a shit about what had happened. The bastard had raced back to Foxworth, saved the people, and now his task was complete. Why was he even with them? He didn't care about Reese. Didn't care about her at all.

Rylan fisted his hands at his sides, longing to drive one of them into Sloan's impassive face.

"It sounds like our only opportunity is if they move her," Connor spoke up.

"Yes." Dominik paused for so long Rylan wondered if the connection had dropped. "They're going to execute her, old-city style, at the base of the council building as a warning to all outlaws."

Hudson covered her mouth to suppress her gasp of dismay. Rylan felt his already weak legs turn to water. He staggered backward until his shoulders found the wall. The asshole Sloan didn't move. It was like he'd turned into a piece of stone.

"When?" Connor asked grimly.

"It'll take twenty-four hours to have the execution order signed. As soon as it is, she'll be brought out and charged for crimes against the Colonies. The sentence will take place at nightfall."

Nope. Rylan refused to accept this. Reese wasn't going to die.

He pushed forward, slapped his hands on the table, and snarled into the phone. "We're coming after her, Dominik. Better say your prayers."

Dominik let out a humorless laugh. "Prayers aren't gonna save anyone."

"We need more details," Hudson begged. "A timetable, location, any weak points. Anything."

"I'll get you what I can, when I can, but you're just gonna have to sit tight until then."

He cut the connection before they could ask another question.

Enraged, Rylan turned to Connor. "She wouldn't be here without Reese." He pointed a finger in Hudson's direction. He couldn't even look at her without thinking of the unfairness of it all. Dominik had saved his sister, but he clearly wasn't risking his neck for Reese.

"I know, man." Connor rubbed the back of his neck. "She's not going to die in there. I'm calling everyone in and we'll come up with a plan, all right? We'll take her when they bring her out."

"Let's go now. We'll plan when we're outside the city walls."

Connor rejected the half-baked idea. "No. They're

not going to try her until tomorrow. Let's wait for Dominik to get back with more details. We'll be able to bring all the right equipment and right people. Besides, you two need to sleep or you're not coming with us."

Rylan opened his mouth to object, but Connor shook his head again. "Not happening, Ry. Whatever you're thinking, stop."

Short of hijacking the chopper, Rylan didn't have any choice. He jacked his hand through his hair in frustration and then spun on his heel. The heat at his back told him that Sloan was right behind him, but Rylan didn't say a single word as he practically sprinted toward his cabin. He waited until the other man had crossed the threshold before pouncing.

"Don't you have any feelings? What the hell is the matter with you?" His teeth ground together. "Did you lose your balls in Reese's cunt? Is that why you're too weak to—"

He didn't get the next word out because Sloan's fist was in his face.

Rylan licked the blood at the corner of his mouth and smiled. Yeah, it was on. He was going to beat this motherfucker who'd left Reese behind. He allowed the righteous fury to drown out his own screaming guilt and launched himself forward, fists out, jaw clenched.

Sloan ducked, but Rylan's arm was quick enough to land a blow. The impact vibrated up his arm and rang his bell almost as hard as he'd rung Sloan's. The man's head snapped back, and then he bared his teeth and drove his shoulder into Rylan's stomach. They crashed into one of the beds, fists flying and adrenaline surging.

Rylan grabbed the man around the neck and tried

to apply pressure to his windpipe, but Sloan was able to push Rylan's head back far enough to prevent him from gaining any leverage. Then Sloan's hand went to the back of Rylan's neck. Rylan saw the action in slow motion—the strong forehead moving toward him, ready to crash into his. He braced himself.

But the head butt that he expected didn't land.

Instead it was a hard, angry kiss that slammed against his mouth, both salty and wet. Sloan was . . . crying, yet there were no sounds in the cabin except for their harsh breathing.

Rylan's heart stopped, and he reared back as far as Sloan's grip would allow.

The other man's tears streaked down his face in an unrelenting downpour. The expression on Sloan's face was gut-wrenching. Pale and tired, full of need and anger and regret.

"I miss her too," he groaned against Rylan's mouth.

"I should've never backed her crazy plan," Rylan mumbled in response.

His outrage had been wiped away by Sloan's grief, replaced by bone-crushing guilt that tightened his throat. He'd been trying to ignore it, using his anger toward Sloan to shroud the real reason he was so fucking destroyed: It was his fault Reese had been captured.

In his reckless desire to be seen as an equal, he'd driven Reese to the outpost when Sloan had tried to hold them back and keep them safe.

If anyone should be livid, it was Sloan. But the man acknowledged Rylan's tortured confession with silence, and in those long quiet moments, Rylan almost broke down in tears of his own.

Since Reese's capture, all he'd kept thinking was that if he didn't get her back, he was worse than his father. Sure, his dad had whored his mother out, but he'd never sent her into a dangerous situation to die. Not like Rylan. Rylan had stood in that room egging Reese on while Sloan had been the voice of reason. And now she was gone, and the two men were lost.

They clung to each other, desperate to find some comfort. Rylan's fingers shook as he pulled at Sloan's clothes. Their shirts came off. Their pants followed, and soon they were rolling around on the musty cabin floor, naked and hard. It was nothing more than a frantic attempt at distraction, Rylan knew that, but his body responded regardless, pleading for relief, for a way to shut off his brain, even if only for a few minutes.

His erection slid against Sloan's, and the heat of their grief-stricken desire burned Rylan like a physical thing. It couldn't have felt more real if someone had held a branding iron to his back.

He gasped when Sloan's hand reached between them to grip him.

"Take me," Sloan growled. "Put your damn hand on me."

Rylan reached down blindly. His knuckles knocked into Sloan's and then he found the other man's hard shaft. Iron sharpened iron. They stroked each other in jerky, uncoordinated movements as they sought their release.

"We're getting our woman back," Sloan snarled against Rylan's lips.

"Damn right we are." He bit at Sloan's mouth, scraped his tongue and teeth along Sloan's chin until the man was arching into his merciless grasp.

"Or die trying."

Release came. Rylan shouted as Sloan bit into his shoulder. Their bodies shook and trembled as their climaxes filled their clenched fists. Then they both groaned and rolled onto their backs, chests heaving with each labored pant.

Rylan sucked in another breath. He wanted to say something, but the stinging in his eyes and the lump at the base of his throat held him back. He swallowed and tried again. This time when Sloan reached for his shoulder, it was a gesture of comfort. And he leaned into it.

He was in love with Reese.

He'd told himself he just wanted a good fuck with an amazing woman, but he'd been fooling only himself. He'd been half in love with Reese since the first moment he'd met her. If all he'd wanted was a good time, there were any number of beds he could've visited. But he'd stayed at Foxworth, leaving his friends behind, because Reese was the brightest star in the entire universe, and he was transfixed.

He rubbed a hand across the hollow space in his chest. "If I'd stayed away from her, I wouldn't feel this way," he admitted.

"Once you met her, you were sunk," Sloan said quietly.

"So were you."

"Yeah." Sloan rose to his feet, then wiped his hand and abdomen off with his shirt and fumbled around in the pocket of his cargo pants. He pulled out a cigarette and lit it.

Settling back by Rylan's side, Sloan took a drag and then passed over the cigarette.

Rylan inhaled for a puff and watched the smoke stream from between his teeth to mix with Sloan's exhalations.

"I think I was just existing before I met Reese," Sloan whispered. "Each foot I put in front of the other was leading me closer to her." He traced a finger over Rylan's collarbone.

"Destiny then?"

Sloan shrugged and plucked the smoke from Rylan's lax fingers. "I don't know what it is. I only know that I never felt complete until I met her. And even though she picked Jake"—he paused and slid a wry look toward Rylan—"and you, being the gun in her holster, the steel at her back, was all I needed."

"That's because you hadn't tasted her, felt her."

"Yeah . . ."

"And now?"

"You know the answer to that. It's not enough. I want more."

Rylan jerked. That was Reese's word, and damned if he didn't want the same thing. "Me too. Which is crazy, because I've always felt this *more* shit was pointless. I didn't want anything deep. Definitely not a commitment. I didn't look at Con and Hudson and think, I really want what they have. I just was happy joining in every now and then." He grimaced. "And now I can't stop my heart from banging double time and I can practically taste the terror on my tongue. I hate feeling this way. I fucking hate *feeling*."

He didn't want to be his dad. Or his mom, for that matter. He didn't want to feel the kind of emotions that could twist him up inside, that could lead him to make decisions that would destroy everyone around him.

Sloan read his apprehensions easily. "Not all love is sick. Connor's not gonna abuse Hudson. And Len would throw himself off a cliff before he'd hurt Jamie. And you are not your father's son."

"How do you know?" He stared at the beams in the ceiling. How could anyone know what kind of partner they'd be until they tried?

"Because I'm here to punch you in the face if I feel like you're going off the deep end."

The corners of Rylan's mouth twitched. "That's generous of you, brother."

Sloan smiled. "I know."

But this man's presence was exactly what he needed. With Sloan there, Rylan could be himself without fear. He'd be able to love without worrying that it would turn rancid and hurt the people he was supposed to care about the most.

He'd be able to have Reese.

And Sloan.

And everything that he'd always believed was out of his reach.

26

Sitting in a cell gave a woman plenty of time to think about her life. The fact that she was facing execution only sped up that process, because Reese literally didn't have much *life* left.

As Ferris had promised, there were no trays of food or bottles of water brought to her. She'd been abandoned, dismissed from their minds, not to be remembered until it was time to face the firing squad. Reese had started her imprisonment sitting in the chair, but after hours had passed, she'd finally admitted defeat and curled up on the small cot.

It was kind of fitting that she was spending her last hours alone. That was the way she'd lived ever since she'd escaped the city when she was thirteen years old, after she'd climbed into the back of that supply truck, hidden under a blanket, and hadn't moved a muscle during the eight-hour drive.

She'd been alone for an entire year before encountering another outlaw. She taught herself how to make snares, how to build fires. She'd hunted her own food and slept in abandoned buildings and barns. She'd thrived on her own. And even when she got older and began letting other people into her world . . . even after she came across Foxworth and decided to form a permanent settlement there . . . even when she became friends with people like Bethany and Arch . . . even when she'd let Jake into her bed and Sloan into her confidence . . . she'd still considered herself alone.

But Reese hadn't realized, not until this very moment, how much she depended on all those people. And how much they depended on *her*. She could picture them sitting around and planning a rescue, fully prepared to risk their lives to save her. She knew with bone-deep certainty that they would try to come after her, and that knowledge made her think back to Ferris's questions earlier. How she'd doubted herself, questioned whether she would let her people die if it meant securing her revenge over the council.

The answer to that was . . . no. She *wouldn't* let them die. She'd take a bullet for any one of her people, give her life before she let the Enforcers hurt them.

But there were two people she'd give more than her life for. She'd give them her heart and her soul and every goddamn thing they wanted from her. She would give up anything, even her vengeance, just to see them again and tell them that she was wrong.

Love *did* exist. She knew it did because she felt it. She didn't feel it for one man, but two, and maybe that made her a really messed-up individual, but it was the truth.

She would die before she let anything happen to her men. Which meant she needed to find a way to get a message to Sloan and Rylan. A signal for them to abort whatever foolhardy rescue plan they were putting in motion, because any march on the Enforcer compound or the city itself would result in their deaths, and she could *not* have that on her conscience.

But she also couldn't get a message out when she was trapped in this room. No one had come in or out since her interrogation, and she had no idea when Ferris was planning to execute her.

Her groan of dismay echoed in the quiet room. She closed her eyes, but sleep didn't come. Instead, she lay there on the cot for what seemed like an eternity, and she was still in that position when the door finally creaked open.

A burst of hope went off inside her when she saw Dominik in the doorway. He was alone, but Reese could hear the murmur of voices in the hall.

Fuck. She needed to be quick. "Dominik," she started.

"Shut up," he snapped. His face was expressionless as he stalked over to the cot.

"Please," she whispered urgently. "I know you're still in touch with—" Warning flashed in his eyes, and she quickly amended, "I know you still have contacts. I need you to get a message to my people. It'll be for both our benefits, because trust me, you don't want them laying siege on you guys, so please—"

"Shut up," he said again, sharper this time. Then he nodded at the door and two Enforcers marched inside.

They hauled her off the cot and the next thing she knew her hands were yanked behind her back and a pair of handcuffs was snapped into place. Her stomach lurched when she glimpsed the item in one of their hands.

"Is that really necessary?" Reese muttered, but no one answered.

The Enforcer swiftly put the hood over her head.

Darkness.

And with the darkness came a spark of fear. She'd seen pictures in the old prewar history books. Hooded figures being led to the gallows . . . a noose tied around their necks.

Her own neck started to itch, even though she knew that wasn't her fate. Ferris had made it clear he wanted pomp and circumstance for her execution. Reese envisioned dozens of uniform-clad men lined up with their rifles drawn. Citizens being forced to watch. Or hell, maybe they wanted to watch. Maybe they were so brainwashed by the council that they truly believed the outlaws were the real danger.

She squeaked when her feet suddenly gave out from under her. Someone tugged her forward, but she didn't know where she was supposed to walk. She moved one foot in front of the other and prayed her death would be as painless as her mother's. She'd heard the doctor say that Sylvia hadn't felt pain from the overdose. It was as if she'd died peacefully in her sleep.

But Reese doubted that dozens of bullets shredding into her flesh could be considered peaceful.

She was dragged forward again, and then she felt a whisper of breath through the thin cloth covering her face. "Don't try anything stupid." Dominik's voice, low and raspy. "It'll be easier if you don't fight."

A choked "fuck you" squeezed out of her throat.

His grip tightened on her arm. "Do what I say and it'll all be over soon."

Reese's heartbeat was surprisingly steady as they walked for what seemed like forever. Her boots thudded softly against the floor of what she suspected was a hallway. A few minutes later, a gust of cold air hit her, cooling her face even through the hood. Gravel crunched beneath her boots. Eric hadn't blindfolded her last night when they'd driven through the huge electric gates of the Enforcer compound, and she remembered seeing gravel in the courtyard. She wondered if that was where they were now.

She heard male voices but couldn't make out what they were saying. The conversations were muffled by the hood and the sound of her pulse now shrieking in her ears. Her sense of equilibrium wavered as someone pushed her onto what felt like the seat of a car. Doors slammed, and there were so many footsteps in the courtyard that she wondered if the entire Enforcer compound was coming to watch her get shot to death in the city square.

Once again, she clung to Hudson's insistence that Dominik was a decent guy. "Your sister is a good woman," she blurted out.

There was a sharp hitch of breath, followed by another command. "Quiet."

Reese kept going. "I wasn't sure I could trust her, even after she donated almost all the blood in her body to try to save a dying man. I still thought she might have an agenda, that she might be working with you and the council to kill us all."

No answer.

"She asked me to spare you," Reese confessed with a shaky laugh. "When we were attacking the outposts, Hudson was worried you might be in one of them. She begged me to spare your life. I told her I wouldn't make any promises."

Still no answer, so she finally gave up and quit talking. She wasn't sure what she was trying to achieve anyway. Was this her plea for Dominik to spare *her*? Hudson had said he was working behind the scenes, and if that were true, that meant he'd never be able to save Reese without revealing his betrayal to Commander Ferris. Whatever Dominik was or wasn't doing, he'd be crazy to release a high-profile outlaw prisoner. It would instantly make him, as he'd called it, an enemy of the Colonies.

Reese was surprised to feel tears sting her eyelids. She really wished she'd listened to Sloan. She wished she could see Rylan's careless grin one last time. Those two men had made her feel . . . they'd made her feel like a woman. And that was a liberating sensation for a woman who'd always felt as empty as her womb that could never be filled.

The silence dragged on and so did the drive. Based on Hudson and Connor's intel, Reese knew the Enforcer compound was about fifteen miles from the city gates, but it seemed like they drove for a lot more than fifteen miles. Or maybe time had just slowed to a grind. Maybe each minute was no longer sixty seconds but a thousand of them. Maybe that was what happened when you were on your way to die.

Eventually she closed her eyes, but she didn't sleep. She listened to the sound of the engine and felt the bumps of the road beneath the tires. The handcuffs dug into her wrists but she ignored the discomfort.

She just wanted to get this over with. Maybe it would be better this way. Maybe Sloan and Rylan were better off without her. Without her callousness. Her tendency to shut down whenever she started feeling a little too much. Not to mention that she couldn't give them a future, at least not one that involved cherub-cheeked infants like Bethany's.

Her heart twisted painfully as she remembered Sloan and Rylan's insistence that she was a mother to everyone in Foxworth. They could be right, but it didn't matter anymore.

A low voice sounded from the front seat of the vehicle. "We're all set," someone said.

"Good," Dominik replied. "Send a text to Vin to let him know."

Who the hell was Vin? And why hadn't anyone mentioned Ferris this entire time?

The car came to an abrupt stop, and once again Reese was being jerked around like a doll. Her boots hit the ground with a squishing noise, as if she'd stepped in a puddle. Or soft, wet earth. Either way, it didn't feel like she was standing on a road.

She instinctively tensed when cold hands brushed her wrists. There was a jingle of keys, and the handcuffs popped off at the same time the hood was pulled off her head.

Light assaulted her vision. Not bright sunlight, but the glow of dusk. She blinked rapidly to adjust to it, and her mouth fell open when she glimpsed something in the distance. Three somethings, actually. Gleaming military choppers.

Reese blinked again. What the hell was going on?

The frantic internal question was answered when Dominik appeared in front of her. His gray eyes were hard, but the corners of his mouth lifted up in an almost smile.

"I hope you're not scared of flying," he said.

27

"You're a crazy son of a bitch, you know that?" The metallic roar of the helicopter rotors made it difficult for Reese to hear her own voice. She was sitting in the back of the chopper with Dominik and six other Enforcers, still marveling at this turn of events.

"Not as crazy as you," Dominik retorted. "What the hell made you think that you and a handful of people could take out an outpost of thirty Enforcers?"

"There weren't supposed to be thirty there," she grumbled. "It was a trap."

"It was a trap you should have anticipated," he said with a smirk. "Any military leader worth his salt would have accounted for that."

She bristled, even though he was right. She'd made a stupid decision based not on intelligence and strategy, but emotion. She'd been on edge because of the threesome and the feelings it had roused in her, and instead of listening to sound advice, she'd acted on her own revenge-driven urges, fueled by the need to run away from her feelings.

"Ferris will kill you for this," she informed Dominik. He flashed a grin. "Only if he finds me."

"You? This isn't just *you*." She waved a hand around the cramped cabin. "You brought a goddamn party with you." Reese had counted at least twenty-five Enforcers boarding the three choppers in the clearing. "Why would you do this?" she demanded. "Why defect now?"

"Didn't exactly have a choice," he said dryly. "We had a plan in motion, a schedule for when we would desert, but your capture sped up our timeline." He cursed under his breath. "My sister begged me to help you. And if you know Hudson like you claim you do, then you know it's impossible to say no to that woman. She's a stubborn little thing."

Reese experienced a pang of guilt as she recalled her conversation with Hudson, when she'd told the woman in no uncertain terms that she wouldn't cooperate with the Enforcers or spare Hudson's twin brother if it came down to it. And she'd been so damn resentful after Hudson's warnings about Rylan.

But the woman was an ally, and Reese had refused to see it. It was just another mistake to add to her growing list of screw-ups.

She stared at Dominik. "What's your end game?" she asked suspiciously.

He rolled his eyes. "Would it kill you to say thank you?"

She narrowed *her* eyes.

"I just saved your life, lady. And in the process I put my own life in danger, not to mention my men's. I helped the queen of Foxworth escape—Ferris is not going to take that lightly. And he already hated me to begin with. He suspects that I helped my sister escape too."

"You did help her escape."

"Yeah, but he doesn't have any fucking proof. You'd think he'd trust the word of his most loyal servant." Dominik looked genuinely offended.

Reese had to laugh. "Who are you loyal to now?" she asked after a moment.

"My sister," he said steadfastly. "And by extension, my sister's man. Family's the only thing that matters in this world. The people you love—those are the only ones who deserve your loyalty."

She swallowed hard. "Yeah, I think you're right about that."

"I'm always right," he drawled.

She gestured to the other men, none of whom had spoken a word to her. They were all watching Dominik as if waiting for him to issue an order even when they were thousands of feet in the air. "And who are they loyal to?"

Dominik opened his mouth, but the man to his left beat him to it. "We're loyal to Dom," he said gruffly. "And we're loyal to each other. This"—he gestured toward the other Enforcers—"is *our* family."

A family of killers, she almost said. But who was she to judge? She'd killed dozens of Enforcers during those outpost attacks. She'd killed bandits. She'd killed Jake.

She was a killer too.

She suddenly remembered the other bit of information Hudson had given her. "Are you guys still taking those drugs?" she asked warily.

Dominik shook his head. "We've been off the cocktail for several months now. Took a while because we couldn't have the men going off them all at once. And I wasn't sure who was loyal to me and who was loyal to Ferris." A dark look crossed his eyes. "Some of those men that you shot and blew up, they were loyalists, Reese. They didn't deserve to die."

She didn't offer him an ounce of sympathy. "Yes, they did. It doesn't matter if they were drugged these past few years—they weren't drugged before that, when your father was in charge. They may not have killed as many outlaws back then as they're doing now, but they still killed people."

He sighed in acknowledgement. "We all kill people," he agreed, echoing her own thoughts.

"Twenty minute ETA," the pilot, who hadn't said a single word in the last hour, suddenly barked.

Dominik twisted around to pat him on the back. "Thanks, Jose."

Reese's heartbeat accelerated. The prospect of reuniting with . . . God, with who? She didn't even know who had survived the outpost attack. She'd been too scared to ask Dominik before, but now she had no choice.

She took a breath and met his gray eyes. "The people who were with me at the outpost . . . do you know if they survived?"

He nodded.

"Who?" she whispered.

"Most of them, I think. I didn't catch any of the names Hudson told me, except for someone with a D? David maybe?"

"Davis." Relief hit her. Davis had been with Nash,

so that boded well for Nash surviving. But what about Beckett? Sam?

Rylan.

Sloan.

"Did Hudson say exactly how many survived?"

"Five or six?"

"Was it five or was it six?" Reese demanded, swallowing her panic.

"I don't know," he said irritably. "I'm sure you'll find out soon enough."

The chopper dipped to the right as the pilot changed course slightly. As far as Reese could tell, they'd been traveling west for most of the flight. Now it seemed like they were going northwest. Her heart dropped, because that meant the mountains. Connor's place, she deduced. But why not Foxworth? Her people would be *there*.

I'm going to set your little town on fire . . .

Her pulse sped up as Ferris's words returned to her. Was Foxworth gone?

She peered out the window, but they were too high up to make out any distinguishable landmarks down below. She didn't see any plumes of smoke to indicate a fire, but for all she knew, her town could be burning.

It became hard to breathe in those last minutes of their journey. The helicopter started its descent, and sure enough, she saw the snowy mountain caps. She'd been to Connor's camp only once, but she recognized the landscape. As the chopper dropped lower and lower, she glimpsed the roofs of wood cabins peeking from the trees.

The helicopter set down in a clearing that appeared to be several miles from the cabins she'd seen from the sky. There were no vehicles or people waiting. Reese gulped again, because if Sloan and Rylan were alive, they'd be standing there waiting for the chopper to land.

The bird lurched as it touched down. One of Dominik's men threw open the doors, and everyone climbed out. The still-spinning rotors created a tornado of wind that whipped Reese's hair around her head.

Twenty feet away, the second Enforcer chopper was landing. Beyond that, the third. Enforcers streamed out of the birds, and for a second she found herself reaching for a gun that wasn't holstered to her hip. She had to remind herself that they weren't her enemies—they were her saviors. These men, these deserters . . . they were outlaws now.

Dominik had a phone to his ear and was murmuring into it. She was tempted to yank it out of his hand and demand to speak to Sloan. Or Rylan. Or, hell, even Connor, just so he could tell her whether her men were alive. But Dominik ended the call before she had the chance.

"We're two miles out, but we have to get there on foot because the trail is too uneven for vehicles to drive on," he told her. "This was the only place we could land."

She nodded.

"Are you up for it?" he pressed.

"What do I look like, a pussy?"

He chuckled. "No, you look like a woman who hasn't had a real meal in twenty-four hours."

Reese shrugged. They'd given her an energy bar on the chopper and she'd chugged at least two bottles of water, but even though she was still hungry, a two-mile hike wasn't going to kill her.

"Let's go," she said, already charging past him.

Still chuckling, Dominik followed her toward the brush.

There wasn't much talking during the trek toward Connor's camp, but it wasn't quiet. Thirty-odd men walking through the slush in heavy boots created a lot of noise: twigs breaking, rifles pushing away branches, the undergrowth of the forest cracking beneath their feet.

The men matched her rapid pace. They were all eager to reach civilization, but Reese wondered if the Enforcer deserters knew what they were in for. They certainly wouldn't encounter the same luxuries they had on their compound. Connor's camp had a generator. It had lights, plumbing, lots of game in the woods. But those weren't the kind of conveniences that these men were used to, and if the generator ran out of fuel, all those luxuries would go away.

The woods thinned out about a mile and a half into the hike. After another quarter mile, Reese saw the first cabin. And then another one. She walked faster, feeling energized despite the fact that her stomach now hurt from exertion and no sustenance.

She stumbled through the trees and reached a path that winded past several more A-frame cabins that looked abandoned. She knew this had once been a wilderness resort where families had come on vacation. As the path widened, she suddenly heard voices. Far more than she'd expected, since Connor ran a small camp of less than ten people.

This sounded like a lot more than ten people.

She sprinted toward the noise, then stumbled to a stop when she saw the people. *Her* people. Or most of them anyway, milling in the huge courtyard. Several hundred yards away was a large log building with a sign that said THE LODGE. Reese spotted Christine and her brothers sitting on the steps, talking with some of the other Foxworth teens—Randy, Sara, Ethan.

She shifted her gaze and glimpsed Pike standing twenty feet away with his pet wolf at his feet. Sam was with him, down on her knees as she patted the adorable wolf pup.

Reese's gaze moved again, and that was when she saw them.

Sloan and Rylan.

Sloan saw her first. He broke away from his conversation with Connor. Almost simultaneously, Rylan disengaged from Connor's other side, and then the two men were racing toward her.

She wasn't sure which one of them caught her, but the next thing she knew, she was sandwiched between them both.

The moment she was in their arms, the tears finally started to fall.

28

Reese's tearful reunion with her men lasted all of five seconds. She'd barely had a chance to hug and kiss them before Connor was marching over and announcing they were holding a meeting in the lodge.

"Now?" Sloan said irritably, and Reese hid a smile at his grumpy expression. It was rare for him to reveal his unhappiness to outsiders.

Connor nodded. "We need to run a few things by Reese. We'll make it quick." He glanced at her. "Unless you're not up for it?"

She looked from him to the men, but the urgency in Connor's eyes trumped the impatience in theirs. "Yeah, let's get all the business out of the way now, because once my head hits a pillow, I won't be waking up for two days."

The foursome headed for the large wooden porch, where some of the kids were still congregated. Christine immediately dove off the steps and into Reese's arms.

"I'm so glad you're okay!" the girl cried out, burying her face against Reese's chest. "I was so worried."

"Ah, you know I'm invincible," Reese said lightly,

but the lump in her throat made it hard to maintain the careless tone. Her voice cracked as she added, "I'm just glad *you're* okay."

Christine pulled back, her eyelashes glistening with unshed tears. "We all are." She looked at Sloan and Rylan. "They got us out."

Gratitude flooded Reese's belly, spurring her to place a hand on either man's arm. "Thank you," she told them, but her gaze was focused on Sloan. "You kept your promise."

"Always," he said gruffly.

She was perilously close to tears herself, so she gently stroked Christine's cheek and said, "We'll talk later, okay? I need to meet with the other leaders right now."

"You should come see my cabin when you're done," Christine said with a beaming smile. "It's really pretty."

Reese's throat tightened even more as she watched the fourteen-year-old scamper off. She'd never seen Christine happier. The girl was changing. They were all changing.

Inside the lodge, a small group was already gathered at one of the round dining tables. There were dozens of those tables in the wood-paneled room, along with a large kitchen in the back, and a raised section off to one side that featured a huge fireplace and cozy sitting area.

The change in scenery was jarring. Her perfect little town, with its Main Street and brick buildings, with the town square and the gorgeous gazebo and Graham's restaurant . . . it was gone. She didn't know if Ferris had kept his promise to burn it to the ground, but it didn't matter if he had. They could never return to Foxworth now that its location had been compromised.

Despite the ache in her heart at losing the town she'd built, she knew that Foxworth wasn't truly gone. The community lived on. A place where freedom thrived . . . The *idea* lived on.

And luckily, Connor's camp had plenty of space to accommodate her people, as well as the Enforcer deserters.

She wasn't surprised to see that one of those deserters was being included in the meeting. Dominik sat next to his sister, once again drawing Reese's attention to the eerie resemblance between them.

But it was the familiar face on the other side of the table that made Reese gasp. "Tam! When did you get back?"

The tall, beautiful brunette gracefully rose from her chair to give Reese a warm hug. The two women had been friends for years. The smuggler and the outlaw queen.

When Tamara planted a quick kiss on Reese's lips, a strangled groan came from Rylan.

"Seriously? Did you really have to do that?" he griped. "Now I'm gonna have a hard-on for the whole meeting."

"You always have a hard-on," Sloan muttered, but his lips were twitching with amusement.

"Got in this morning," Tamara told Reese. Her dark eyes twinkled with mischief. "Thanks for not being here to greet me, asshole."

"Gee, I'm sorry. Next time, give me a heads-up when you're coming and I'll make sure not to face execution that day."

Dominik snorted.

They all took their places at the table, with Rylan and Sloan on either side of Reese. She hid a smile when she noticed their protective postures.

Connor rested his forearms on the wooden table-top and glanced at Reese. "Brynn and Mick checked in last night. All their outpost attacks were success-ful."

"What about Garrett and the north?"

"No word yet, but we weren't expecting to hear back yet," Pike spoke up in his gravelly voice.

There was a flicker of movement, and Reese real-ized Pike's wolf pup was sitting in his lap. For fuck's sake. The man brought his pet to a debriefing?

"I gotta imagine Garrett is having success too," Connor said. "His people are good fighters, better than Brynn and Mick's."

Reese turned to Sloan. "What about the Foxworth people we lent them?"

"On their way back as we speak. They have the coor-dinates for Con's camp. Should be here in a few days."

Good. Soon all her people would be under her watch again. She turned to Dominik. "And the city? Ferris?"

"Won't be a problem for much longer," Dominik said with a savage smile. "There are still loyalists inside. They're going to take out Ferris the moment I give the word . . . ?" He left that hanging in an unspo-ken question.

Connor and Reese exchanged a long look, and then Con's gaze shifted to Dominik. "Give the word," he said briskly. "The sooner the commander is eliminated, the sooner we can make a move against West City."

"Every city," Tamara corrected, her throaty voice capturing everyone's attention.

Reese glanced over in surprise. "What?"

"The outlaws in South Colony are on board. Same with the ones in the east. I didn't get a chance to hit the north yet, but I assume that once the other three colonies start rebelling, the fourth will join in too. Oh, and the outlaw army in the south? It's a thousand strong."

Everyone stared at Tamara.

"What? Did you think I was just working on my tan?"

Rylan snickered.

Connor sighed.

"I get shit done," Tamara said, tossing her thick, shiny mane over one slender shoulder.

Reese didn't miss the way Dominik's gray eyes tracked the brunette's every move. Hardly a surprise, though. Tamara was the most beautiful woman Reese had ever met.

In a brusque voice, Connor went over a few more details, including the living arrangements for the influx of people who had swarmed his formerly tiny camp. Everyone agreed that they'd take a couple of days to rest before making any more plans for the rebellion, and then the meeting was adjourned and Reese was being ushered to the door with Sloan's hand on her arm and Rylan's fingers laced through hers.

She didn't glance back to check the expressions on the faces of Connor and the others, but Tamara's low laughter tickled her spine. "So *that's* happening now, huh?" came the woman's highly amused observation.

Reese's pulse sped up. Yeah. She supposed it was.

* * *

Before the door to the cabin had even closed behind them, Reese found herself in Sloan's embrace again. He held her so tightly that her lungs couldn't draw oxygen, and she gave a weak laugh as she batted at his rock-hard chest. "Sloan. You're crushing me."

Rylan chuckled and stepped toward them. "Cut the man some slack, gorgeous. He's had a rough couple of days."

She raised one eyebrow. "Rougher than being locked up in the Enforcer compound and sentenced to death?"

Just like that, the relief in Sloan's eyes transformed into overwhelming concern. "What do you need, sweetheart? Food? Water? We'll get you whatever you need."

"First and foremost, a shower," she confessed. "I feel dirty."

Rylan's eyes gleamed devilishly. "Dirty, huh?"

He looked ready to offer a filthy suggestion, but Reese gently touched his cheek. "And I could use ten minutes to myself. I . . ." She swallowed. "I need to collect my thoughts."

Without argument, Rylan firmly led her to the bathroom door. "Soap and towels under the sink. Try not to use too much hot water or Con will freak."

The kiss she planted on his cheek was soft with gratitude. "Thanks. I'll be right out."

Once she was alone, she let out a long, shaky breath. She could hear Sloan and Rylan moving around in the cabin, talking in low voices. Footsteps thudded against the hardwood. A door creaked open and then clicked shut.

Reese turned on the shower, then stripped out of her muddy, sweat-stained clothes and stepped under the spray. She kept it hot only for the few minutes she needed to soap up, then switched the temperature to lukewarm as she rinsed off and washed her hair.

She didn't know what she was going to say to them. She'd done a torturous amount of thinking when she was locked up in that interrogation room. Questioning, obsessing, vacillating. A part of her still wasn't convinced she was the woman they needed or deserved.

The other part of her was smacking her internally for even contemplating letting either one of them go.

When she emerged from the bathroom ten minutes later, she found that Sloan and Rylan had laid out a feast for her. Fresh fruit, cheese, and best of all—bourbon.

"Oh thank fuck," she said as she accepted the glass Sloan handed her. "You don't know how badly I need this."

Both men watched in amusement as she drained the entire glass.

The alcohol warmed her belly and sent a lethargic buzzing through her blood. "Damn, that's good." She flicked up a questioning eyebrow. "You had time to load up the booze before you evacuated Foxworth?"

Sloan nodded. "We took as much as we could. But our priority was getting our people out."

Rylan spoke up in a quiet voice. "And they're all safe, thanks to Sloan," he said, rubbing Sloan's shoulder with his palm.

She didn't miss the gentleness of that touch or the way Sloan leaned into it, and for some reason it brought her comfort knowing that they were able to bring each other comfort.

Adjusting the bottom of her towel so it remained closed, Reese sat on the edge of the bed and grabbed a piece of bread.

Sloan lowered himself beside her. "Teresa . . ." He searched her face. "Did they hurt you? Did they . . . rape you?"

She was quick to shake her head. "No. They just locked me in a room while they waited for the death order to be signed. Ferris decided I wasn't an ideal candidate for torture, that I'd rather die than give up any information." Her stomach churned, and not because of the food she was introducing to her empty system. "He believed I'd let all my people die before I'd talk."

Her gaze locked with Sloan's, then Rylan's. "He's wrong, though. I would never let anyone I care about suffer just so I could exact revenge on the council."

"We know," Sloan said.

"Do you?" She studied his rugged features, seeking any trace of doubt. But there was none. "When I found out Ferris was sending men to Foxworth, I tried to get Dominik to help me, to strike some sort of deal." Her tone became wry. "I didn't realize you guys had already beaten me to it."

Rylan laughed. "Hey, Con's been telling you for months that Dominik could be trusted. You were just too stubborn to believe it."

"I'm starting to think *stubborn* might be my middle name."

"Nah, your middle name is . . ." Rylan paused in

thought. "Sexy as fuck—how about that? Does that work for you?"

Laughter bubbled in her throat. God, she'd missed him. This man with his readily available jokes and sparkling blue eyes, the man who never took anything too seriously.

But just as that thought entered her head, he threw her for a loop.

"I love you," he said fiercely.

Reese's gaze flew to Sloan, but he looked calmer and more content than she'd ever seen him.

"*We* love you," Rylan continued.

Her pulse grew erratic. "I thought you didn't believe in love."

He reached out and stroked her cheek. "I'm a changed man, baby. Ask Sloan—he can vouch for that."

Sloan leaned closer, resting his chin on her shoulder. "It's true. Our man loves the hell out of you." His warm breath tickled her bare skin on a ragged exhale. "And so do I."

29

Sloan felt Reese stiffen, but she didn't pull away. Not from him, and not from Rylan. She remained seated between them, her gorgeous face flushed from her shower, and maybe something else. Maybe arousal, but he hoped it was more than that.

"We love you," he murmured in her ear, and she shivered in response. "So fucking much, sweetheart."

Rylan nuzzled the other side of her neck, eliciting another shiver from Reese. Sloan saw the pulse point in her throat throbbing wildly, and he leaned in to press his lips against it.

This time she shuddered. "You're crazy. Both of you."

He chuckled. "Loving you is crazy?"

"Yes," she whispered.

"You know what made us even crazier?" He trailed kisses from her throat up to her jaw. "The thought of losing you."

"Lost our goddamn minds," Rylan agreed, and then he was kissing her too, a hot, slow path that brought his lips inches from Sloan's.

Smiling, Sloan brushed his mouth over Rylan's, then gave the man's bottom lip a playful bite.

"Fuck," Rylan choked out. "You're supposed to be turning *her* on, brother, not me."

"How about we all turn each other on?" he countered.

Reese released a wheeze of laughter. "You're crazy," she repeated. "Crazy to want this."

Sloan nibbled on the corner of her mouth while Rylan's lips danced over her delicate jaw.

"But I guess I'm crazy too," she murmured. "Because I want the same damn thing."

Sloan lifted his head so he could see her eyes. Those big, beautiful, brown eyes. The emotion he saw shining in them robbed him of breath.

The corners of her mouth quirked upward. "Rylan's not the only one who's changed. I've changed too." She ran her fingers through Sloan's beard, and he almost purred in happiness. "I'm done pretending I don't feel things. I'm done pretending I don't love you."

His breath hitched.

Rylan's did the same when she turned that infinitely gentle touch to his cheek. "And I'm done pretending I don't love *you*."

Sloan took her left hand and entwined their fingers. Rylan did the same with her right hand.

"I'm still going to be a bitch sometimes," Reese confessed. "I'm still going to make decisions both of you might disagree with. I still . . ." Her voice caught. "I still can't give you children."

"I don't want children," Sloan said instantly.

"Me neither," Rylan piped up. "They're a pain in the ass."

Her expression became grave. "You say that now, but . . ."

"It won't change." Sloan's tone was firm. "Kids have never interested me, sweetheart. I don't want or need that responsibility." He laughed ruefully. "Besides, we've already got enough on our plate dealing with the children we have now."

Rylan backed him up. "Yup, we've got a camp full of children to take care of. Or rather, you do. You two can play mom and dad to all those assholes out there. I'll just hide in this cabin until you guys feel like playing a different kind of game."

Sloan reached over and gave Rylan's cheek a light slap. "Bullshit. You don't get to dodge your responsibilities. If you're our man, you lead with us."

"Con might not like having his leadership challenged . . ."

"Nobody's challenging shit. We take care of our people, he takes care of his."

Rylan paused thoughtfully. "Actually, I take it back. I bet Connor would be happy to let Reese lead everyone. He's never wanted the job for himself." He shrugged. "But enough with this business talk—we're talking love, remember?"

Reese rejoined the conversation with a laugh. "This is the weirdest relationship I've ever had." She hesitated. "I'm still not sure it's ever going to work."

"It'll work," Sloan said roughly. "We love each other, it works. There."

"You sound confident of that."

"I am confident. I'm your rock, remember?" He jerked a thumb at Rylan. "I'm his rock too. And you . . ." He brushed his lips over hers. "You're our fire."

"What am I then?" Rylan asked curiously.

Sloan thought it over. "You're the wind," he finally answered.

"No way. That sucks. The wind blows out the fire."

"Naw." He met the other man's eyes, a slow smile stretching his mouth. "It kindles it."

The darkly seductive look he got in return succeeded in turning his cock to granite. "Yeah . . . yeah, you're right." Rylan toyed with the top of Reese's towel for a moment. "I'm really good at stoking fires."

Damn straight he was. And he was fast too—Sloan barely had a chance to blink before Rylan had their woman completely naked, the towel tossed aside.

Sloan's breath lodged in his throat at the vision of pure perfection in front of him. Smooth, pale skin. Long legs and silky thighs. Reese's tits, round and plump, begging for his mouth. But Rylan beat him to it.

Reese moaned when Rylan's lips closed around one puckered nipple. "I thought you wanted me to eat," she reminded them.

"Decided I was hungrier than you," Rylan rasped before flicking his tongue over her other nipple. "Sloan, my man, you look famished too."

A laugh rose in his throat. "Starving," he confirmed, and then he slid between Reese's legs and captured her clit in his mouth.

Her hips shot off the bed. "Jesus. Are you two trying to kill me?"

"Naw, sweetheart, we're just loving you." He sucked on that rapidly swelling bud before licking his way to her opening, where he lapped eagerly at her arousal.

He wasn't sure how or when his clothes came off,

but suddenly he was naked and his lips were no longer on Reese's pussy, but kissing her eager mouth. He chased her tongue past her lips and deepened the kiss, ravishing her mouth with damn near desperation.

A rough hand closed around his cock, stroking and pumping until he was seeing stars, until he wasn't certain who was even touching him anymore. Or who *he* was touching. Soft curves and hard muscles skimmed beneath his hands. Reese's lips, Rylan's lips traveled along his heated flesh. Hoarse groans and heavy breathing filled the cabin.

He fisted his heavy shaft and brought it to Reese's pussy, rubbing the head over her clit in a sensual caress that made all three of them groan. Then he slid inside her tight, wet channel, and a rush of pleasure roared through him with so much force he feared he might come if Reese so much as twitched. She lay sprawled beneath him, legs parted, breasts flushed with excitement as he slowly moved inside her.

"Sloan," she moaned, but he couldn't answer her, because the mattress creaked and suddenly there was a cock in his mouth.

Sweet fucking God.

Rylan groaned as Sloan licked at the piercing on his tip. Then the man drew the shaft all the way to the back of his throat, while Rylan's hips pumped in a fevered rhythm. When Reese reached out and squeezed his balls with one delicate hand, he nearly fell over and had to brace himself on Sloan's rockhard shoulder.

Sloan chuckled around Rylan's cock.

"You're laughing now, fucker, but I'm the one

getting my dick sucked and my balls squeezed," Rylan said. He transferred his hand to Sloan's head, running his palm over the closely-cropped hair.

Sloan responded by swallowing him deeper. The piercing pulled away from the end of Rylan's cock, the deliciously painful sensation making him dizzy with need. He was one hard suck away from coming, but he wanted to be inside Reese. Her absence had filled him with gut-wrenching agony that was only going to be assuaged by fucking her long, deep, and hard.

With a tiny bit of regret, he tugged his dick out of Sloan's mouth, who released him with a scrape of teeth in punishment and a grunt of disapproval.

"I wasn't done there." Sloan frowned, his rhythmic pounding of Reese's sweet pussy halting for a moment.

Rylan slipped his hands under Reese's shoulders. "I know, brother. It felt too good."

"Isn't that the point?" Reese drawled.

"Yeah, but I want to come inside you, baby. I want us both to come inside you." He captured her chin and pulled her up for a tongue-tangling kiss.

Sloan scooted carefully to the end of the mattress, pulling Reese's lithe form with him so they wouldn't be separated. Still embedded deep inside of her, he lifted her slowly while Rylan positioned himself underneath her and palmed her ass. His dick, wet from his own arousal and Sloan's mouth, twitched in anticipation.

"I feel like we should swat this sweet ass until it's red for making us spend almost two days in fucking terror," Rylan remarked.

Reese glanced at him over her shoulder. "By the

touchy-feely act I saw when I got here, it looked like you two had a real tough time of it."

He smacked one cheek in response. "I manned up because you were gone. Somebody had to take on Sloan's aggression so he didn't beast out and destroy our new home."

"Sweetheart, the only way you're going to shut Rylan up is to get his dick in your ass. So open up." Sloan cupped her hips and lowered her over Rylan's quivering tip.

She groaned. "Oh shit. You're killing me."

"You can take both of us," Sloan encouraged.

Rylan's eyes rolled back as he pushed past the ring of muscle into the tight squeeze of Reese's ass. Sloan's cock pulsed against his. He gritted his teeth, summoning up every iota of control he could find. It wasn't much. Reese felt too good. Sloan was too intense. Rylan wanted to plunge inside with a violence that caught even him by surprise.

"Oh baby, you are so fucking hot. With Sloan inside you, it's tight. You gotta make room for me," he begged.

She whimpered, a breathless, ravaged response. Her head lolled back against his shoulder and her arm came up to wrap itself behind his neck. He gently rolled his hips forward and she opened.

"Ohhhh fuuu-uck," Reese hissed as Rylan slid home. "It's too much."

"Never," Sloan said, wrapping a hand in her hair and jerking her mouth against his. "It will never be too much." Over her head, Sloan's eyes met Rylan's. "Let's show our woman how much we missed her.

How much we love her. How much we can't fucking live without her."

He didn't need to be asked twice. He pushed into her with slow, deliberate movements, and Sloan held her up with one hand as the two men worked her over.

Rylan felt the orgasm boiling low and knew he wouldn't last much longer. He reached between them to find Reese's clit, pinching the bundle of nerves until she began to clench around them. Then he gritted his teeth and addressed Sloan.

"Brother, I can't hold on for much longer."

But he would. They all knew he'd hold on for as long as it took for Reese to find her pleasure. Luckily, he didn't have to wait long before she tumbled over the edge, her body shaking between them with the force of her orgasm.

Rylan couldn't help himself. He slammed forward, balls slapping against Reese's ass, sometimes touching Sloan's body. He felt the other man, just on the other side of a whisper-thin web of flesh. They moved in perfect synchronicity, driving each other beyond sanity into the glorious abyss of sensation.

"I love you two. Fuck, I love you," Sloan ground out.

Rylan felt the man come inside Reese, felt the warm rush of moisture as it dripped out to coat his own cock, felt his own release mix with Sloan's.

They collapsed on the mattress, boneless and wasted. Hands slid over sweat-soaked bodies. Mouths traded soft, languorous kisses. And through it all, the *more* that Reese had once been afraid of pursuing engulfed them.

"I love you both so much," she whispered between

kisses that had grown soft and caresses that had grown tender.

"This life . . ." Rylan felt his emotions catch in his throat. He tried again. "The two of you are worth every bad thing that's ever happened in my life. I don't deserve either of you, but I'll be damned if I give you up."

Sloan reached over and grabbed Rylan's hand. Reese laid hers on top of the joined fingers.

"Good thing we're staying together then," Sloan growled.

It was almost more threat than promise, but in this untamed land, wild souls needed fierce promises. Just like the ones they'd made tonight.

Epilogue

Reese slid out of bed just before dawn, before the first rays of light had even sliced through the dark sky. She thought she was being quiet, but Sloan's dark eyes instantly slitted open as her bare feet silently hit the hardwood floor. Yeah, she was silly to think she could make a single move without triggering Sloan's finely tuned alarm system.

"Go back to sleep," she whispered to him. "I'm just going for a quick run. I'll be back before you know it."

He gave a small, sleepy nod, then closed his eyes and nestled closer to Rylan, who was sprawled on his stomach. The blanket had gotten tangled sometime during the night, revealing Rylan's taut, bare ass and the sculpted muscles of Sloan's arm as it lay draped over the other man's broad back.

Warmth spread to every inch of Reese's body as she stared at them.

Her men.

Fuck. She loved them more than she'd ever thought possible.

Wrenching her gaze away from the perfect scene

on the bed, she reached into the duffel bag on the floor. Sloan and Rylan had brought all of her belongings from Foxworth, and her heart swelled even more. The fact that they'd done that meant they'd never doubted, not for one second, that they'd get her back.

She slipped into a pair of stretchy pants, a hooded sweatshirt, and her ratty old sneakers. Then she crept out the door and stepped outside.

The air was cold, but it didn't bother her. Neither did the crisp wind that hit her face and snaked under her ponytail as she took off running toward the path. Foxworth might be gone, but her routine hadn't changed. Waking up at the crack of dawn. Running to clear her mind and prepare for the day.

But, no. Something *had* changed. The weight that usually crushed down on her shoulders was no longer there. The fear in her throat, the ever-present worry that regularly gnawed at her insides . . . it had dimmed, almost to the point of nonexistence.

She didn't have to lead alone anymore. She had Sloan. Rylan. Connor. Tamara and Hudson and, hell, even Dominik. The burden didn't fall squarely on *her* anymore, and holy fuck was that liberating.

She slowed her pace as she neared a few of the more isolated cabins, not wanting the thump of her footsteps to wake anyone. To her surprise, someone was already up. Two someones, actually—Bethany and Archer. The new mother was on the unlit porch, curled up on a wicker chair with a blanket wrapped around her as she nursed her baby.

Bethany looked startled when she spotted Reese, but then she relaxed, smiled, and lifted her hand up in greeting.

For the first time since Bethany had given birth, the sight of the infant didn't bring a deep ache to Reese's heart.

She waved back, then continued down the path. The forest was muddy. Her sneakers sank into the wet earth and made soft plopping noises with each step, so eventually she slowed to a walk, the leisurely tempo allowing her to really take in her surroundings.

Connor's camp was quiet and remote. Peaceful. Beautiful. It wouldn't be so terrible living here, she decided. And it helped that Con's security was top-notch; he and his men had rigged every inch of the huge property with motion sensors, explosives, and security cameras that Xander monitored on his computers.

She wasn't quite sure how Dominik and his men fit into this picture, but she imagined Hudson would be running a lot of interference. She also suspected there were going to be a lot more strategy meetings in the near future. Arguments between her and Mick. Decisions to be made by all the camp leaders. Cities to siege and council members to kill. And she still had to drive back to the farm to check on Scott and Anna, who Sloan said had refused to join them. If they'd survived the appearance of the Enforcers, then she planned on moving heaven and earth to convince them to come back with her.

Yeah, there was a lot of excitement to look forward to. A lot of changes, both good and bad.

But those changes didn't seem so terrifying anymore. When Reese had told Christine she was invincible, she'd only been joking. And yet that was exactly how she felt at the moment. Invincible. Strong. *Free.* She felt as if she could face any challenges that came her way, any storm that threatened to knock her down, any enemy that threatened to destroy her.

She could face it all, conquer it all, because she wouldn't have to do it alone. Sloan and Rylan would be there with her. Her right hand. Her left hand. The rock and the wind. Unshakable strength and soothing sunshine.

As long as the men she loved were by her side, she could handle anything the future decided to throw at her.

Don't miss seeing how
Jamie and Lennox got together in

ADDICTED

Available now.

"I miss our house." Sighing, Piper nestled her head against Lennox's shoulder and curled one arm around his chest. "Are you sure it's too dangerous to go back?"

She'd been asking that same question for weeks now. Lennox was getting tired of answering it, but of all the people he'd extended his protection to over the years, Piper was one of the few he had a soft spot for. She'd turned twenty a few months ago, and despite the hard life she'd lived, her youth and innocence had been preserved. Well, maybe not the innocence— even as she voiced the question, her hand was drifting seductively toward Lennox's waistband.

"It's too dangerous to go back," he confirmed. Then he chuckled and intercepted her hand before it could slide inside his pants. "And what you're doing is equally dangerous, love."

Her laughter warmed his ear. "Aw, come on, Lennox. How long are you going to hold out on me?"

Hmmm. Probably until he could look at her without seeing the bedraggled sixteen-year-old who'd shown up at his doorstep four years ago. He'd been twenty-three, and lusting over a teenager hadn't felt right. Sure, Piper had grown up since then, but it was still hard for him to reconcile the skinny kid he'd taken under his wing with the gorgeous woman she'd become.

Which was ironic, because he had no problems lusting over his best friend, and he'd known *her* since they were both in diapers.

As if on cue, a blond head across the room swiveled in his direction, and the object of his thoughts flashed him a mischievous wink. It was as if Jamie always knew when he was thinking about her, and he had the same sixth sense about her. Growing up together had created a bond between them. They knew each other inside and out.

Though in a moment, another man would hold claim to the *inside her* part.

He'd known it was bound to happen after he and Jamie moved to Connor Mackenzie's camp. In a world filled with danger and uncertainty, it was important to form alliances, and Connor was a valuable ally to have. Lennox was damn grateful for the man's assistance.

Connor's right-hand man, on the other hand . . . Lennox liked the guy, he really did, but Rylan's flirtation with Jamie was starting to wear on his nerves.

It was Rylan who was sprawled on his back right now, his chest bare as Jamie's fully clothed body straddled his on the frayed couch. He reached up to cup Jamie's breasts through her shirt, summoning a moan from her rosebud lips. Even though her blue eyes went hazy with pleasure, they stayed locked with Lennox's.

If any other woman were looking at him like that, all heavy-lidded and visibly turned on, Lennox would have sprinted over there and joined the party. But he knew Jamie wasn't sending an invitation. She simply got off on being watched.

Watching was all he was capable of doing anyway. Jamie had been his best friend for more than twenty years. She was the only person in this fucked-up world who he trusted implicitly, who he could confide in and count on. After everything they'd been through, their friendship was rooted in feelings. Respect, admiration, affection . . . all those pesky emotions were too dangerous to bring into a sexual relationship. Sex was fun, but it was complicated as hell when feelings were involved.

And these days, life was already complicated enough.

For twenty-seven years, Lennox had lived and struggled in the free land, labeled an outlaw by the Global Council that ruled the Colonies with an iron fist. In order to prevent another war and ensure that the remaining natural resources weren't squandered, the council was all about population control and enforcing rigid restrictions on its citizens. If you didn't live in one of the four council-run cities and follow their rules, then you were considered a threat.

Lennox had never been too good at following rules. Except one: keeping his hands off his best friend. He'd already suffered too much loss. His parents, his friends, and now, thanks to an ambush by the Enforcers, his house. Jamie was important to him—he'd be damned if he lost her too.

He shifted his gaze from Jamie and Rylan, focusing

instead on the back corner of the barn, which was stacked to the rafters with furniture and other random junk. The rest of the room had been cleared out and cleaned, the large space empty save for a couple of couches and an assortment of ratty old armchairs.

It was a far cry from the setup at the old place. Lennox didn't want to depress Piper by admitting it, but he missed their house too. It was hard to consider any place "home" in the free land, but that cozy split-level had come damn close. He and Jamie had stumbled upon it after Enforcers ran them out of their camp on the coast. They'd fixed it up, scrubbed it down, and turned it into a place where other outlaws could come and bask in the little freedom they had left. Booze, sex, conversation. Simple joys, really, but thanks to the war that had devastated the globe forty years before, joy was hard to come by these days.

"I'm serious," Piper insisted, and then her lips brushed the side of his neck. "The sexual tension is killing me."

Lennox chuckled again. "Xander and Kade are in the lodge," he told her. "I'm sure they'd be happy to help you relieve some tension."

She sighed again, her fingers absently tracing the raven tattoo on his forearm. "You're no fun, Lennox. You never want to entertain me."

He reached out and tweaked a strand of her brown hair. "I'm not here to entertain you, love. I'm here to take care of you."

"Yeah, I guess that's true." Her voice softened. "And you've taken really good care of me, Len. I can never repay you for everything you've done."

"Seeing you happy and safe is the only repayment I've ever wanted," he said gruffly.

That got him another kiss—a loud smack on his cheek. "Ha, you're such a softie. I don't know why you bother acting like a badass all the time. Everyone can see right through you."

He could have corrected her, pointed out that he didn't *act* like a badass—he *was* a badass. He'd killed. He'd stolen. He'd betrayed people he'd cared about. Because that was what it meant to be an outlaw—you did everything in your power to survive.

Piper had never seen that side of him, the one that valued self-preservation above all else. He'd done his best to shield her from it, leaving her at home when he went out on supply runs, sending her away when he needed to put a bullet in someone's head. He hoped to keep shielding her, but like with everything else in this world, he knew that was probably hoping for too much.

"Anyway, since you insist on being mean to me, I'm going to track down Kade," she added, hopping off the couch. "Night, Lennox."

"Night, love."

As she headed for the door, he fought the urge to go with her, reminding himself that she would be fine trekking through the camp in the dark. She was armed, and Connor and his men had secured the hell out of the wilderness resort. The huge property was hidden in the mountains, rigged with motion sensors and explosives, and monitored by security cameras, which trumped all other luxuries. If the generator was low on fuel, Connor ordered everything else to be powered down—lights, heat, anything would be sacrificed to keep the security system operational.

Even so, it was hard for Lennox to accept that this place was truly safe. The Enforcers who policed the cities and searched the Colonies for outlaws were an ever-present threat, and one he never under-estimated. Even when he was balls deep in a beauti-ful woman, he was still painfully aware that an Enforcer bullet could strike the back of his head at any moment. He just hoped those bastards had the decency to let him climax before they pulled the trigger.

"Rylan," Connor called from the door. A second later, the camp leader strode into the barn with a scowl on his face.

Without missing a beat, Rylan untangled himself from Jamie, his scuffed boots hitting the barn floor as he rose to his full height.

Lennox was impressed by the way Connor's men obeyed him on instinct. The man was a natural-born leader and protector, even if he was a prickly asshole a lot of the time. Lennox knew that if anything ever happened to him, Con would protect Jamie and the girls, no questions asked.

As Jamie's companion abandoned her for his leader, Lennox saw a slight pout form on Jamie's lips, but she didn't voice a complaint. Con and his woman had been away from camp since dawn, and everyone had been on edge awaiting their return. The two of them had gone to see Reese, the leader of a small town several hours east, with whom both Connor and Lennox had a reluctant alliance.

Reese was unpredictable on good days and downright vindictive on bad ones, so Lennox never knew what to expect when he paid a visit to her self-proclaimed kingdom.

"I need you," Connor barked at Rylan. Then he glanced Lennox's way. "You too, if you've got the time."

Lennox rolled his eyes. "What else do I have going on?" He'd been bored to tears since he and the women joined up with Connor's group.

Before, they'd been surrounded by people. Nomads who stayed at the house for a while before traveling on, strangers who needed a bed for the night, friends from other outlaw communities in West Colony.

Here, Connor discouraged visitors. He wasn't keen on letting anyone *leave* the camp either, unless it was for a meeting with one of their allies, or a supply run. But they'd stocked up on enough shit to last them through the winter, so as far as Connor was concerned, there was no reason to step foot outside camp.

Lennox, on the other hand, was itching for action. And sex. Christ, he needed a good lay. With Piper and Jamie off-limits, Layla was the only available woman at the camp, and though he'd screwed around with her several times already, he enjoyed a little variety in his life. He'd been tempted to finagle his way into Connor and Hudson's bed, but the couple didn't seem inclined to include anyone but Rylan in their bedroom activities.

Fuckin' Rylan. The man got to screw the delectable Hudson *and* the woman Lennox had fantasized about for years. Some guys were just born lucky.

As he stood up, Jamie marched in his direction. Her pale blond hair fell over one shoulder, hovering right above her cleavage. She had fantastic tits—which she never failed to remind him of, probably because he'd spent a good portion of their adolescence ragging her about her flat chest. She'd had the last laugh, of course, transforming from a scrawny girl to a curvy, sexy-as-sin woman right before his eyes.

Truthfully he would've screwed her back then, flat chest and all. Jamie had been his first crush. He sure as hell hadn't been hers, though. She'd had all the boys in their camp panting over her, and she'd known just how to keep them wrapped around her little finger.

"I want to come to this meeting," she announced.

Lennox smirked. "You weren't invited."

"Screw that. We're a team. I go where you go."

"Things are different now, love. You and I don't run things anymore. Connor does."

Her blue eyes flashed. "Screw that," she repeated.

"You're just pissed because you didn't get to sit on Rylan's dick." He chuckled.

That got him a hard slap on the arm. "I don't care about Rylan's dick right now. I just don't want to be kept out of the decision-making process. Blind obedience isn't my thing, Len."

She was right—she'd always had a mind of her own, and that was one of Lennox's favorite things about her. The woman was outspoken, smart, and stubborn as fuck.

"It's not mine either," he admitted. "But we're playing by a new set of rules. Connor took us in, and now we've gotta do what he says." He tipped his head. "Unless you want to take off on our own? Because I'll do it, if that's what you think we should do."

She went quiet for a beat. He could see her shrewd

brain working. Then she raked one delicate hand through her hair and sighed. "Not this close to winter. If we want to find a new place, we're better off waiting till spring."

He nodded. "Agreed. But that means we defer to Con until then. Ergo, you need to go to your cabin while I find out what he has to say."

"I hate it when you *ergo* me."

A grin sprang to his lips. "Bullshit. You love everything about me."

She responded with a grudging smile of her own. "Yeah. I do." Then she reached around him and smacked him on the ass. "You better hustle, babe. Don't want to keep our mighty leader waiting."

Lennox was still grinning to himself as he left the barn. Darkness instantly enveloped him, the smell of pine and earth filling his nostrils. The camp was too damn rustic for his liking, but hey, at least the cabins were clean and cozy, the security was top-notch . . . and Jamie was here.

She was really the only thing that mattered, if he was being honest. He could be living in a volcano, inhaling ash and bathing in hot lava, and he'd be perfectly content with it as long as Jamie was by his side.